Vargr-Moon

Bernard King

NEW ENGLISH LIBRARY

First published in Great Britain in 1986 by:
New English Library, Mill Road, Dunton Green, Sevenoaks, Kent.
Editorial office: 47 Bedford Square, London WC1B 3DP

Typeset by:
Hewer Text Composition Services, Edinburgh.

Printed and bound in Great Britain by:
Biddles Ltd, Guildford and King's Lynn.

British Library Cataloguing in Publication Data
King, Bernard *1946–*
    Vargr moon.
    I. Title
    823'.914[F]   PR6061 I43/

ISBN: 0 450 06145 0

To Colin, Mary and Paul,
with gratitude and affection.

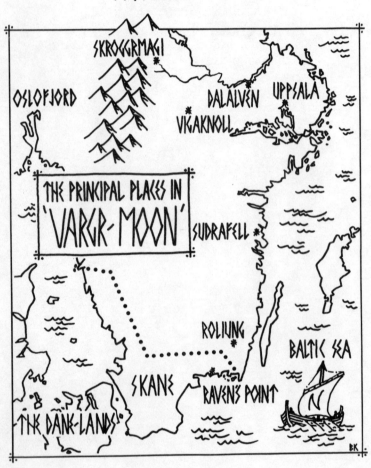

SWEDEN ABOUT 990 AD

SKROGGRMAGI

OSLOFJORD

DALALVEN   UPPSALA

VIGAKNOLL

THE PRINCIPAL PLACES IN
'VARGR·MOON'

SUDRAFELL

ROLIUNG

BALTIC SEA

SKANE

RAVEN'S POINT

THE DANE·LANDS

BK

Hart er i heimi, hordomr mikill,
skeggold, skalmold, skildir ro klofnir,
vindold, vargold, adr verold steypiz;
mun engi madr odrom þyrma . . .

There shall be evil upon the earth, a time of fornications,
of biting swords and clashing shields, an age of the wind,
an age of the *vargr*, until the world is ruined; and no man
shall show mercy to another . . .

VOLUSPA, THE SYBIL'S PROPHECY

Contents

THE THIRD PART: OF KILLINGS AND THE GLIMPSES OF
   THE MOON

Author's Note

The sagas claim that many strange things happened in the dark ages of Sweden's past, before the fall of the mighty Yngling dynasty brought the country's story into historical times. The legend of Starkadder, the old, accursed warrior who killed King Oli, was one of them.

There is a word in Old Norse, *vargr*, which has no modern equivalent. It was a word that raised goose-flesh upon the skin of the most hardened listener. It meant murderer, and wolf, and shape-shifter, and strangler, and sexual monster and oath-breaker. It signified carnage and madness. And still it had other meanings as well.

The same scholar who relates *vargr* to ergot, a fungus which attacks rye and is a naturally-occurring form of lysergic acid, shows that at one time Jesus, the *hvitakrist* or 'white Christ' of the north, was regarded as a vargr.[1]

The above is simply offered to show what a complex word *vargr* was. The meaning it takes on in the following episodes bearing upon the life of Hather Lambisson, Starkadder's young friend and companion through the last days of the reign of King Oli the Great, will become clear in due course.

[1] Mary R. Gerstein, 'Germanic Warg: The Outlaw as Werewolf', in G. J. Larson (Ed.), *Myth in Indo-European Antiquity*, University of California Press, 1974.

This story is not merely a sequel to *Starkadder*. It is a tale that the skalds might have sung of Hather and his service to King Omund, Oli's son. It is a story of the Yngling dynasty in its own right.

B.J.H.K.

A hound in the night before Uppsala's gate

THE DOG snarled at him, flashing yellow-white teeth in the darkness.

Around him the proud city of Uppsala slumbered through the hours before the dawn. The night sky was dark and clouded, starless and heavy with the threat of rain. Behind him the stockade-wall which surrounded the royal palace ran with dew, making the tangled weeds about its base heavy with the moisture of the night. The timber uprights stabbed into the ground for several feet, unbreachable, forbidding entrance to the place where King Omund kept his court.

Yet the traveller had come there, undetected by the sentinels, unseen.

She sat awaiting him, her back, unfeeling, to the dampness of the timber wall. There was no face to see, nothing to know her by. She sat and waited covered by the fur cloak which was itself heavy with the night-time's moisture.

Still, somehow, without eyes, she knew that he was there.

'Be still, Garm!' she hissed. 'It's only a traveller. Only someone who wants to hear his runes. That's all. Hold your noise, dog!'

1

The dog growled. It eyed him with suspicion. Then it fell silent and lay down, folding its forelegs beneath its tooth-heavy jaws.

'Am I right, stranger?' she asked him, seeming to look through the dew-wet cloak to where he stood watching her. Her arms made corners beneath the covering. Old, gnarled hands, hands like the knotted branches of some dead, forgotten tree, appeared to clasp it, to move it, to reveal her face.

At least, to reveal what should have been her face.

He peered at the old woman, as if he were trying to discern her features beneath the heavy, wadmal veil which shrouded them. How she could see through such homespun was a mystery in itself. Yet those who knew the runes were always mysterious. And their mysteries could often be broken by a little investigation.

She'd heard his footfalls, his breathing. It was that simple. Easier still, she'd heard the dog and known that it signalled someone's approach. At that time of night, in such a place, it was likely to be someone without a bed, a traveller, and a traveller was more likely to be a man than a woman.

No mystery here. Only an old woman and her tethered dog.

'You haven't answered me, stranger. Am I right? Do you want to hear your runes?' Her voice was soft and ancient. It crept into the ears like the insidious, demented whisperings of some lurking, perverted dwarf inciting acts of lust and murder. Yet it was gentle in its enquiry, almost discreet.

The veil didn't move, but somehow he knew that she had seen him. She knew how tall he was, and that he was travelling on foot. She knew that he was wrapped in a long, blue, fur-lined travelling cloak, pulled tight around him against the chillness of the night. Probably she couldn't see his features, for he stood with his back to what little light still burned from the settlement outside the palace walls, and he wore the hood of his travel-cloak up, almost shrouding his features in the same way that her veil of wadmal covered her own.

2

The dog was still watching him. It growled softly. He grinned at it where it lay, showing his own teeth, and it whimpered into silence.

'No, little mother,' he replied. 'I haven't come to hear my runes.'

She giggled beneath the veil. 'I thought not,' she said. 'You're one who knows your runes already. Well, then. The runes of another, perhaps?'

'Are you that skilled?' he asked her. The question was plainly asked, in a voice that betrayed no surprise that she might have such a skill, that she might be able to cast for one who was days, perhaps weeks, of travelling away.

'One who has tethered the mighty Garm, the Hound of Hel, has done many things, has many skills, traveller,' she told him.

He looked at the dog again. It was brindled brown, long-legged, with a box-shaped, heavy head. It had sufficient teeth and gape to its jaws to make the tearing off of a man's head the act of a single leap, yet it shifted uneasily beneath his stare, re-crossing its forepaws, trying to pretend unconcern by a force-born yawn.

The Hound of Hel?

'Is that truly what you've done,' he asked her. 'Is that Garm, tethered there, little mother? The Hound of Hel itself?'

She shrugged beneath the veil. 'And if it's not? Can you not allow an old woman her fantasies, stranger? There's so little left when you grow old, you know. Only dreams and memories.'

'And the runes?'

She sniggered. 'And the runes. Whose would you have me tell you?'

'Do you know the name of Hather Lambisson?'

'Hather of Sudrafell?' She paused, completely still. Then she nodded. At least, the veil of wadmal moved as if she were nodding beneath it. 'I know the name of Hather. Who doesn't? Who hasn't heard of the man who, in his youth, killed the one called Starkadder?'

3

The traveller nodded. 'Well then, old witch-wife, can you tell me his runes? Or is that beyond your skill?'

He felt her smile. The veil prevented him from seeing it, but he knew that she was smiling. Somewhere, he thought, I have seen that smile before.

'That depends,' she said, blandly.

'On what?'

'On who's asking me, for one thing.'

'And for another?'

'That depends upon the first.'

He returned her smile. 'Some call me Grim,' he said.

'Grim? That simply means *the hooded one*. I can see that from your cloak. You're going to have to do better than that before I tell you Hather's runes. Try again, traveller.'

'Very well, my name is Svipall.'

'And that means *the changeable one*. It's a good answer, for a second answer. Whoever taught you to play such games taught you very well. Now then, a third try. Tell me your name, before I tell you Hather's weird.' She paused, and he felt her eyes upon him through the veil. 'Well?' she demanded. 'I'm waiting for you.'

'I've told you the truth already,' he replied. 'Both times I've told you what I'm called by some. They also call me by many other names. What would you like next, little veiled mother? Harbard, perhaps, or Bileyg? They call me both, and many other things.'

She nodded. '*Greybeard* and *One-eye*. True, like the others. I knew you before you came to me, you know.'

He smiled again. 'I know. Now, will you tell me Hather Lambisson's weird?'

'You want a prophecy?'

'Not a prophecy. I simply want the truth before it turns into fact and history. That's all.'

'Is that not prophecy, sometimes-called Harbard?'

'Not at all, little mother. Prophecy is something that men get from sybils.'

'And are you not a man, Bileyg? And am I not a woman?'

4

The traveller said nothing. Around them the silence deepened. The night, unspeaking, drew closer to its end.

'Must you really have such answers, Mother Skuld?' Odin asked at length. 'I'm not a man. And a Norn could never simply be a woman. Not even a woman who was a prophetess. So it's not a prophecy I've come to you to have.'

'Where did you leave your wolves and ravens, Odin?' she demanded. 'You've hidden them well, this time. Are they close by?'

'Close by, Skuld. They're waiting for me.'

'Surely you know Hather Lambisson's weird already, Allfather? You have the power. I know you have the power.'

'I know what I've seen,' Odin replied. 'I always know what I've seen. But that isn't always everything there is to see. I know the power of your sisterhood, Mother Skuld. I know what you can do to what I see, to the future I descry. This time I'm asking you to let it be, to stay out of the future of this one man. That's all I want. Just this one time. Nothing more.'

Beneath her veil Skuld giggled once more. Then her laughter stopped and her voice became serious as she asked: 'Do you really fear my skills that much, Allfather?'

'Only when there's a chance you might employ them,' the god replied. 'And I can see your hand in the future of this one man. Didn't you do enough before? Is he to have no peace at all? Yes, he brought about the death of the one called Starkadder, and in doing so he lost a friend. Since then he's built himself a life once more. He's earned his happiness. Must you really take it from him?'

Her eyes were twinkling beneath the veil. 'I, Odin? Do you have no hand in this? Are you really so blameless of the shape of Hather's weird? Or do you simply seek to push the blame onto me before your own intentions happen, Allfather?'

'That isn't true!' he snapped. 'You know that isn't true.'

5

'But you're the one who isn't going to leave him in peace. Your precious Yngling dynasty will founder and be lost for ever if you don't disturb him. We both know that. King Omund's weak. If Starkadder had been allowed his way then Omund would never have been king at all. But you had to save your precious Ynglings. So, let it be. What will happen will happen. If Hather Lambisson of Sudrafell means so much to you, Odin, you save him.'

And you know you can't do that without my help, she thought, mischievously.

The one-eyed god turned away.

'Wait, now,' Mother Skuld called to him. 'Don't be impatient. It might be possible to keep the Ynglings on the throne a little longer. It might even be possible to preserve some little of Hather's hard-won happiness. After all, you knew he had the seeds of future greatness within him when you chose him to ride beside Starkadder for the last days of that hero's life. Didn't you, Odin?'

When he turned back to face her, there against the palace wall at Uppsala, Allfather was smiling beneath his hood.

'So, what do you propose?' he asked the Norn.

'A term of happiness and preparation,' she replied. 'Will fifteen years suffice? After all, he'd lived fifteen years before he met and killed Starkadder. You could say they were fifteen years of preparation. Well, let him have another fifteen. Then we'll play the game out, Odin. How does that sound to you? A compromise, Allfather. You were always good at compromises.'

He stared at her, trying to see through the veil once more. Eventually he gave up and looked across to where Garm was dozing into sleep, a little way away.

Slowly, deliberately, Odin walked across and planted his booted foot full in the Hel-hound's ribs. As Garm howled into wakefulness he stepped back, beyond the reach of the fetter which bound the dog. Garm stopped howling and began to snap at him, straining against his tether.

6

'A compromise, Mother Skuld,' Allfather grinned. 'That will serve quite well.

'For now,' he added, as he walked away.

She watched him go, walking down into the sleeping huts and houses of Uppsala. She knew, although his back was turned, that he was smirking, congratulating himself on the outcome of their encounter. She also knew that they hadn't seen the last of one another, that perhaps they never would.

And, after all, she hadn't promised him very much. Not very much at all.

She reached out a gnarled hand to fondle the fretting Garm's ears. 'You'd like to bite his heart out, wouldn't you, boy?' she asked. 'It mustn't be, though. It's not your weird to tear up Allfather. But perhaps we can manage something almost as good for one of your descendants.

'A taste of one of Odin's favourite mortals, Garm? Would that be nice, do you think?'

If it's possible for a dog to smile, then Garm smiled in that moment. He nuzzled his massive head against Mother Skuld's hand in an attitude which expressed both contentment and anticipation. His long, pink tongue, steaming slightly, flicked wetly about her fingers.

'We'll see about Hather of Sudrafell,' she comforted. 'We'll see what we can do for him in a few years' time. Did I agree with Allfather, Garm? Did I really say that Hather should have his fifteen years? Could I have been so foolish?'

She sighed. 'No matter. It's not for Odin to set terms with me. I think perhaps that I can cheat a little. We mustn't have you losing patience, Garm, must we? No. No, no, that would never do.'

The night turned into dawn. The dawn grew, strengthening from a sky-born eastern redness into the bright, strong herald of a fine spring day.

It shone with vibrant life. It woke the birds to song and flight and hunting for their food. It woke the city of Uppsala, clustered in hovels and halls about the wooden walls of Omund's palace, to trade and work and idleness

7

and love. Eventually, as the sun began to rise, dark shadows deepened long and rich upon the ground.

The first strong rays caressed the palace wall. Yet long before they touched it the Hound of Hel, together with the veiled old woman known as Mother Skuld, had vanished with the night.

The coming of the vargr

CHAPTER ONE

Looking for Tyrfing

THEIR EYES eyes shone, pale, smouldering reflections of the full moon glistening in the night-black sky above them. They shone yellow like a cat's, save for the dark slit of the pupil. That was wide, adapted to make the most of whatever light was available at any time.

Moonlight. Torchlight. Lamplight. The phosphorescent gleamings of their damp-bright underground world.

Never sunlight.

Occasionally one of them would break off his scrabbling and return to the entrance to the burrow, glancing warily towards the eastern horizon of the plain called Roliung, looking for those tell-tale streaks of roseate dawn. When they came, when the brightness in the east proclaimed the coming day, Thrudnir and Illugi would dig in and cover themselves, hiding away until their instincts told them that the sun had fallen in the west and night's safety was resumed once more.

'Still dark?' Illugi called from the depths of their excavation.

Thrudnir nodded, his clay-heavy hands hanging brown-stained by his sides, weighted by the earth clogged under his taloned fingers. 'Still dark,' he said, realising that his fellow dwarf was too deep into their digging to see his nod. 'Plenty of time yet.'

Illugi grunted. He was the older of the two and his hair, when clean, was ivory-white in token of his years, his centuries. Thrudnir, at approaching a hundred and thirty, was still a mere youth, his hair still glimmering with traces of that red which made younger dwarfs so fearsome to look at. Under their beards and thick thatches of matted hair their faces were sharp, almost starved, their noses hooked and their eyes bright in sunken sockets.

As he thrust his hands deep into the loam Illugi felt the talons on the thumb and index finger of his right hand bend with unexpected resistance. Leaving that hand where it was he withdrew his left and clawed away the earth around it, throwing handfuls behind himself, back into the tunnel they had created. Slowly, almost lovingly, his broad mouth drawn back in a smile which revealed his wolfish teeth, the talons of his left hand traced the outline of a broad, flat stone. Then another. And a third.

An inner wall of stones. Through that, and their mission would be completed.

'Thrudnir,' he hissed. 'Get in here, you lazy young crow! I'm through to the tomb lining.'

The younger dwarf ducked back into the tunnel and scampered eagerly towards his companion, his short legs permitting him to move on all fours like the burrowing creature he was.

Nearly done. Through the wall, then back to Trollheim.

Together they scraped away the earth, exposing more of the carefully-interlocked stones, working in a darkness which would have been almost total for humans but which passed for little more than twilight for dwarfish eyes. At no point in his digging did Thrudnir attempt to remove any of the stones. Illugi would say when they were to start that phase of the work. He was in charge of the job.

More and more of the wall was exposed, earth being clawed away and thrown behind them until it threatened to block the tunnel and prevent their escape from the grave-mound. Finally Illugi stopped digging and his younger companion followed his example. They sat together in the darkness, the only sound the labour of their breathing.

Through the wall and they were done.

Come on, Illugi, Thrudnir fumed to himself. Let's get on with it, you senile old dwarf. Whilst there's still enough dark to get back across the plain and into the tunnels in the hills. Get that first Frey-damned stone out!

Illugi turned his head and glared at him, almost as if the words had been spoken aloud. Then he nodded and reached out. His talons dug deep into the clay which mortared the stones together, levering and prising. The muscles in his short, powerful arms strained through the rents in the sleeves of his dirt-stained grey tunic.

With a slight scraping and a faint sucking of wet loam the first stone came away.

Thrudmir reached out for one of the adjoining stones, only to find Illugi's hand clamping onto his wrist in restraint. 'Supposing it isn't there?' Illugi demanded.

'It will be,' came the reply. 'It has to be. Come on, now. Let's get in there and take it, like King Alvis ordered us to.'

Illugi nodded and released his grip. Thrudnir tore the second stone away, permitting a slight trickle of wet gravel to spill from the aperture they were creating.

'A double skin,' Thrudnir muttered. 'Outer wall, gravel, inner wall. Hather Lambisson had this tomb built well.'

'He built it for a great man,' came the reply. 'Now shut your mouth, unless you're breathing through it. You're the one who's so eager to get on with this. Remember?'

They pulled away a third stone, a fourth, piling them against the cleared areas of wall to either side, sweeping the spilling gravel beneath their knees, clearing a hole which would give them access to the inner lining of the tomb-chamber. Like the outer, the inner wall was con- structed of interlocking stones. Unlike the outer, the clay mortaring the stones of the inner lining seemed to be solid and dry. Illugi strained through the aperture they had

13

created, but even his practised talons were unable to find a purchase that would permit sufficient leverage.

'Hand me one of those stones,' he ordered. 'A big one. If I can't pull this out, then I'll batter a way in.'

He struck once. Then again. Then a third time. The reverberation of stone against stone almost deafened them in the confined space of the tunnel.

Thrudnir wondered about a quip about waking the dead with all that noise. But, like Illugi, he was beginning to be a little afraid of what exactly they were going to find. Even the dwarfs could sometimes revere the mysteries of the chambered dead.

At the fifth blow Illugi's chosen stone fell inwards. Immediately the two dwarfs fell back, choking and gasping before the miasma of decay which issued from the tomb-chamber. Thrudnir, his eyes rolling, cast a desperate glance behind them to make certain that the tunnel wasn't blocked, giving the gases some means of escape. Illugi, older and more practised, though closer, held what breath remained in his lungs from before the breakthrough and raised a hand to his throat, massaging his windpipe against the choking pungency of the exhalation. As Thrudnir wiped at his streaming eyes, beginning to think that his reeling head would burst, together with his stinging lungs, the gases dissipated along the tunnel and out into the moonlit night beyond.

'You were right,' Illugi wheezed. 'Hather Lambisson built this tomb very carefully. The tomb-chamber must have been airtight.'

Together they forced sufficient stones out of the inner wall to allow them access. Illugi climbed in first. As Thrudnir joined him their pupils widened further, almost blacking out the yellows of their eyes completely.

Even for a dwarf's eyes the tomb-chamber was almost as dark as blackness.

Slowly they began to pick out details of their surroundings. The chamber was small, about eight feet long and a little over half as wide. Its roof would have been about five feet high at the apex of the rough stone vaulting, high enough to permit a dwarf to stand but too small for a man. Along the centre of the stone floor rested a handsomely-carved wooden bier, the side-members carved with dragon-heads at both ends. Upon the bier, still dressed in the black armour it had worn in life, the skull-mouth open in a mocking death-grin, rested a cadaver.

When they had placed him in the tomb they had taken time to lock his fingers together over the wound in his stomach. The contractions of decay had forced them apart in the darkness, giving the stretched-parchment hands the appearance of clawing at the slitted abdomen. The fabric of the clothing had rotted and fallen away, what fragments remained draping the sides of the bier with their tatters. Only the metal of the mail remained, together with some mouldering articles of leather.

'One of the two last mortals to enter Trollheim and leave alive,' Illugi muttered, his tones almost reverential. 'Hather Lambisson was the other.

'Look on him well, Thrudnir,' he continued. 'Cursed by the gods, mocked by the Norns, hated by his fellow men. Hather Lambisson was his friend, but Hather killed him. Hather Lambisson killed him in a duel before the fortress at Dalalven, but he raised this tomb above his one-time friend here on the plain of Roliung. You know, they say this warrior showed no fear, not even when he stood at night before our late king, Dvalin, on the balcony of the highest tower of the castle in the burning lake. They even say he forced a bargain from Dvalin, then tricked the king into keeping his word, though Dvalin was prepared to die to thwart him.

'He did all this.'

Thrudnir shuddered. Any being who could defy a dwarf-king was a creature to be afraid of, even in death. After all, it was their own fear of their king which had brought them here.

'Speak his name, Illugi,' Thrudnir said softly to the darkness. It was neither entreaty nor demand. Simply a manifestation of awe.

To do all this, and now to sit in Valhalla with Odin, the

15

Allfather, was almost beyond Thrudnir's conception and belief.

Illugi swallowed hard and made sure that his mouth wasn't too dry. Some names could be dangerous if you had them sticking in your throat.

'Starkadder.'

The name echoed gently about them. The cadaver on the bier grinned unmovingly on.

'This is why we had to come when the moon was full,' Illugi muttered. 'So that his ghost would remain quiet. If we'd been foolish enough to come when the *glimpses of the moon* were abroad, when the moon was new, his ghost might have risen and attacked us. And you know as well as I do that the only way to lay a human ghost is to wrestle it back into death. That takes time, and probably more strength than even we could muster between us.

'Now, let's find Tyrfing and get out of here.'

Thrudnir regarded his companion with renewed respect. Knowing everything that he did about the fearsome partnership which, albeit briefly, Starkadder and the sword Tyrfing had forged, a partnership which had brought King Oli of Sweden to bloody death in the waters of his bath, a partnership which had killed Hather's father, Lambi Nef, and ultimately brought about even Starkadder's looked-for death, Illugi could still speak both names aloud, here, in the old mercenary's tomb. That took courage of a kind Thrudnir doubted he himself possessed.

'What're you standing there dreaming for?' Illugi demanded. 'The night's passing. Do you want to be bottled up in here all tomorrow? Get on with it. Find that sword!'

His reverie broken, Thrudnir crossed to the cadaver and bent over the rotting leather scabbard. Then he looked up, his eyes wide with surprise.

'It . . . it's not there,' he mumbled.

Illugi mumbled a curse and pushed him aside. The scabbard was empty.

'Freya's tits!' he grunted. 'Well, it has to be in here somewhere. Everyone knows that Hather had Tyrfing

16

buried with Starkadder. Look in the grave-goods beneath the bier.'

Thrudnir got down onto his hands and knees. With eager, trembling fingers he thrust aside the pitchers and boxes, spilling the tangle of leprous white, shrivelled tendrils which had germinated in the darkness from an offering of grain, scattering gold, 'that yellow shit,' King Dvalin had called it, questing the dwarf-forged sword which Alvis had commanded them to bring back to Trollheim. In his desperate haste Thrudnir briefly recalled that night, hard weeks before, when King Alvis, Dvalin's successor, had summoned them up from the dungeons where they awaited sentence of death for raping a mortal woman captive their commander had kidnapped for himself. Not that they feared death, but dwarfs knew many ways to kill. Some, like the hideous ritual of the blood eagle, had found their way out into the world of men. Others, longer and more painful, some even lasting a month or more in the hands of a skilled executioner, could keep the victim babbling for a mercy that would never come until immitigable madness dulled the separate sensations into a constant, blinding, throbbing single hurt throughout the entire body. Or what remained of the body.

Alvis, tall for a dwarf at almost four and a half feet, sat hunched inside his voluminous robes, the purple silk giving his pallid features an even more unhealthy cast in the torchlight. His chained captives stood before him, Thrudnir with his head bowed, fighting the tremors of terror in his limbs, Illugi more erect, more defiant.

About them stood the guards, their weapons sharp and bright, the plumes of human hair on their helmets waving in the night breezes which wafted through the unglazed windows.

'Slow petrification, I think,' Alvis wheezed. His voice was never more than a whisper, little louder than the rustle of the silks that pampered him.

Thrudnir swallowed against the bile which threatened to rise in his gorge. Illugi's tongue probed the corners of his mouth for something to spit, but found it terror-dry.

17

'If you fail me,' King Alvis added.

As one, as if rehearsed, as if they didn't truly believe their own ears, the prisoners looked up, then at each other, then back towards the king.

'What . . . do we have to do?' Illugi asked uncertainly.

With a flick of the taloned, bejewelled little finger of his left hand Alvis indicated that their shackles should be removed. As they rubbed the sore, chafed bands about their wrists and ankles another flick brought finely-wrought goblets of wine before them.

Their king knew that he already had their unspoken agreement. Slow petrification, the controlled exposure of small areas of their bodies to the destructive power of sunlight, was the most hideous death any dwarf could face. The parts exposed turned to stone. The flesh around them suppurated and became intolerably painful. If knocked the petrified areas would snap away, eventually leaving shambling, then crawling, but carefully nurtured creatures that first lost the use of their limbs and finally, one by one, their senses. The petrification preventing them bleeding to death, leaving them at the last one open, gibbering, *knowing* sore.

Alvis licked his lips, then smiled. 'Listen to me carefully, if you want to save yourselves. You doubtless recall the sword Tyrfing, which was stolen from us by King Svafrlami of Skane. My predecessor, King Dvalin, cursed the weapon that it would always kill whoever owned it. And it did,' he grinned. 'Svafrlami died by his booty's edge. So did those who came after him. But when the sword came into the possession of Hather Lambisson of Sudrafell it was taken from him by his friend Starkadder and brought back here to Trollheim. Starkadder exacted a promise from King Dvalin that he would be the last person to be killed by Tyrfing. At the end Starkadder tricked the king into keeping his promise and the curse passed from the sword with Dvalin's death.

'Now, this is what I want you to do to save yourselves. Tyrfing was buried with Starkadder on the plain of Roliung. You are to leave Trollheim tomorrow night. All

18

sentinels will be informed that you are only to be allowed back if you have the sword Tyrfing in your possession. Whatever tunnels and caves exist beyond Trollheim you may use, but the sanctuary afforded by this place is denied to you until you bring me the sword. I don't mind how long it takes. My patience is almost beyond limit. But if you attempt to re-enter Trollheim without Tyrfing your original doom of slow petrification will not be deferred again. Do you understand me?'

They nodded and drank their wine. Then Illugi asked: 'Sir, if the curse has passed from Tyrfing, then why do you want it back?'

'Should not a dwarf-forged blade belong in Trollheim?'

'Yet it's three years since King Dvalin and Starkadder died. Why wasn't Tyrfing sent for before now?'

'What is my name, Illugi?' the dwarf-king asked.

'Al . . . Alvis, sir.'

'Good. And what does it mean in the Norse tongue?'

Illugi thought for a moment. 'All-knowing,' he replied.

Alvis nodded. 'Very nearly right. A literal translation would be *all-wise*. Does that answer your question?'

He wanted to shake his head, to tell the king that he didn't understand at all, but such prevarication could be dangerous. Instead he held his tongue and made the most of his new-found liberty.

That was how he and Thrudnir came to be here now, grubbing about in the darkness like grave-worms for a dwarf-forged blade called Tyrfing.

Which wasn't there.

'It must be,' Illugi growled.

'It isn't. See for yourself,' Thrudnir snapped in reply. 'There's no sword under here.'

'Very well. Then there's only one place left it can be. Lift him up.'

Thrudnir felt his eyes bulging. Looking at Starkadder's cadaver was one thing. Actually touching it, let alone lifting it off the bier so that Illugi could look underneath, was a different matter altogether.

'Go on. Get on with it. We haven't got all night.'

19

Swallowing hard Thrudnir slid his arms beneath the withered husk. For a moment he thought Starkadder was going to snap like a dry twig beneath the weight of his armour, but the remains of the skin had stretched over the bones and hardened to the consistency of leather, leaving the cadaver light but surprisingly strong. With an effort more of will than of muscle he held the body clear of the bier on a level with his face.

'All right,' Illugi said dejectedly. 'Put him down again.'

As Thrudnir returned Starkadder to the bier he looked across at his companion. Illugi's hands were empty.

'Then . . . where is it?' he asked incredulously.

'Thor's prick, you idiot! How the Hel should I know? I doubt if even our *all-wise* king can answer that one!'

'But . . . but . . .'

'You sound like an old billy-goat. But, but, but, but! I know what you're going to ask me. But what do we do now? Right? We keep on looking. That's what we do now. We look anywhere and everywhere. Norway, Sweden, the Dane-Lands, Frankheim, everywhere. We wait. We listen. We search.

'And above all, whatever else we do, Thrudnir, even if it takes us centuries, we don't go back to Trollheim without Tyrfing!'

CHAPTER TWO

Goodbye to Sudrafell

'YOU . . . KNOW leechcraft and the power of potions . . .'

White-haired and brown-eyed, wrinkled into an age that should have been fragile and pitiful, but which somehow lent her strength and dignity, Old Tisti studied the wary silhouette framed against the open doorway of her hut.

She smiled and slowly bowed her head. 'I know these things, little mistress,' she replied. 'And so perhaps will you, one day. For now though, little Astrid, you have a need, a deep need. I know it already. I saw it today, upon the beach. I saw it in the lapping of the waves against a prow. I heard it in the shrieking of the sea-birds about a sky-stabbing mast. I heard it in the slash of oar-blades in the water as a ship went past.

'I can help you, little one. Only Old Tisti can help you.'

Her visitor exhaled, its sound somewhere between the catch of laughter and a sigh. 'I . . . need something . . . to bring on sleep, Tisti,' Astrid said. 'Can you . . . really help me?'

'You shall have it by nightfall, little Astrid. By the time it grows dark it will be ready, Hather's wife. Come to me for it then, Svipdag's mother.'

Astrid exhaled again, more heavily. Only then did she realise that she'd been holding her breath all the time the old Lapp had been speaking.

21

'Thank you,' she said, her voice heavy with relief. 'Thank you, Tisti.'

She turned away, out of the doorway, and was gone.

It isn't working, Tisti thought to herself. Little Hather will be crying for her soon. That's one of the curses of mortality. We are, at so many different times, with so many different people, so many different things.

She blames him for a revenge he couldn't take. She wants to visit Oli's sins upon his son, but my Hather cannot do that.

If they part, they part.

Hather Lambisson had wedded Astrid, Thorstein's-daughter, a little over three years before. The marriage had taken place as soon as the period of mourning following his father's, and Starkadder's, obsequies permitted. With Lambi Nef's death Hather had inherited the estates at Sudrafell and become a wealthy chieftain in his own right. Though still a few months under twenty he managed his property well, helped and advised by his father's steward, Thorkel Tongue. His mother Hervara had survived in her madness long enough to see, but not understand, the birth of Astrid and Hather's son, Svipdag. Yet her mourning for the dead Lambi Nef brought on a species of insanity which never left her, and she had finally been laid in her grave-mound some three days after Svipdag's head-sprinkling. That was a year before.

Astrid and Hather were about the same age and came from similar backgrounds. Both were the children of retainers of King Oli of Sweden. But whilst Lambi Nef had plotted successfully against the king, Thorstein of Nerike had been betrayed and suffered death by the blood eagle. Astrid had been forced to watch before finally being dispossessed and cast to the mercy of an uncertain world. Hather and Starkadder had discovered her in bondage to a blacksmith shortly before the fateful events at Dalalven, which had resulted in the deaths of Lambi Nef, King Oli, and Starkadder himself. Even at that first meeting Hather and Astrid had felt the tugging of something approaching love, a tugging which ensured

22

beyond question that they would one day marry. And they had.

And they had been in love. Deeply so.

But it was dying.

Early shadows were beginning to mar Astrid's slender beauty. Her dark, rich hair now hung in rats-tails when she released it from her braids. In their caresses it whipped at Hather's face instead of floating against it as it had done. Her eyes, once bright and the colour of nightshade berries, a brown so deep that it was almost purple, were ringed with tiredness and red with secret tears.

For the first two years they had been as happy as any couple known to the watching eyes of the world. Their love had grown and strengthened, surviving its first youthful rush into a mature and stable relationship in which each delighted equally. They rejoiced in little Svipdag's conception, greeting his growth within Astrid with daily rituals of tender vigil and wonder at first kicks and movements. Old Tisti, once Hather's nurse, had taken charge of the welfare of both mother and unborn child, massaging Astrid's belly and buttocks with scented oils to smooth her skin, easing off unwanted milk in the later stages, and finally supervising a labour which, beneath her ministrations, was both short and relatively painless.

The baby was perfect. A strong, healthy boy. His hair dark like his mother's, his eyes the ice-blue of his father Hather. Two young lovers and a healthy baby. A family that could grow and endure. Wealth aplenty to cushion them from the harsher realities of the world.

Then it began.

It was almost as if the death of Hervara, Hather's mother, signalled the destruction of their happiness. Against her better judgement Old Tisti relented to Astrid's pleading and found a wet-nurse for the baby. Sometimes a day would pass without Astrid seeing the child. Longer if the nurse or Tisti didn't make a deliberate effort to bring mother and child together, if only for a few precious moments.

'You must talk to her, little Hather,' Tisti said sternly. 'You are the master. Besides, little Svipdag's your son as well as hers. Talk to her. She must see more of him. They're growing apart and, what's worse, Astrid's growing into herself.

'Talk to her.'

And so he did. He went in to her, deliberately, and asked her what was the matter. Nothing was, she told him. Leave me alone. I'm all right. I'm happy. I love you. Now leave me be.

But something was the matter and they both knew it. Their love was failing, and Astrid never mentioned her son. After several weeks had elapsed Hather tried to make love to his wife again.

She lay in their bed-closet, breathing in sighs, staring wide-eyed at the roof-beams.

'Make her drunk.'

He did as Tisti told him. She prepared an infusion of hemp which he slipped into her wine. She drank it all. Then she told him.

'You don't love me,' she said calmly, though the wine and the drug it carried must have been coursing through her veins like liquid fire.

'That's nonsense,' Hather replied gently. 'I love you more than I love anyone. You're my wife. You're everything to me.'

She turned eyes on him that were more alive than he had seen them for months, but they were alive with the fire of anger, not with love.

'If you loved me my father wouldn't lie in his grave-mound unavenged.'

Hather felt his mouth hang open. King Oli had killed Thorstein of Nerike, and Starkadder had killed King Oli in his bath. He'd been there. He'd seen the sword Tyrfing flashing as it plunged again and again into Oli's twitching body. Up. Down. Up. Down. Murderous.

'Listen to me, my love,' he began, reaching out to stroke her hair. 'Oli killed your father. Oli's dead. Starkadder killed him.'

She pulled away from his touch. 'Oli might be dead, but there's still an Yngling on the throne. His son Omund's

24

succeeded him. You know that. You helped to put him there.'

'Are the actions of one man reason to destroy an entire family?' Hather asked. 'Oli was mad. If we hadn't killed him he'd have killed Omund as well as Starkadder and myself. He was mad, my love. He wasn't responsible for what he did. Would you have me wipe out the entire Yngling dynasty because of him? A dynasty they say was founded by Odin himself? I can't do it. I *won't* do it. Omund's ruling well. He started weak and young, but he had good people around him, men like Thorvald Brotamad and Vermund Bjarnisson.'

'Men who stood around and watched whilst Oli had my father killed.'

'There was nothing they could do. Too many were afraid of him. Even I would have been afraid of him. I was. Right up to the moment when Starkadder killed him. He wanted us all dead. He was going to kill me as well, but I doubt if I could have done what Starkadder did. Not even to save my own life.'

Astrid made no reply. She smiled faintly, then the force of the drug took hold and the fire began to sing songs in her ears. For a little while, as the drug was working on her, it didn't matter any more. She closed her eyes and kissed Hather gently. Her hand reached out for his and she led him to their bed-closet.

It was the last time they made love.

Throughout the following months Hather frequently despaired, but he never gave up hope completely. Some day, somehow, things would be once more as they had been in the beginning. They had to be.

They slept badly together and finally agreed to sleep apart. Even so, neither slept well and Tisti wouldn't have been surprised if either had asked her for something to ease their sleeplessness long before Astrid came to her hut that afternoon.

All in all it was to be a day she would remember to her death.

About mid-morning the look-outs on the point had sent

25

a message that a ship was approaching their little harbour. Hather and Astrid, together with Thorkel Tongue and Old Tisti, had ridden down to see if it would dock. The vessel, however, a twelve-oared knorr, remained in deep water, standing off with the oars raised. A single figure, its skin seemingly as dark as the brown robes it wore, stood in the prow. Hather considered the possibility that it was a Christian missionary, perhaps even the one he had met at Dalalven, the Englishman called Brother Gerard, but the absence of any kind of cross on the figure's breast led him to reject the supposition.

He looked at Astrid. She was smiling slightly for the first time in weeks. His gaze lingered there for some moments, then travelled on to Thorkel Tongue's puzzled visage, and finally to Tisti.

There were tears in the old woman's eyes.

For several moments the vessel stood off, then as if by some unspoken command the oars were lowered and the knorr, its square sail furled at the masthead, back-watered and turned off along the coast. At the last moment the dark figure in the prow waved to them. Without understanding Hather and Thorkel Tongue waved back.

So did Astrid.

So did Old Tisti.

When Astrid came back to the hut, at the appointed time, for the sleeping draught, Old Tisti handed it to her with a sad smile.

'Will the stars go out tonight, little Astrid?' she asked.

Hather still ate his meals with his wife, though her own appetite had faded dramatically and her clothes hung from a frame that was old before its time. Occasionally they forced a few words to pass between them, and once that evening Astrid filled a cup for her husband and handed it to him. Their fingers touched and, for once, she didn't pull away. Afterwards, for the first time Hather could remember in months, she went and bade their year-old son good-night.

Yawning, suddenly weary, Hather took himself off to his solitary bed. In her own bed-closet Astrid undressed and sat listening to the noises of the night, to the singing of night-birds and the creaking of beams and timbers within the stockade at Sudrafell. She had known for some time what she had to do. Now all that remained was for her to do it.

The fires burned out and the torches were extinguished. The household retired for the night. In the morning Hather would sleep late and probably awake thick-headed. It wouldn't take him long to realise that the draught Tisti had prepared for Astrid had found its way into his own drink. By then, though, it would be too late.

There were no sentries on the stockade gates. Sweden was at peace, still basking in the peace which, paradoxically, Oli's madness had forged for it to enjoy. She passed through them, naked and alone, and made her lonely path down to the beach.

The surf was washing gently at the shoreline. Here, a little over three years before, Hervara had given her son Hather a birthday present. Its wrapping of Byzantine silk had flapped unnoticed up the sands as the young Hather held and admired the proud sword, the famous sword, Tyrfing, for the first time.

Astrid turned and looked back as the water washed her feet. On the hill above the shore the bulk of Sudrafell's stockade stood out against the starry sky.

'Good-bye,' she whispered. That was all she said.

She waded in as far as she could. When the water began to lap about her breasts she launched herself forward and started swimming. Her wet hair slapped her face with every stroke.

The water was becoming surprisingly cold.

She swam on, oblivious of all save the water beneath and the stars above. Her muscles ached. Her arms grew heavy, as if they had been weighted down with lead. Her breaths came in panting gasps, taking in almost as much water as air with each mouthful.

For a moment she turned and looked back, treading water. The shore was so far away now. Too far to swim back, even if she wanted to.

With a supreme effort Astrid continued swimming, each stroke lancing sharp agony through her weary joints, bringing her ever closer to the total oblivion of death by drowning.

As she faltered in mid-stroke, as her feet began to sink down beneath her, Old Tisti's words came true.

As if some giant bulk had been interposed between Astrid and the heavens, the stars went out.

CHAPTER THREE

The massacre at
Raven's Point

IT WAS the gulls, wheeling and screaming above the cliffs,
diving and plunging and feasting with unholy glee, that
first told Atyl Skin he might find the answer he sought
around the next headland.

Not right, though. Even if it was the answer it could
only be a part of the truth. It was in the wrong place.

He cupped his hands to his mouth and called back along
the knorr to where the captain was standing with the
steersman. 'Pull her close in around the next headland,' he
ordered.

The captain shrugged and nodded to the steersman.
Their vessel had been built for trade and, indeed, it carried
a cargo of wool wrapped in oiled bales amidships. Even
so, the crew were picked fighters and, unlike that of a true
merchantman, they had orders to abandon the cargo at the
first sign of it impeding their progress. Wool was cheap
and plentiful in Danish warehouses, and Atyl Skin's orders
from Jelling made it perfectly clear that their mission was
far more important than worrying about a little trade to
cover their activities.

With the practised gait of an experienced seaman the
captain left the steersman and made his way forward.

Whilst this stranger in the prow bore no military rank he carried a short runestaff commanding obedience to his orders in the name of their king.

'You think this is it, Master Atyl?' he asked when he drew close enough not to have to shout.

Atyl Skin drew his cape closer against the wind which skimmed the peaking of the waves. Spindrift clung to his hair from the knorr's progress across the waters and droplets hung from his shaggy eyebrows. Beneath them his grey eyes were bright and intelligent, set in a face tanned by the better part of forty summers. There were deep laugh-lines around the eyes and mouth and his nose jutted high like an eagle's neb. His beard was the same yellow-blond as his hair, and his upper lip was carefully scraped bare of moustache by a wickedly-sharp bronze razor at his belt.

For the most part he was handsome. Only a scar dragging down the outer corner of his right eye marred his features.

'It shouldn't be what we're looking for,' he replied. 'We're off north-east Skane by my reckoning. The *Bright Eagle* should be west of here, somewhere on her course towards Oslofjord. Still, maybe it's another ship altogether.'

But it won't be, he thought. It's the *Bright Eagle* all right. It has to be a large vessel to keep that many gulls happy for three weeks on human carrion.

'There!' called the look-out perched at the mast-head.

They looked up to him, then back, following the line of his pointing finger. Above the lapping waves, partially hidden by the rocky headland they were approaching, jutted the dragon-headed prow of a Danish longship. Some little distance away, fire-charred, black against the grey-blue of the water, the mast stabbed skywards like a broken javelin in a sea-clad fist.

'As close as you can, now,' Atyl Skin called to the steersman.

A gentle pressure on the steerboard and a few more powerful oar-strokes brought the knorr almost alongside.

30

Atyl Skin and the captain exchanged glances. Neither was smiling.

'Look at the dragon's head,' Atyl said, trying to keep emotion out of his voice. 'I don't think there's much doubt about that. Do you?'

The captain shook his head. 'That's the *Bright Eagle* all right. And there, on the beach.'

'Feeding the gulls.' Atyl spat. 'Can you get in close enough to land?'

'I think so. Clear the wreck, then helm hard around,' the captain called aft. 'Ship oars. We'll drift in.'

The crew obeyed him with professional precision. As the knorr cleared the sunken stern of the *Bright Eagle* it twisted into the little bay beyond the headland.

'Do you know this place, captain?' Atyl Skin asked.

'I've sailed this way once or twice. That headland's called Raven's Point.'

'Still in Skane?'

'It is. This is Danish territory for some miles up the coast yet.'

It didn't make any sense. There was the *Bright Eagle*, fire-scuttled in Danish waters. Beyond it, on the shore, even the weakest eyes aboard the knorr could now make out the decomposing, gull-scavenged bodies of the long-ship's crew. The breeze blowing along the beach carried occasional foul gusts to the approaching sailors' nostrils.

The knorr beached and ran out a boarding plank. Abandoning his position in the prow Atyl Skin mounted the gunwale and half-ran down the length of springy timber. Splashing through the last few feet of shallow water he crunched onto the sandy shore and moved straight over to the nearest corpse. Behind him the captain and two of his crew followed closely.

They were battle-hardened men, used to scenes of carnage and destruction. Atyl Skin himself, so named from the Lappish coat he wore under his travelling cloak, a tight-fitting jacket of whalebone plates sandwiched between a tough outer leather and a softer leather lining, was one of King Gorm of the Dane-Lands' most competent and valued agents, equally at home in the professions of trade, bribery and assassination. Yet this was a scene of such magnitude as to churn even their stomachs with a confusion of emotions and revulsion.

They moved from one corpse to another, sometimes uttering a cry as some feature or token of the gulls' leavings identified a friend or former comrade. Most of the flesh was gone from the bones, and in almost every case the soft, accessible jelly of the eyes had been stolen as a preferred morsel. What remained was blackened by decay, contrasting strongly with the matted, sun-bleached hair which straggled into the sand from bone-ivory brows. Beneath the bodies the sand was discoloured, mixed with blood and other fluids, baked into unholy cakes by the vanished heat of a past autumnal sun.

The captain knelt beside a twisted corpse, turning the amulet which had hung about its neck in his fingers.

'Did you know him?' Atyl asked gently.

The seaman looked up with tear-bright eyes. 'My nephew,' he replied in a harsh whisper.

Atyl Skin squatted beside him and studied the body. The position of the head, twisted unnaturally back, was similar to many of the others. The open mouth of the gristled skull grinned upwards, its fleshy parts long since torn away to feed the carrion scavengers. Beneath it the neck was arched, its vertebra showing through the remaining flesh.

'His throat was cut.'

The captain looked at Atyl Skin with questioning eyes.

'The muscles at the front were cut through,' he explained. 'When death's stiffness set in the remaining ones contracted at the back, pulling the head up and bending the neck like that. For the most part the rest were killed that way as well.

'Listen to me, captain,' Atyl continued, standing up. 'Your work is over now. We've found the *Bright Eagle* and we know what's happened to its crew. All that remains for you is to bury the bodies and return to Jelling. The king's going to want a full report on this. The *Bright Eagle*

32

was carrying arms and gold to support a rebel faction in Oslofjord. It seemed an easy way of extending our mainland territories to the north-west.'

'Is that it? We just bury them and turn around and sail back?'

'You do, yes. My job isn't going to be that simple. I've got to try and make some sense out of all this. There are several things that don't fit together in this puzzle. For instance, when the *Bright Eagle* sailed from Hedeby she should have kept the Danish coast on her left to make course for Oslofjord. She didn't. She sailed east through the islands instead of north. No seaman makes a basic error like that and the crew of a thirty-oared longship is usually selected from the best available men. After all, we're talking about a mission for the king, not just a simple little private enterprise. That's one thing.

'Another is that the attack on the *Bright Eagle* must have come from landward. There's no room to anchor two longships in this bay, and a little knorr like ours couldn't have held enough men to work this butchery. Now, we're still in Danish territory, on the coast of Skane. The border with Sweden, established by Oli the Great some fifteen, sixteen years ago, and it must be about that because his son Omund's been on the throne for about thirteen years now, is almost a half-day's ride north of here. So, we have a choice. Either these men were killed by Danish rebels, or else the Swedes have made a particularly lethal incursion into Danish territory. Either way it's something that King Gorm's going to want to act upon.

'I expect you noticed that the arms and gold the *Bright Eagle* was carrying are nowhere about. Chances are they were the object of the raid. Now, I'd have thought that there'd be enough there without the killers needing to strip weapons from the dead as well. But look around you. The only weapons on this beach are broken. They took coin, they took weapons, they took armour.'

'Pirates, perhaps?'

'Setting a land ambush for a ship which should have been sailing in the opposite direction? Leaving items like

33

that Thor-hammer amulet around your nephew's neck? Pirates would have ripped that off before cutting his throat, not left it there.'

The captain thought for a moment, then nodded and stood up. 'Get the rest of the men ashore except for sentries,' he called. 'We'll bury what's left of our countrymen.'

He turned to Atyl Skin. 'What will you do?' he asked.

The Dane shrugged. 'There must be some sign left for me to follow. The worst of the winter hasn't set in yet, and the number of men it took to do this can hardly move without leaving any traces. To begin with I'll move inland and see if I can buy a horse. Then I'll find the killers' trail and follow it, wherever it goes. If they're rebels, I'll try to raise forces locally to deal with them. If they're Swedes, then it may mean war. Either way you can tell the king I'll get a message back to him.'

'Good luck to you, Atyl Skin. I'll make sure King Gorm knows what you're doing, and what's happened here.'

They clasped wrists. Then Atyl left the captain and his crew to bury the dead and raise a mound of protective stones over their remains. He found quite a reasonable path up the cliffs, a fact which tended to reinforce his theory that the attack had been mounted from landward. On the top he paused and looked down towards the activity on the beach. One or two of the dead were people he recognised as old friends, but it wasn't his place to mourn over them there as the captain would mourn over his nephew. There would be time enough for that afterwards, once he'd found the killers and ensured a swift and punitive vengeance.

Later that day he found a small farmstead and paid well over its value for a mount. He questioned the farmer and his wife about the massacre at Raven's Point, but if they knew anything they were unwilling to pass it on. Returning to the cliffs he explored the area around the path, checking it from several angles until he found a place where the grass wasn't lying properly beneath the wind from the sea. Dismounting he pulled tufts aside, examining the individual blades for breaks and tears, feeling the ground beneath for the impressions of horses' hoofs. Until he reached the plains to the north it was likely to be a long, difficult trail to follow.

The trail was there, though.

To unskilled eyes it would have been invisible, but Atyl Skin was an expert in such matters. He had to be. His life had depended upon such skills as these so many times before. Yet even Atyl Skin, diplomat, hunter, soldier and assassin, had never faced a force as formidable as that which awaited him in the terrifying days to come.

Days when Denmark and Sweden would stand upon the very brink of war.

CHAPTER FOUR

The man who didn't kill Starkadder

HE LOOKED at the messenger, noting the man's laboured breathing and the glistening sweat-tracks streaking the dust which clung to his features. Outside the hall Thorkel Tongue, now more a supervisor than a fully-working steward, was finding servants to prepare somewhere for the messenger to sleep and to stable his lathered horse.

In the light from the long fire, in the flames which flickered in their cressets about the wooden walls, he examined the object which the messenger had handed to him. It was a piece of carved birch, cut to the shape of a small sword and bearing two words in runes.

The first word was *eda*, return. The second, though it had no style preceding it, was the name of the king, the name of Omund Olisson, King of Sweden.

Hather's fingers felt the smooth finish of the wood. The little wooden sword had become darkened and polished through years of use, years of passing from hand to hand, of travelling in leather pouches or tucked inside tunics against the sweaty chests of those who carried it. Such

36

objects served two purposes, one wartime, the other in times of peace. In war they were used as safe-conduct tokens for those who had messages to carry between the opposing camps. In peacetime they constituted a royal summons to whoever received them. Here, in Hather's hall at Sudrafell, its meaning was clear and unambiguous.

King Omund wanted him.

'How soon does the king want me at Uppsala?' Hather asked.

'He set no time or date, sir,' the messenger replied. 'He asks that you return the token to him as soon as you may find it convenient to do so. That's all.'

The Master of Sudrafell nodded. 'Does King Omund give any indication of the reason for this summons?'

'No reason that he saw fit to tell me.'

'Then I'll have to bide my curiosity until I arrive in Uppsala,' Hather smiled. 'Very well. My men are preparing somewhere for you to sleep tonight. And we'll feed you well after your journey, naturally. When you return you may tell King Omund that I shall be with him inside a week.'

The messenger bowed and withdrew. Hather, alone in the hall, continued to turn the token in his fingers, but his eyes were upon the long fire burning in its pit down the centre of the hall, and his thoughts were in other times and other places.

He was twenty-eight. His hair was straw-blond, framing features that were slightly too dark for it, even though the suns of all those summers would have tanned it brown. His eyes were a cold, piercing ice-blue and beneath his nose, a nose slightly too large for the rest of his face, a full, thick moustache and beard swept down onto his chest.

The eyes were crumpled into slits against the brightness of the fire. The mouth was set to begin with, but as his thoughts progressed the lips parted slightly and began to tremble. His was a past he often thought of, a past that was known to many others besides himself. Once more he stood upon the plain before the fortress of Dalalven, north of Uppsala, on the banks of the river whose name it bore.

37

Once again it was dawn on a day some thirteen years before. He was fighting then, as he had done some few times since, for his very life.

He was fighting a man called Starkadder.

King Omund's father, Oli the Great, stark mad and diseased, had been killed by the old Norwegian mercenary that Hather was facing. They had been friends. They had ridden together, the old killer and the fifteen-year-old Hather Lambisson. They had freed the young Omund from the imprisonment to which his mad father had confined him. Hather had helped Starkadder to bring about King Oli's death. Unfortunately, in the berserk rage brought on for Oli's murder, Starkadder had also killed Lambi Nef, Hather's father, creating a blood-feud between the youth and his ancient comrade.

So they fought together in the dawn, before the fortress of Dalalven.

Despite the disparity in their ages the match had not been too uneven. Starkadder was using the dwarf-forged sword Tyrfing, but Hather had knocked it from his hands, sending the blade up, up into the air, up high above them.

Tyrfing fell.

They looked up, following its descent. With a sudden, sick feeling Hather Lambisson knew where Tyrfing was going to land, whose flesh it was going to impale in its descent.

His own.

The others, standing in a semi-circle watching that duel, had known as well. Brother Gerard, the Christian missionary from England, Dalalven's commander, Askel Horsetail, Oli's marshal Vermund Bjarnisson, the mercenary captain Thorvald Brotamad, Hather's mother, his old nurse, Thorkel Tongue and the others, the soldiers and servants and . . . poor, vanished Astrid, now ten years gone. All of them had known where Tyrfing would strike. flesh.

And Starkadder had known.

In a sudden, unexpected remembrance of the love that he and Hather had once borne for one another Starkadder pushed forwards. Hather's sword transfixed his stomach in the same moment that he pushed the youth back, away from Tyrfing's falling path, exposing himself to the descending weapon's point.

Tyrfing struck his open mouth, passed through his lower jaw, out at the throat, then re-entered behind the rib-cage, crossing Hather's own sword, now released by the youth, in the old mercenary's body.

'And still they call me the man who killed Starkadder,' Hather whispered to the fire. 'I didn't kill him. No one killed him. It was Tyrfing which killed Starkadder.'

So it happened. Starkadder fell dead upon the plain before Dalalven. Hather had his body carried to Roliung and interred with the sword Tyrfing. He raised a mound above the fallen mercenary, a man who had been to Hather Lambisson almost a father and always, even at the moment of his death, a friend.

Then he returned to Sudrafell.

The years passed on about him. His mother, Hervara, died at the early age of thirty-three some three years later. He opened his father's mound before the gates of Sudrafell and buried Hervara there, beside her husband, his father, Lambi Nef. He had runestones carved and set up to honour them upon the mound.

His love for his wife, Astrid, was doomed to fade and die. They married and she bore him a son, Svipdag, now ten years old and Hather's greatest pride. Yet Astrid couldn't forget the part the Yngling dynasty had played in her early life. She urged Hather to exact a terrible vengeance upon King Omund, a vengeance which Hather knew to be both unreasonable and unjust. All that they found of her after she'd vanished were her footprints upon the beach, leading out into the Baltic Sea.

He married again. Hather was a chieftain in his own right. His father, Lambi Nef, had been one of King Oli's chief retainers and their estates at Sudrafell were extensive. Hather was a rich man. He might have been a powerful man in the kingdom if he'd chosen to be, but he stayed away from the court unless he was summoned, as he was now. He raised levies for military service and fought himself, showing himself to be a brave, though not reckless, champion. Yet always in his heart he wondered if Omund resented the part he had played in his father's death. Whilst Oli was mad, whilst Oli had threatened Omund's life and would have had him executed if Starkadder hadn't murdered him, Hather could never be sure of Omund.

Kings were strange animals. They had power, and power had a way of corrupting those who wielded it. Power could go beyond reason, as it had eventually done with King Oli.

So Hather stayed away from the court. Except when Omund summoned him. And Omund summoned him now.

He stood up, leaving the little wooden sword upon the trestle table before him. He had a good life, a quiet life. He was well-liked at Sudrafell and tried to be a good master to his people. After the violence and adventure of his early years all he wanted was peace, to be left alone to be his own man. For someone who had helped to save King Omund's life and set him upon the throne it didn't seem a great deal to ask.

Even if he hadn't killed Starkadder.

Yet still the myth persisted. They had seen his weapon enter Starkadder's body before Tyrfing struck. They vowed that the old Norwegian mercenary had died then, that Tyrfing buried itself in someone who was already a corpse. They didn't know, as Hather knew, that Tyrfing was the only weapon which could have killed Starkadder, that Hather's own blade wasn't even felt. And so they came from time to time, banging upon the gates of Sudrafell, the young and not-so-young, looking for the man who had killed Starkadder, looking to enhance their own reputations by taking revenge for a man they hadn't even known. Starkadder had no living kin, but that didn't stop them. Pretend cousins, brothers, sons both bastard and legitimate, sought Hather out and claimed a blood-feud. Mostly he disarmed those he couldn't talk out of their folly. Some lost an arm, a hand, a finger or so. Others, the better ones, the more persistent ones, he had to kill. Five mounds, smaller than his father's and unmarked, stood before Sundrafell's gates, mute testimony to the fools who wouldn't listen.

All he wanted was to be his own man, to be at peace. Was it so much to ask?

He walked out of the hall, through the vestibule which guarded its entrance from the elements, and out into the evening. The messenger was already quartered for the night and Thorkel Tongue, his father's steward before his own, was standing beside the open gates, looking out to where the twin runestones stuck up like fangs from his parents' mound against the night-grey of the distant sea.

The old man didn't turn as Hather approached. He simply asked: 'When will you be leaving, little master?'

The term was a misnomer. Hather stood very nearly six feet tall. In his youth, before Starkadder's death, he had resented being called 'little'. Now, with maturity and the surety of manhood, he allowed his two oldest servants, both friends, to use it to him. Thorkel Tongue was one of them. The other, Old Tisti, his strangely knowing childhood nurse, was the other.

'Probably the day after tomorrow,' Hather replied. He paused, standing beside the old steward who was almost as tall as he was himself. Thorkel Tongue had been grey-haired in Hather's youth. His hair and beard were now the pure white of deep-lain winter snow and a crippling disease had left him lame in one leg. The only duties he still retained in full were those of priest to the family temple, an office he had shared with Hather's father whilst Lambi Nef had been alive.

'I don't want to go, Thorkel,' Hather admitted. 'I don't like the feel of this summons. There's something not quite right about it. Besides,' he added, 'I don't like leaving Old Tisti at this time. Is she any better tonight?'

Thorkel Tongue shook his white hair. 'I've followed her instructions about how to treat her, and I've made sure that the fire's well-tended in her hut. But she's not good, Hather.' He shrugged. 'Probably she'll be dead before you

41

have to go. She can't last much longer. The fever's taken hold of her. I can't understand what she's trying to tell me any more. Do you want to see her?'

Hather tugged at his beard half-heartedly. Then he nodded.

Tisti's death was both inevitable and expected. She had already been old when first she appeared, brown and wrinkled, bearing in her colouring the unmistakable taint of Lappish blood, to take charge of him after Hervara had given him birth. Since then she had been confidante, friend and prophetess, reading the runes for Hather each year upon his birthday, guiding his steps and actions by her hints and intimations, slowly but certainly playing her part in moulding him towards a fine, befitting adulthood. Even before Hervara's death Old Tisti had been more like Hather's mother than Hervara had. Now, though old, almost blind, wrinkled beyond the count of seeking fingers, she still guided him, still counselled his actions, even as she had done in the childish days before Starkadder's dying. Possibly she alone of those watchers on the plain before the fortress of Dalalven had known the truth of Starkadder's death, for it was Old Tisti who had warned Hather of the sword Tyrfing's power, of the way it might be directed by the dwarfs to betray those mortals rash enough to seek to use it.

That was why Hather had buried the fine, gold-hilted weapon with the old mercenary at Roliung. Tyrfing was a sword with power and, like most things with power, it wasn't a sword that could be trusted.

Starkadder had known that. Starkadder had saved him with such knowledge.

Thorkel Tongue placed a thin arm about Hather's shoulders and walked with him towards the circular wooden hut near the centre of the compound. It was built in the same shape as the temple Thorkel tended, but with a smoke-hole at the apex of its hide-covered roof, unlike the thatch, turf and wooden shingles which roofed the other buildings on the Sudrafell estate. Its rough-plank door opened outwards upon plaited leather hinges, hinges that

42

held it tight and made it grate against the frame in dry weather, yet left it sagging and crooked in the damp when the leather stretched. Hather had offered to replace those hinges many times, to fit new ones of cast bronze that would keep the old woman's dwelling secure and warm whatever the weather, but each time he had offered she had refused him.

'That's how we make hinges where I come from, little Hather,' she would say. 'That's how hinges are made in my homeland. What need have I to give them up for new wonders? Should I abandon my gods and runes as well?'

He didn't entirely understand her questions. There were many things about Old Tisti that Hather didn't really understand. Many of them would remain mysteries for ever with her death, though over the years she had tried to teach him much.

'The eight steps of runecraft,' she told him once, 'are something you have to know. They will serve you well one day, little Hather. Remember them.

'Know how to cut runes,
Know how to read runes,
Know how to stain runes,
Know how to prove runes.
When you evoke runes
Know how to hallow runes.
Know how you cast runes,
Learn how to send runes.'

It took him a while. The verse was in a form he wasn't familiar with, one that even the skalds who knew the incantation metre didn't understand. Yet the verse, once mastered, was a useful mnemonic. Runes had to be cut, stained with the blood of the runemaster, and hallowed by an incantation to make them powerful for magic. For divination strips of wood, *kefli*, were cast down onto a cloth. Each strip was marked with a rune. Three strips were picked up and their meanings interpreted into an oracle. In order to master the runes you had to know how to read them. You must also be able to prove them, which meant understanding their meanings in words, sequences and various other strange combinations. Evoking them meant being able to tap the power inherent in the basic symbol, and sending the runes was the synthesis of all the former knowledge, the ability to make their magic work.

'Sorcery?' she asked, her eyebrows lifted, in answer to his question. 'Witchcraft? Perhaps, little Hather. But there is nothing either good or bad about using the runes. What matters is the use and the way the runemaster sees that use. Perception is the secret, not the purpose of your runecraft.'

He didn't really understand that either. But he loved her, and somehow that in itself was sufficient for Hather Lambisson. That's why he listened, why he questioned, why he struggled to make some sense out of her words.

And now she was dying, and there was nothing anyone could do.

Thorkel Tongue pulled open the door and they stepped within. The floor of the hut was strewn with rushes, like the main hall and Hather's bed-closet. The other servants and members of the family made do with the coarser covering of straw, but Old Tisti, surrogate mother that she had always been, had rushes like her master.

On the other side of the hut from the door, against the bundle of bedding which wrapped the old woman round, on the other side of the fire which burned in the pit at its centre, stood a chest of old, dark oak, the only piece of furniture Tisti had ever wanted to have. This was where she kept her clothes and the secret things she had accumulated throughout the years, however many they had really been. Here was kept the leather bag of *runakefli*, the rune-strips with which she worked her divinations, and the white cloth onto which they were cast.

The fire was burning brightly, worrying the eyes of the two newcomers as they tried to see past it to the old woman lying beyond. A small figure, kneeling beside the hides and fur rugs beneath which Old Tisti lay huddled, stood up as they entered and stared at them through eyes as blue as those of his father. Ten-year-old Svipdag was dark and slim, with a smaller nose than Hather's. In his delicate features he favoured his mother, the vanished Astrid.

'How is she, son?' Hather asked the boy gently.

'Still hot, Father,' Svipdag replied. 'And she keeps talking, but I can't make any sense of what she's saying to me.'

Hather nodded. He'd seen delirium before. He knew what a fever could do to the mind much better than his son did yet.

He turned to Thorkel Tongue. 'I want to be alone with her,' he said quietly. 'Take Svipdag to bed. It's time that he was asleep.'

'Do I have to go?' the boy asked. Hather could see the twin trails of moisture from his eyes that streaked his cheeks. No one had told him that Tisti was going to die, yet somehow he knew it for himself.

'For tonight,' his father answered. 'You can sit with your old friend again tomorrow.'

Thorkel Tongue took Svipdag back to his bed-closet behind the main hall. Alone with the sad, dying remains of the old woman who had been one of his greatest friends throughout the whole of his life so far, Hather felt the tug of tears behind his own eyes. He walked past the fire and knelt down beside her, feeling beneath the coverings until he could take one of her thin, wrinkled hands in his own.

'I love you, Tisti,' he said softly. 'I want you only to get better, to be strong with us once again. I don't want you to die.'

Her lips were moving. Sounds came from them that he didn't understand. Her own tongue, Lappish, perhaps.

'Don't leave us, Tisti,' he urged.

Her forehead was beaded with sweat. He wiped it off on his sleeve, trying to dry the wet, matted grey hair above it as well. Her mutterings continued. Her brown, rheumed eyes were tightly closed.

'Stay with us. Stay with those who love you.'

Stay with me, Tisti, he thought. I need you. I still need you. . . . I love you.

45

The sweat broke out again, but this time the mouthings, the unintelligible words in Lappish, stopped. Slowly, seen first as a flickering of her almost-vanished lashes, the old woman's eyes opened.

They didn't move. They didn't need to. They were staring straight at Hather Lambisson.

'I . . . knew you'd come . . . tonight . . .' she croaked, her voice the dry, cracked husk of sun-forgotten wheat.

'Did you?' he asked her. 'Even in your fever, Tisti? Did you know that?'

She managed a dry, rasping laugh. 'Fever?' she demanded. 'Do you really think I can't master a little fever, Hather? Will you get me something to drink, to ease my throat?'

Some wine stood in an earthenware pitcher nearby. In a leather bottle beside it was some water. Close to the two vessels, on its side, lay a horn beaker. Hather tempered some of the pale wine, from the banks of that river south of Jutland they called the Rhine, with a little of the water. He raised the beaker to Tisti's lips and forced some of the mixture down her throat. She swallowed, coughed and dribbled. Then she waved feebly for him to take the beaker away.

'That's better,' she said, a little more strongly. She was still sweating but she seemed calmer, more in control of herself. For those few minutes she was once again almost the Tisti he had known for the past twenty-eight years.

'Listen to me, little Hather,' she began. 'There's nothing about you Old Tisti doesn't know. You've learned that much, haven't you? In all the years you must have learned that much . . .'

'Shhh,' he urged. 'Don't try to talk. Save your strength for getting better.'

She closed her eyes for a moment and smiled. When she opened them she said: 'You might fool yourself, little Hather, but you're the only one in here you'll fool tonight. Even little Svipdag knows I'm dying. Even your ten-year-old son. Now, don't interrupt me. I have things to say whilst I'm still capable of controlling my tongue. I know that a messenger's come for you from the king. I know

46

Omund wants you at Uppsala. There's nothing magical about my knowing. Little Bjorn told me. One of the servants told him. By now the entire estate of Sudrafell must know that you've been summoned to Omund's court.

'There's a . . . piece of advice . . . I have to give you.' Her voice was starting to break up. The coherence she had struggled to possess for those last few vital minutes was slipping away. They both knew that her death was coming soon.

'No,' she continued, squeezing his hand with her precious, vanishing strength. 'Listen to . . . me whilst I can still . . . talk to you. I have to tell you . . . this, little Hather. If you survive you may bless my memory for it . . .'

If you survive. If you survive, Hather. If you survive.

Odin's blood, how much does the old witch really know?

'My . . . oak chest . . . is yours. Remember your runes. . . . You must remember your runes. Take . . . my chest. There . . . are things . . . in it that may be . . . useful . . . to you . . .'

'Things, Tisti? What things? What's going to happen to me?'

'You . . . will have . . . to fight . . . for Omund. His reign is being threatened . . . by powers he . . . doesn't . . . understand. You . . . have to fight . . . for Omund. For Omund, little . . . Hather. No matter what he says, no . . . matter what he does or . . . tries . . . to do to you . . . you must keep him safe. Save him . . . from the wolf . . . in the golden mask . . . Hather. Save Omund. Save . . . Omunnn . . .'

She struggled to rise. The horny, talon-like nails of her knotted hand dug deeply into his own beneath her effort. Her eyes were wide, staring disquietingly into his own, a fearsome, hidden knowledge still burning in their dying depths.

'Beware . . . the . . . dogs . . .'

She fell back.

47

He leaned over her, droplets of perspiration from his forehead falling and breaking against her relaxing face. 'Tisti?' he demanded. 'Tisti? TISTI?'

For a moment her eyes widened with the effort of thwarted speech. Then they began to glaze.

'TISTI!'

The echoes of his cry provided their own answer. Blinking back his tears he freed his hand from her death-grip and kissed her lightly on the lips. Then he pulled one of the fur rugs up over her face.

CHAPTER FIVE

Old friends and new enemies

WHILST ATYL SKIN was following a difficult trail north towards the Swedish border, Hather Lambisson had Tisti's grave-mound raised before the gates of Sudrafell. The runestone, her monument, he would carve himself upon his return from Uppsala, using the knowledge she had taught him to perpetuate her memory.

As they laid her in the damp earth of autumn many cried. In their own ways they had feared and loved the difficult, mysterious old woman. With her passing something was taken away from them, something that would never be restored.

Hather, without any assistance from his household, removed the oak chest from the old Lapp's hut and carried it to his bed-closet. A brief examination of its contents showed little that might be of any use. Her rune *kefli* were there, together with several bags of various dried herbs. In addition there was an ancient bronze box, its lid pierced with a hole the thickness of a man's thumb. Forcing the lid upwards Hather found inside a plaited rope of a substance he didn't recognise, lying on top of a hide-bag, apparently stuck against the brass with some tacky black matter. Inside the bag was a dark, gritty substance with a folded sheet of vellum, discoloured with age, lying on top. It bore words in the monkalpha, the book-hand or Latin alphabet which the Christians used, which Hather didn't know. However he recognised some of the symbols, and read aloud: 'C . . . R . . . A . . . S . . . Y . . .'

At the bottom, wrapped in an old shred of goatskin to which some of the original hairs still adhered, was a heavy gold finger-ring, its face carved in an intricate and unusual design of rayed lines with fork-like projections:

The mount was plain, as was the ring itself, and the gold was old and red, of the kind which used to be called *Dwarf-gold*, because it had been mined and smelted in the north. Southern gold, the kind that came up from Byzantium and across from England, was paler and more pure, refined by the more exact techniques taught by the alchymistical masters of Greece and Rome.

Hather slipped the ring, still wrapped in its goatskin, into a pouch at his belt. Then he closed the chest and walked across to Old Tisti's hut. Wetting a finger with his tongue he held it up to check for wind-direction, making certain that it was blowing away from the other buildings within the Sudrafell stockade. Inside, the embers of the previous night's fire still glowed red.

Taking a length of smouldering firewood sufficient to act as a torch, Hather swung it around until the glowing end caught flame. Trails of thin smoke hovered in twisted patterns in the still interior, weaving transient, mystical symbols known only to the unspeaking fire, symbols which somehow reminded him of the arcane Lappish design on the ring in his pouch. With his makeshift torch well alight he looked about the hut for the last time.

He'd come here many times. Always, on the anniversary of his birth, Old Tisti told his runes for him here. It was here that her casting had sent him off on that quest which had led him to Starkadder, then through the gates of

Trollheim to stand before King Dvalin, and finally to that fateful duel upon the plain before the fortress of Dalalven.

So many years. So many memories. And now the king wants me again.

Goodbye, Tisti.

Moving outside he touched the brand to the walls and roof of the circular hut. Beyond him his second wife, Gudrun, and Thorkel Tongue, together with young Svipdag, stood by the waiting horses, one saddled for riding, the other loaded with provisions for the journey. Throwing the torch back through the open doorway he crossed to join them.

They stood watching together. The roof fell first, its blazing hides collapsing inwards, leaving beams like blackened tusks to tremble and glow before they followed. Flames licked between the joints of the wooden walls, flames that touched at first like searching fingers, clasping fingers, before becoming straining, destroying fists of orange fire.

He kissed his wife and son in silence and clasped wrists with Thorkel Tongue. As servants swung the stockade gates open he took up the reins of the pack-horse and mounted his own. Several times he looked back and waved, watching the figures of those who were left to him grow smaller, watching the mounting plume of black smoke rising in thick, lazy twists into the air above his home. Then they became too small to see and the smoke blurred and dissipated in his sight, and the path through the mountains, the path towards Uppsala, called him on.

He remembered the journey so well. True, he'd made it several times now, but each time it was with recollection of the first time. Then he was a fifteen-year-old boy with an accursed sword, an unworldly youth seeking an ancient and accursed mercenary called Starkadder. Two curses to fight with the little knowledge he had of a hostile and uncertain world. That journey had taught him so many things. Lessons of faith and betrayal, and the terrible knowledge that man was nothing more than the futile, passing plaything of the gods and the Norns. Yet there

51

had also been good friends, friends that had grown closer through the passing years, men like himself who had met and mastered fear and now found pleasure in each other's company.

They would be there, at Omund's court.

He always camped in the same places, those places which held special memories for him. He always broke his journey, once he was through the mountains, at a place where two streams, running parallel, crossed over and then resumed their separate courses. Here he had first met the ancient mercenary he had only seen before on a visit to the court of King Oli with his father. Here he had first learned two truths which were to save his life. The first was the true nature of the curse King Dvalin had placed upon Tyrfing, that it would always kill those who owned it. The second was that Starkadder, the man he had set out at his mother's urging to kill, was to be a truer friend than his legend might admit.

Over thirteen years had passed since then, but there are some things a man may never forget.

The misted path which led to Trollheim was gone for ever. Each time he passed the place where he thought it might begin there was nothing there but a pile of fallen rock. The gates were closed, and they would never open to him again.

Four days after leaving Sudrafell he rode into Uppsala, picking a weary path up through the tangle of hovels, huts and houses that sprawled before the palace complex. At the gates he announced himself to the sentries and was asked politely to dismount and wait. A messenger was sent off into the geometrical arrangement of longhouses which occupied the centre of the massive stockade. Around the inside of the earthworks, dug out beneath the wall and reinforced with strong timbers, were the stabling and guard-quarters. The central longhouses were reserved as guest-quarters for the king and his retainers.

Hather's father, Lambi Nef, had kept a residence here, but Hather had relinquished it, preferring to spend his time at Sudrafell with his family, rather than surrounded

52

by the etiquette and protocols of court life. At home he was his own man. Here, despite his reputation and position, he was the king's.

The figure which came striding across the compound to greet him was both familiar and unmistakable. Though time had shot grey through his thick dark hair and the hairline was receding it was still dressed as it had always been, with a plait hanging down to either side in front and the rest gathered behind to hang down in a long horse-tail. This was what gave the short, heavy-set, moustachioed warrior both his distinctive appearance and his name. Born Askel, son of Sigurd, few called him Askel Sigurdsson. To almost everybody the veteran commander was known as Askel Horsetail.

With a broad laugh he clapped Hather in an embrace which threatened to do permanent damage to the younger man's ribs. As the grip relaxed and they drew apart the two friends grinned at each other, genuine pleasure shining in both their eyes.

'Don't leave it so long, next time,' Horsetail said with mock severity. Then he heaved an arm about Hather's shoulders, no mean feat in view of the difference in their heights, and snapped an order to the waiting sentries.

'Right. First, you obey Lord Hather as you obey me. Second, have his horses stabled and his packs taken to the quarters which are prepared. The guard commander will tell you where they are.'

He propelled Hather towards the central longhouses, leaving the guards to carry out his orders. 'They're all here,' he said. 'The whole crew of 'em. Vermund, Thorvald Brotamad and the rest. There's one or two you haven't met yet, Leif Half-Foot for one, but I think you'll get on with them all right.'

'Wait up, there,' Hather laughed. 'Supposing you tell me what's going on before we end up in front of Omund, Horsetail? There has to be more to this than the king hosting a reunion. Doesn't there?'

The older man stopped and stood facing his friend. His face had clouded and his manner was suddenly serious.

53

'There is,' he said gruffly. 'There's trouble, Hather. Omund's not brought us here just for the fun of it. He's raising a special force.'

'To do what?'

'It's probably better if he tells you that. I've sent a man to tell King Omund you're here. For now, though, come along to my quarters and clean up a bit. There's some good ale and some of this new-fangled pork that's been fire-roasted as well. Have you tried it yet? It makes the boiled stuff rather poor after you've tasted it.'

Hather nodded resignedly and followed his friend. As they made their way between the longhouses he couldn't help but feel that there was something Horsetail wasn't telling him. Omund wouldn't raise a special force for no reason. That cost money. And Horsetail had said there was trouble. What sort of trouble could only be told him by the king?

Horsetail steered him through a vestibule and into the wide hall of one of the longhouses. Servants produced food and drink and prepared a wooden tub of hot water. Hather bathed first, thankful to rid himself of the clinging dirt of his journey. Though it was late autumn the ground was still dry and dusty after an unusually warm summer, and the water quickly turned an unappetising shade of earth-brown.

Later, after they'd eaten and Horsetail had carefully kept their conversation to reminiscences and matters of little consequence, a messenger summoned them to the central longhouse where King Omund held his court. They entered together to find that most of the retainers had already assembled. A fact which Hather couldn't fail to notice was that this was primarily a gathering of warriors, with most of Omund's higher-ranking commanders present. Many he knew and some he had fought with. Those who didn't know him introduced themselves respectfully. Not for the first time did the Master of Sudrafell reflect that his part in the killing of Starkadder still hadn't been forgotten.

Starkadder was a legend in his own lifetime, he reflected. But that was almost three hundred years long. At the age of twenty-eight am I already a legend in my own right? I didn't kill him. Those who were there must know that. I didn't kill Starkadder. Tyrfing killed Starkadder.

A tall figure, its once-blond hair now white cascading ringlets, moved forward to greet him. His left eye, or rather its empty socket, was covered with a patch of finely-tooled leather and a long, waved beard swept down across his mailed chest.

'Hather, my friend,' he said, embracing the newcomer.

'Odin be with you, Vermund Bjarnisson,' Hather replied, matching the embrace. 'Still here? Still in command?'

Vermund nodded. 'Still the king's marshal,' he answered. 'But it's not easy. Not with louts like this to contend with,' he added, gesturing with a gnarled thumb towards a scarred figure behind him.

Thorvald Brotamad grinned evilly at the insult and clasped Hather's wrist. Slightly taller than Hather, Thorvald had earned his nickname by his prowess in battle. *Brotamad* meant 'disrupter', and the broad scar which ran down the right side of his face and into his dark beard proved that it had been properly earned. Unlike Horsetail and Vermund, Thorvald was a Norwegian mercenary who had served King Oli before Omund came to the throne. A hard man, inclined to be moody and at one time notoriously self-seeking, it was his boast that he had only ever given ground before one man.

Starkadder.

Good friends. Good memories. But they all go back to that one man. Thirteen years dead, Hather thought. And he haunts me still.

Whilst they were talking guards had filed into the hall, guards dressed in the mailed shirts and plain black leather surcoats of Omund's personal household. The idea of the king taking picked men into his own service was still novel in the north. It had been carried up from Byzantium, where the Emperor's guard, the elite Varangians, was composed entirely of exiled Norsemen. Each man held a halberd as well as carrying a broadsword at his belt. Their helmets were of plain, polished metal, the noseguards

55

spread and curling back to form a mask over the upper part of each man's face.

A lur sounded, the signal that King Omund was coming into court.

The assembled company formed ranks. Hather's natural inclination was to hang back, but Vermund and Horsetail steered him forward, positioning him between themselves in the line nearest the raised dais which held the throne.

Alone, dressed in trousers and tunic of pale green silk beneath a cloak of emerald, fastened on his left shoulder with a heavy box-brooch of gold set with carnelian and emeralds, King Omund strode through the partition door at the end of the hall and mounted the dais, which was set against one of the longer walls. He was slender, as he had been in his youth, and his large grey eyes were set in a thin face slightly too small for them. His fair hair was lank, though clean, and a straggly beard and moustache struggled to conceal the lower half of his features. The stark, evil majesty of his dead father, Oli the Great, was completely absent.

He smiled along the ranks of captains, warriors and lords assembled. When his eyes met Hather's they flicked quickly on.

He remembers, Hather thought to himself. He remembers the first time I saw him, when he was a frightened prisoner of his father in the fortress at Dalalven. He remembers that time, when he was sentenced to death by his father, as I was, as Starkadder was.

He remembers, and he cannot forgive me for my own memories. We saved his life, and he holds it against me.

Omund seated himself upon the throne and began to speak. His voice was thin and weak, yet it held some promise of cunning, some threat of a destiny which he intended to fulfil.

'My lords,' he began, 'I have assembled you here for a purpose. A dreadful purpose. Some of you know it already, but for those who do not I shall explain. . . . A vargr has come upon this land of ours.'

56

Hather felt himself blink. He must have misheard. Behind him a voice asked: 'Sir, did you say a vargr?'

'I did,' King Omund replied, smiling faintly. 'A vargr,' he repeated.

The incredulity which met his statement was both unmistakable and embarrassing. *Vargr* was a word of legend, a word relegated to myth and the singings of the skalds. It had shades of meaning which were both difficult to describe and to comprehend. In common parlance it could mean 'murderer', but that was too weak, too shallow a term to be synonymous. It held taints of berserk rage, of bestiality, even of *shape-shifting*. The fantasies of excessive intoxication and the delirium which came of eating bread baked with rotten rye were embraced within it, as was slaughter, horror, cannibalism and death. It was curse and plague. It was disease and terror. It was . . . vargr. It was witchcraft and sorcery and the power of the runes and hatred and lust and cruelty.

It was vargr. That's what King Omund had said.

Inwardly Hather smiled, though his face remained impassive. It was werewolf. A wolf in a golden mask. Odin rot you, Tisti! Why did you have to die?

'There have so far been killings at Birka, Sigtuna, and Skara. Others have been reported as well. Villages, steadings, even towns have been attacked and destroyed. As you are aware, whilst Skara is far to the west both Sigtuna and Birka are within striking distance of Uppsala. There is every possibility that whoever is behind this has designs upon the throne and the security of this land. For the most part we have been able to maintain the peace and stability established by my illustrious father, King Oli the Great. . . .'

Illustrious father, indeed! The madman wanted you dead, Omund.

'. . . but these attacks are beyond my power to ignore. Indeed, were I to do so it would be a disservice to my subjects. I thus propose the raising of a special force to seek out and destroy this vargr before it does irreparable damage to our future security.'

Vermund Bjarnisson stepped forward. 'Sir,' he asked,

'how do we know it is indeed a vargr and not just some confederacy of outlaws and malcontents?'

'By their deeds are they to be known, Marshal Vermund,' came the reply. 'By burnings and killings and slaughter, and by the fact that no matter what the savagery no gold or jewellery is taken. The dead may be mutilated, indeed several have had their hearts cut out, one can only assume for eating by the beast, but they are not robbed. That is how I know it to be a vargr, and not simply outlaws.

'In service to your king,' he continued, 'you will remain here until such time as the constitution of the force has been decided.'

Omund rose, signifying that the audience was over. The assembled warlords bowed.

'Hather Lambisson,' King Omund commanded, 'attend me.'

Hather followed Omund towards the partition. Before he could follow him through the doorway three of Omund's personal guard interposed themselves. A further three brought up the rear, effectively separating Hather from the king. Whilst the assembly behind them dispersed, Omund's small procession left the court-longhouse and crossed to the king's private apartments. Once inside Omund dismissed the guards and motioned Hather to sit opposite himself, separated from him only by a small, low trestle table.

Servants brought a glass decanter of wine and crystal goblets. Frankish workmanship, Hather decided. Once they had filled the glasses Omund waved them away.

Hather sipped the Rhenish wine and waited. Omund moistened a finger and ran it around the rim of his glass. Then the huge grey eyes looked up, fully and disquietingly into his retainer's.

'I want you to lead this force, Hather,' he said quietly. 'I want you to hunt down the vargr and destroy it.'

His words weren't entirely unexpected. Of the reasons which Hather might have postulated for this private audience the leadership of the special force had been most likely.

'You're very quiet. Will you do this for me?'

Hather looked back into the grey depths. Oli's eyes had been so black that they seemed simply to be whites with an enormous dark pupil at the centre. Omund's were less disturbing, but they still held fires that spoke of a weak will bolstered by desire, and desire could always lead on to treachery.

'Why me, sir?' Hather asked.

'Who better than a man who is universally admired?' If the question was ironic, then the irony was very carefully hidden. 'You're the best-known warrior in my kingdom, Hather. The man who killed Starkadder.'

Odin, is that to haunt me for ever? Is there no way I can break free of this myth?

'But I didn't kill Starkadder, King Omund. The sword Tyrfing killed Starkadder.'

'You're too modest, Hather Lambisson. Your own blade transfixed him before ever Tyrfing struck his flesh. I was there. I saw it.'

It has to stop, Hather thought. It has to stop here, and now. It can't go on any longer. I won't live out the rest of my life as the man who slew his friend. Better the legend fades than a lie goes on for ever.

He shook his head. 'I'm sorry, sir,' he replied. 'I can't do it. Let Vermund or Horsetail or Thorvald Brotamad lead the force. I can't.'

'You won't save Sweden for me?' The grey eyes were calm, holding no trace of frustration or anger or disappointment. Only the voice asked the question.

'There are others who can do it as well as I. Probably better. I have enough to live with as the man who killed Starkadder. I don't want to be the man who killed the vargr as well. Get someone else.'

He drained his wine and stood up. 'Custom requires that I ask your permission to leave the court, sir,' he said calmly.

'You have it,' Omund replied. But the grey eyes, holding their own secrets close, burned on.

59

CHAPTER SIX

The passing of
Thorkel Tongue

HATHER LEFT King Omund's court at Uppsala the following morning. On the afternoon of the fourth day of his return journey he cleared the mountains and started down towards Sudrafell. Long before he saw the heavy pall of smoke which hung above his home he smelled the burning on the wind. He slapped the pack-horse across the haunches, driving it ahead of him as he galloped on, around a rise at the foot of the mountains, until he could see the atrocity which had been wrought in his absence.

The shape of the stockade was still there, to distant eyes, but it was black like a silhouette. As he rode closer cold sweat broke out upon his brow and trickled from his armpits.

Broken teeth. The charred, ravaged wall of the stockade stuck up like broken teeth.

And the smell grew stronger. Fire death. Burning flesh, timber. Burning home. Burning family.

The horse almost stumbled as he vaulted from its back. He fell to his knees upon the ash-strewn ground and scrambled to his feet, rushing towards the fallen gates, their heavy timbers lying charred and futile before him. Could the wind have shifted? Had Old Tisti's hut wrought some unhallowed revenge for its burning? Surely the place hadn't been burning for nine days? Someone would have noticed. Someone would have sent for help and fought the blaze. This was Sudrafell. There were villages around on the estate, villages that owed allegiance and friendship to Hather Lambisson, villages that blessed his name in prayers to Thor and Frey and Allfather Odin.

When he saw the first body he knew that it wasn't eight days old. And he also knew that Old Tisti's hut hadn't caused all this.

Fire killed cleanly, in its way. At least, it didn't rip the heart from a young man's body.

He wanted to vomit. An upright from the main hall had fallen across the servant's legs, setting light to the clothing and half-cremating the body, but the damage had been done long before that. The hair was gone and the flesh had begun to bubble. The eyes, staring sightlessly up, had cooked after they rolled up in death. But the ruined chest, cut open and torn outwards by heart-seeking hands, or paws, told the story of death in terrible detail.

Steeling himself Hather pulled off a riding gauntlet and reached down to touch the mutilated body. It was still warm, almost hot.

If only he'd ridden a little harder. An hour, perhaps two . . . and he'd have been lying dead as well. And then he thought about his family. His wife. Little Svipdag. Thorkel Tongue.

The bile in his gorge receded, replaced by a cold, deathly calm. His face set, his eyes blazing with fear and fury, Hather Lambisson began to walk towards his ruined hall. The vestibule built onto the side had collapsed, but there was a path through, almost as if one had been cleared, leading inside.

Had it been cleared? Could someone have actually survived this carnage? Had the vargr actually allowed someone to survive?

It had to be the vargr, the eater of hearts, the one who butchered for unknown, mysterious purposes of its own. No outlaw would tear out a human heart and eat it. No

61

bandit or pirate bothered with that. Other cruelties, perhaps. The slow death of the blood eagle. Dismemberment. Burning alive.

But not the eating of a human heart.

They said that he who ate the hearts of young men prolonged his own life. That's what they said. But few could steel themselves to such an abomination. Eating a wolf's heart for courage, perhaps, but a wolf was an animal, a hunted animal. It wasn't man.

But a vargr . . . a werewolf . . .

All things pass, Hather. Even grief and terror pass. Yet when you're feeling them you forget how transient they are. Then they go on for ever.

In the ruins of the vestibule he found his wife. She hadn't been raped. Or unduly mutilated. Her death had come quickly, if knowingly. From her position and wound it was easy for Hather to tell that her arms had been pinioned from behind, preventing her from struggling whilst her throat was cut. Her hair was gone and her clothes had burned off against her flesh, but she'd died long before that happened. And the vargr hadn't taken her heart. She'd been spared that much at least.

Somehow the inner door still hung upon its hinges, forced ajar. Hather picked his way across the roofless hall, searching through the mass of fallen timbers and charred furniture for the pathetic little body of his son. It had to be there. There was nowhere else for it to be. Anything that would eat human hearts and butcher his wife wasn't going to spare a ten-year-old boy. It didn't work that way. Not even when you were praying as you walked.

Yet little Svipdag wasn't there.

Somehow the partition which divided the bed-closets from the rest of the longhouse was still standing, or most of it. The gable was burned away where the scorching heat of the burning roof had attacked it, and the centre-beam had fallen against it, not completely burned through, threatening to push it over with its weight. The doorway was gone, reduced to a blackened hole with only one upright remaining, and smoke curled lazily, a gentle, slow contrast to the devastation the burning had created, through the opening.

As Hather approached, ash from the air sticking to his sweat, his heart pounding, his ears heard something above the cracking of fire-dried timbers. He heard a voice. Old and husky, and in pain. A human voice. Thorkel Tongue's voice.

Then he remembered the other horse, the one which wasn't his own or the pack-animal, the one which had been tethered beside the open, fallen gates.

Two voices.

Hather Lambisson slipped the keeper-thong from the hilt of his sword and slid it silently from the oiled leather scabbard. His left hand held out to balance the blade extended in his right he moved warily towards the remains of the doorway, then through.

'Tell . . . the master . . .'

'Tell me what, Thorkel?'

He lay upon the remains of a bed in the nearest closet. Strong hands held him propped up, the strong hands of a fair-haired man in a Lappish coat.

The hands were strong, but they were also gentle. Hather sheathed his sword.

'Who are you?' he asked the stranger.

'That can wait,' Atyl Skin replied. 'This man is dying.'

Hather nodded and dropped to his knees in the ashes beside the bed. His hand reached out for Thorkel Tongue's. Only then did he notice that it was pressed to a deep, slowly bleeding wound in the old man's abdomen.

'Belly cut . . .' the steward muttered through clenched teeth. 'They wanted . . . you . . . to find me . . . alive, Hather . . .'

'They wanted me to? Odin's eye! What is all this?'

'They have . . . little Svipdag. . . . They told me that. They . . . want you . . . to follow them.'

'Who are they, Thorkel? Who did this to you?'

Painfully the aged steward shook his head. As he gritted

63

his teeth a trickle of blood ran down his chin. Atyl wiped it away with a charred rag Hather recognised as a fragment of one of his wife's dresses.

'I don't . . . know. The leader was small . . . dressed in wolf-skinggggg . . .'

His body arched with a sudden spasm of pain. As he relaxed again he struggled to continue. 'And a . . . golden mask . . . shaped like a wolf. There . . . was another as well. A . . . giant . . . with five, perhaps six, giant dogs . . . cross-bred Dane hound and . . . wolf . . . I think. He took his orders . . . from the other . . .'

The wolf in the golden mask. The vargr. And the dogs. And Tisti in her grave.

'Where have they taken my son, Thorkel?'

'With . . . them. That's all they said. They came this morning. They . . . waited for hours . . . with us prisoner. Nobody killed . . . except young Bjorn. . . . They took his heart and gave it to the wolf-mask. . . .

'They want you to follow them . . . Hather . . .'

There was no sign to show the passing of Thorkel Tongue. No death-rattle. No exhalation. No slow, flickering closure of the eyelids. Just the certainty that death had come to one who had served Hather and his kinfolk long and well. Even the eyes retained their misty brightness, the brightness of age fighting to live, until Atyl Skin spread his hand and closed them with a gentle movement of his thumb and forefinger.

Hather stood up, his hands upon his hips, and threw his head to the sky. 'They kill my wife!' he shouted. 'They take my son! They want me to follow them!'

'And they killed an old man slowly to make certain he could give you their message,' grunted Atyl Skin.

Hather nodded and lowered his head. Through escaping tears he muttered: 'You're not well met, stranger.'

A corner of the older man's mouth twitched in a brief smile. 'No,' he agreed. 'I'm a long way from being well met. But it's as well we have, Hather Lambisson.'

Before Hather could interrupt the Dane continued: 'No mystery. The old man told me your name. My own is

Atyl Sighvatsson. They call me Atyl Skin. Because of the coat,' he added, holding out his wrist.

Hather grasped it absently and weakly. This wasn't true. In nine days his wife was dead, his home had been burned and his little boy kidnapped. 'And they waited until I was nearly home,' he added, absently.

'They're raiding both sides of the border with Skane,' Atyl Skin said slowly. 'I've tracked them north to here from Raven's Point. There they killed the crew of a long-ship. Nearly forty men in all. Throats cut. Just like here. If I'd been a few hours earlier . . .'

'You'd have been as dead as my wife and household!' Hather snapped. 'This way at least there are two of us after them. And I know where I can get more. And the best Sweden has, at that.'

He stared at the Dane, taking in the weatherbeaten face and scarred right eye. There was a strength and openness in Atyl's features which Hather immediately trusted, despite the inauspicious circumstances of their first meeting.

'Will you ride with me, once we've done here?' he asked. 'Will you come with me, Atyl Skin, back to Uppsala?'

CHAPTER SEVEN

The vargr in Uppsala

'I'VE CHANGED my mind, King Omund.'

It had been a strange, alien, disturbed return to Uppsala. Atyl Skin could be a good companion but Hather was hardly in a mood to explore the new friendship. They rode together, the last part on failing horses, past old sites and over the crossing of the streams. All that mattered to Hather was reaching Uppsala and recruiting a force which could track down the wolf in the golden mask, the vargr, and win his son back.

Both his wives were gone now. Astrid, those ten years before, into the waters of the Baltic. Now Gudrun, the second one, killed by the vargr in those moments whilst he was riding out of the mountains towards his home, his ruined home.

All gone. Tisti, Gudrun, Thorkel Tongue, even his son, even little Svipdag. Nothing but ashes and bodies to be buried. Or sought.

Was it possible? Could he find little Svipdag alive? If the vargr wanted him to follow it could only be for an ambush of some kind. That's why it had taken Svipdag. To make sure he followed.

All right, he'd follow. He'd go after his son. He had to. But he'd do it with picked, trusted men. If Atyl Skin wanted to come along, that was fine. He wanted the vargr for reasons of his own. But the hunt was Hather's. The rescue, if rescue there was to be, was Hather's. If not, then bloody vengeance, retribution, payment for his murdered son, was also to be Hather's.

And as he rode into Uppsala, as he kicked his way past the elite personal guard and stormed into King Omund's apartments, for the first time in Hather's life Starkadder was forgotten.

'I'm pleased to hear it, Hather Lambisson. I had a feeling you'd come back to me.

'Well now, I've not been wasting my time. The force is ready. As mighty an army as ever a king of Sweden put together. No place will be safe from the vargr now. Supplies to last three months. One thousand men and ten times that number standing ready. Almost enough to invade Denmark with, and in a month or so there will even be enough for that. I'm recruiting, Hather. If your estates hadn't been razed I'd be calling on you for men as well, but they're better employed rebuilding Sudrafell for you.'

Hather shook his head. 'No army, sir,' he replied. 'Too many men take too long to move. There's no point chasing a highly mobile band with an army. And they are mobile, as you know. Sigtuna, Birka, Sudrafell, west, north, south. They can cross the country almost in the wink of an eye. But it's not magic. It's not the power of the vargr. The vargr isn't so powerful that it can do without hostages. It's something else. Organisation. The ability to travel fast and light. Perhaps some central base or stronghold from which they operate, radiating outwards like the rays of a sun-wheel. Not an army, sir. Not to go after them. When we find them, perhaps. But to find them, a small, carefully chosen group. Five, six men at most.'

Omund closed his grey eyes. When he opened them he nodded. 'Very well. Name the men you want. They're yours.'

'It's that simple?'

'That simple. Now, who do you want?'

'Vermund. He's old and creaky, but his mind's still

good. Horsetail. Thorvald Brotamad. That's three. With myself, four. I need one more.'

'Take Leif Half-Foot. He's Norwegian, like Thorvald, but he's proven his loyalty well. And his disability's hardly noticeable. Certainly no more so than Vermund's missing eye.'

'Then that's settled. When we need the force we'll send for them. Once we have the vargr's stronghold located the rest will be comparatively simple.'

'You're sure that five of you will be enough?'

'Six, sir. There's a man I want to take along who's not been mentioned yet. A Dane called Atyl Skin.'

'The man who's waiting outside?' Omund asked, his eyes glowing strangely. 'Let's have him in here.'

He motioned to two of his guards, who opened the vestibule door and escorted Atyl Skin into the royal apartments. Hather noted with silent surprise that, once inside, the sentries remained either side of his new friend.

'A Dane called Atyl Skin,' Omund repeated. 'And where did you meet this new friend, Hather? In the ruins of your home, perhaps?' The king raised his arm and pointed towards Atyl. When he looked back his arm remained outstretched and his face was contorted with fury. 'Where he was left behind by his Danish friends to worm his way into your confidence and betray your every move?' Omund demanded.

Hather felt himself gaping as the guards seized Atyl Skin and others detached themselves from stations against the wall and held their halberds to his throat.

'Move and you're a dead man,' Omund sneered to the prisoner.

'Sir!' Hather demanded. 'Have him released. This man is my friend!'

'This man is a treacherous spy of the Danish vargr!' Omund stormed in reply. 'Hold him fast! You,' he continued, motioning to another of his sentries, 'have the chest brought in for Lord Hather to examine.'

They waited in silence whilst the man complied, Omund grinning in triumph, Atyl Skin motionless inside a ring of steel, Hather looking from the man he thought was his friend to his king and back.

Within moments the guard returned. Behind him two servants struggled to carry a heavy chest of ancient oak, one side fire-scorched and blackened. At the king's command they set it down upon the low trestle table and threw open the lid.

'Items collected from the vargr's victims,' Omund said softly. He reached inside and lifted some of the contents, tossing them onto the rush-strewn floor at Atyl's feet.

They were Danish coins. Bright, new, Danish coins.

Atyl Skin looked down at them. So he was right. The vargr was responsible for the massacre at Raven's Point. Those coins could only have come from the *Bright Eagle*. But King Omund was in no mood to listen to more atrocity stories. He had enough of his own to worry about.

'He was with them, Hather,' Omund said gently. 'They left him behind, knowing he'd be able to get close to you. If the vargr isn't Danish then its support most certainly is. If I'd let him go with you he'd have led you round in circles, just wasting time. Do you deny that, Dane?'

'It's difficult to deny anything with steel at your throat,' Atyl Skin replied wryly.

'Get him out of here,' King Omund ordered.

Before Hather could protest the Dane was hustled out.

'Here,' the king called, compelling Hather's gaze to return to him. His jewelled hand reached inside the chest and pulled out another coin. This one he tossed to Hather.

It wasn't as bright as the rest.

'Some of them even have their victims' blood dried on them,' Omund rasped. 'And none of them would have possessed Danish gold themselves. These coins were spilled from the over-full pouches of their rapacious murderers.'

He slammed the lid of the chest down and leaned upon it, thrusting his thin face close to Hather's. 'The Danes are behind this vargr,' he muttered, his eyes unhealthily bright. 'That's another reason why we have to find and destroy it, Hather. It constitutes an unofficial Danish

69

raiding party. Breaching our territory. Killing our people. That's why I'll let you have your men. Because it makes sense. Impossible, as you say, to track the vargr with an army, but the five of you may stand some chance of success.

'If you fail, though, we may well find ourselves at war with the Dane-Lands.'

The words were spoken slowly, enunciated carefully. There was no possible doubt as to the exactness of their meaning.

Hather studied the bloodstained coin in his hand. There had been none at Sudrafell. But if indeed Atyl Skin had been left behind as a spy there would have been no need of them.

Even so, he found it difficult to believe that the man who had ridden with him to Uppsala would have deliberately walked into Omund's court to face evidence of his own guilt. Atyl Skin was an intelligent man. He would know of the uproar which the vargr's raids were causing. He would expect the king to be collecting evidence which might help to identify those responsible. And if, as King Omund believed, he was truly one of them, he'd know that by accompanying Hather he was placing his own head in a noose.

That he'd not attempted to speak in his own defence weighed for little. The mood Omund was in, Atyl Skin would only have been shouted down by the king. Yet he showed no surprise when he saw the coins, and there was, after all, only his word that he'd not been involved himself in the massacre at Raven's Point, if indeed it had happened at all.

'Will you grant me one more thing, sir?' Hather asked.

'What is it, Hather Lambisson?'

'Take no action against Atyl Skin until we've tracked down the vargr.'

Omund stroked his straggly beard for a moment. Then he said: 'Very well, Hather. But he remains, and is treated as, a prisoner. Is that understood?'

'It's all I could ask of you, sir.'

70

'Then that is how it shall be. I'm depending on you, Hather. I know you won't fail me. For me it's the security of my kingdom that's at stake. For you, though, and this is why you won't fail, it's the life of your son.'

He was right, of course. Hather would be working to save little Svipdag. Yet he would also be working to save other sons for other parents, perhaps even the sons that Omund himself cherished, the sons which would ensure the continuation of the Yngling blood-line.

'Now, how do you propose to begin?' asked Omund.

'It will take too long to return to Sudrafell and track them from there. Besides, their trail will be nine days cold by the time we pick it up. I know that they have Svipdag, and that they want me to follow them. Why, I don't know, but they do. I think that they'll provide me with a fresh trail quite soon, and for that reason I propose to do absolutely nothing until they do.'

'Very well,' Omund replied. 'I hope you're right, for all our sakes. We mustn't forget that there's an aspect of this matter that hasn't been fully considered so far.'

Hather had been frowning down at his feet whilst he explained his proposal. At the king's response, however, he looked up, his ice-blue eyes glaring.

'If it really is a vargr,' he grunted. 'It could just be some grisly imposture. Especially if the Danes are raiding into our territory. My steward saw the vargr figure, dressed in wolf-skins and wearing a gold wolf-mask. No one's actually seen it eat one of the hearts yet.'

'We can't take the chance, Hather,' Omund snapped. 'The legend is that it takes three months, three moons, for the vargr to come to its full power and transcend humanity completely. The first raid, near Sigtuna, took place shortly after the glimpses of the moon two months ago. The next new moon is in eleven days. That will be the third new moon, the time when the full power of the vargr is unleashed and it becomes unstoppable. By such weapons as we have, anyway,' he added. 'At that time the Danes will have created an invaluable weapon to assist them in any intended invasion of our lands.

'We know they have territorial ambitions. King Gorm has been supporting rebels in Oslofjord against their lawful overlord. He wants to push the frontier of Skane as far northwards as he can. If he can control Oslofjord he has our western coast in a pincer. It won't be too difficult for him to push down from the north and up from the south into Smaland and Vastergotland. Once he has those it would be comparatively simple to push east into Ostergotland through Sudrafell and Sodermanland.

'And then he'll be at the gates of Uppsala itself.'

Hather nodded. It made sense. With the vargr ravaging the Swedish countryside the territories would have an enemy at their back as well as the Danes pushing from the south and west.

And there was another consideration as well. If there was a sorcerer left capable of creating one vargr, then others could be created.

He'd been trying to shut the possibility out of his mind. Even Omund had been frightened to mention it. Where there was a vargr there was also someone with the un-hallowed knowledge, believed lost for generations, who was capable of creating more.

But why had they taken little Svipdag? Why did they want him to follow? What was there about this vargr that made him so important to it? And even if he found the vargr, even if somehow he managed to defeat it before the glimpses of the moon came again, before the vargr-moon, how could he hope to defeat the sorcerer behind it?

Tisti, why did you have to die? I need you now. I need you so badly.

He'd searched the ruins at Sudrafell before he left for Uppsala with Atyl Skin. The old Lapp's chest had gone. Somehow the vargr had known better than Hather the import of its contents and removed even that slender chance of defeating it.

So I follow it. So I find it, what then? he asked himself. Even with the best, most experienced fighters in Sweden behind me, even with men I trust with my life, how do I defeat it? How?

72

You die trying, Hather. For your son and your country, for the sons of others, like King Omund, you die trying.

Hather spent the rest of the day with his chosen companions in the search. The only one he didn't know well was Leif Half-Foot, who'd gained his nick-name by the painful method of losing three toes from his right foot in battle. He walked with a slight limp as a result, but in a mock combat against Horsetail he proved himself an able and competent fighter despite his slight disability.

Leif was about Hather's age. Unlike Horsetail or Vermund he wore his hair cut short. Whilst the style was unusual to Hather, whose own hair grew long behind and was plaited into two at the front to keep it away from his eyes in combat, it struck Hather as intensely practical for a fighting man. The same was true of Leif's accoutrements and dress, which consisted of an unornamented, serviceable broadsword in a plain leather scabbard, ring-mail and leather surcoat. He wore wide trousers, as did most fighters, permitting his legs unrestricted movement. These were tucked and tied below the knee to prevent them from tripping him. Tending towards fat, his face, beneath the full beard and moustache, was round and florid and seemed to be permanently creased into a broad smile. His iron helmet had a long nose-guard which came down in a broad blade which protected his mouth as well, and blue eyes shone intelligently to either side.

Whilst the five discussed the possible courses of action open to them in one of the longhouses, Atyl Skin languished in one of Omund's underground, wooden-walled dungeons. These were positioned against the northern part of the palace stockade's circular wall, close to the guard quarters. They consisted of circular, wood-lined pits, roofed over except for a small, grilled trap which opened to permit entrance and the meagre rations supplied to those incarcerated beneath. A shallow depression against part of the wall served as a latrine, and few prisoners survived through hot summer weather without contracting some unpleasant illness or infection in the badly-ventilated cells.

At least it's autumn, nearly winter, the Dane thought.
I may be cold, but I'll live longer. And whilst there's life
there's a chance of getting out of here.

He settled down for the night as best he could, half-
crouched against the wall with his cloak spread over him.
In his frequently-dangerous occupation he'd been in worse
situations than this before, and he knew that concern about
it would only be a misdirection of energies better spent on
devising some means of escape.

Even so, with guards patrolling overhead on the walls
of the palace, positioned so that every angle of the wooden
walls could be viewed at short, regular intervals, escaping
from the pit was only going to be the first of his problems.

Around him the palace began to grow quiet. The sounds
of noisy entertainment issuing from some of the nearer
longhouses slowly faded into silence. As the darkness
deepened only the padding of leather boots on the wooden
walkways of the royal palace at Uppsala came distant and
muffled to his ears.

The moon was waning on its slow way towards last
quarter. Tonight, with the promise of rain or snow in
the clouded skies, it was hidden away, leaving only dim
silhouetted shapes and the occasional pallid square where
feeble lamplight shone through a vellum-paned longhouse
window.

He tried to sleep, but the long, underground minutes
lengthened into hours, beaten slowly out by the feet of
Omund's guards. Occasionally the muted voices of sentries beginning their duty came to his ears as they walked
from the nearby guard quarters, or returned at the end of
their patrols. Then even the softly-padding feet faded
away as well.

Yet despite the total silence Atyl Skin knew himself to
be wide awake.

The silence deepened disturbingly. It was too deep. Too
heavy. His eyes opened in the darkness, slowly beginning
to make out the faint line of light around the edges of the
trap. No noise anywhere. Something up there, beyond his
tiny world, wasn't quite right.

74

Then he heard the snuffling. The trap opened, and he saw the nightmare peering down, dripping mingled blood and saliva from its slavering, silent jaws. A faint click sounded, then a ladder was lowered silently down to him and the face was gone.

For the first time since Omund's men had seized him Atyl Skin began to know real fear, but his chance had come and it was a chance that had to be taken. Pulling his cloak aside he scrambled to his feet and began to climb the ladder, knowing that once he was outside anything was possible.

From Raven's Point to the burning of Sudrafell. From Sudrafell to imprisonment in Uppsala. From Uppsala . . . to what?

As his head drew level with the trap Atyl hesitated. In his cell he at least had some relative form of safety. Outside, in the palace compound, anything could, and probably would, happen.

A hand grasped his hair and drew him up the remaining length of the ladder. Only when he stood upon firm ground once again did it release him. Whilst it held him he caught only impressions of what the situation above ground really was. As the clutching fingers let go, as the tugging at his scalp gave way to relative freedom, he saw his liberators properly for the first time.

Three men, if they were truly men, and other things as well. Two were of medium height, with the untidy, cluttered appearance which characterised successful outlaws. Both wore long swords with fancy hilts inlaid with semi-precious stones and plates of embossed gold. One wore his beard long and plaited. The other, beautiful to the point of femininity on one side of his face, had the other eaten away as if by some terrible disease. They wore heavy ear-rings and black-iron helmets. Their leather surcoats were heavily studded with iron that could turn a blade, reducing a disembowelling stroke to a simple scratch. The half-pretty one had three long knives in leather scabbards hanging from his belt down to his crotch. The other, plait-beard, had two, hanging in their scabbards at each shoulder.

75

They stood back, giving place to the third, the giant, and to the beasts which prowled about his legs.

'They kill in total silence,' the giant whispered. 'They can kill you just as easily as they tore the throats from your guards.'

Atyl nodded. One glance was enough to convince him of the truth of the big man's words. Their outsize feet, wolf-like in proportion to their bodies, bore savage claws that were more appropriate to bears than dogs. Their muzzles, long and vicious, slavering unpleasantly, were lupine, with strong, yellowed teeth that still were flecked with the blood of their victims. Luminously red eyes blazed above the ominously silent mouths.

Two of them. Giants like their master. Dane-hounds crossed with wolves to bring out the fidelity of the one and the ferocity of the other.

He stood above them, above his companions, almost seven feet tall. He wore no helmet. None would have fitted over the mass of plaits that covered his head, greased and bound into horn-shapes. Neither did he bother with a surcoat or tunic. The upper half of his body, above the wide trousers bound beneath the knee and the metal-plated belt with broadsword and war-axe, was naked except for wrist-bands. Apart from his heavy gut the torso was well-formed and heavily muscled. The dark eyes, small and sunken into black pits, matched the black hair and long, sweeping moustache perfectly, leaving his face in the night little more than broad dark strokes and splashes against the sun-browned flesh.

Whilst all three men were heavily armed none of them held weapons. They conducted themselves, here in the royal palace at Uppsala, as jauntily as in the heart of their enemies as they did in the vargr's stronghold. Total confidence. A complete absence of fear. Probably that was the most terrifying thing about them, except for the brute power of the dogs.

Whilst he might stand some chance of outrunning, if not of outfighting, the men, the prowling killers about the giant's legs put all thoughts of flight out of Atyl's mind.

76

Only a fool would challenge creatures like those, and Atyl Skin wasn't about to become that fool. Besides, he didn't really want to run.

'Shall we go, or do you want to stand here all night?' the giant asked.

Atyl Skin grinned. Fear was the only emotion you didn't show to men such as these. Anything. Anything at all. But not fear. No matter how much your legs might feel like giving, no matter how your lower lip might tremble, or want to tremble, when you spoke to them, you had to project the same confidence, the same innate ferocity.

That's why he grinned. That's why he said: 'What took you so long to get me out, Hundermann?'

CHAPTER EIGHT

The fates of men

'WHOSE GAME is he playing, Allfather?' she asked him.

They watched from beside the gates as Hundermann and his companions set Atyl Skin upon the horse they'd brought for him and tethered just outside the palace. She sat, veiled, as she had sat when she cast the runes for Hather Lambisson some thirteen years before. He stood beside her, wrapped in his pale blue travelling cloak against the chill of that autumnal evening, leaning against the long spear Gungnir which was never far from his hand, peering through his single eye after the retreating horsemen and the dogs which padded silently behind them.

Odin shrugged. 'Yours. Mine, perhaps even their own,' he replied. 'They have their part to play, even as you or I do, Mother Skuld. But it was unfair of you to break our agreement like you did.'

He couldn't see her expression beneath the veil, but he suspected that the seated Norn was smiling. His suspicion was confirmed by the edge to her voice as she questioned: 'Thirteen, fifteen years. Does it matter, Lord of the Aesir? Hather would have to face this sooner or later. That's the way of things. Isn't it better that he does it now? Would you have him live another two years, become two years older, two years less skilled? Doesn't he have more chance now? At least his son is still alive. I've left him that much.'

78

Odin scowled. 'I could finish this now, you know. It wouldn't take too much effort, Mother. Where would you be then?'

'You should be asking yourself that question, Allfather. If I'd had my way your precious Yngling dynasty would have finished with mad Oli. I'm tired. I'm bored with playing these stupid ritual lives out to their petty endings. We've lived too long, Odin. The White Christ is spreading up from the south. Your days will be over in a century or so. Why can't you let us die now. Or at least rest?'

'We have responsibilities, Mother Skuld. You and your sisterhood of Norns have inherited the fates of men. You control their weirds. And I have some control over how they reach to them. Not a great deal, because you never tell me how their weirds will end. That's why I have to fight you. I don't know how Hather Lambisson will die, or when. Even when I take my champions from the fall of the slain, even when I set up a betrayal to snatch a hero for Valhalla, I don't know until he's safely in the hands of my Valkyries that I'm actually going to have him.'

She nodded. Or, at least, the veil moved as if she was nodding beneath it. Then she asked: 'Tell me, Odin. Why is the Yngling dynasty so important to you? Oh, I know that the legends claim you founded it, and even to you that must be at least a little flattering. But why are you fighting so hard to preserve it? Its moon is waning. Oli was mad. Omund's weak and unstable. He has a son, Helgi, and two others, but they may well show the same taint of madness as Omund has inherited, albeit in small part, from his father. So, why are these mad kings so important to you? Tell me that.'

The one-eyed god sighed. 'Do you want all my secrets without giving me any of your own?' he demanded wearily.

'Perhaps there might be some trade we can arrange.'

'Such as?'

'The rules of this game, perhaps. Possibly even Hather's life, though it might eventually come down to a choice between the champion of the Ynglings and the Yngling dynasty itself. Why is it so precious to you?'

'It isn't,' Odin replied with a cryptic smile slashing his grizzled beard.

'Then I can end it now?'

He shook his head. 'The dynasty itself isn't important at all, Mother Skuld. What is important is the time it will buy for man.'

'You care for man? Even knowing that the doom of the gods will come, that the White Christ will eventually supplant you? You care for those who, in a mere handful of generations, will turn away from the worship of the gods who've nurtured them? I don't understand you, Allfather. I don't understand you at all.'

'Sometimes I don't understand myself. Dwarfs, gods, men, even Norns. I didn't create them, and I don't know who did. I simply discovered them. To be more precise I discovered that I had mastery over them. But I need the Ynglings for a few years more. They afford time for the north to grow strong, to become a monument to things I hardly understand myself. And it will, Mother Skuld. Sooner or later they'll be born. Sooner or later those which will mould it into powerful shape will come. They won't be Ynglings. As you say, the dynasty is tainted. But they will come. They'll know your power, and mine, and they won't thank us for the gifts we give them. Yet they will be there, and we shall both be proud of them. I, as I fight you for their lives, and you as you snatch them from my hands. I am their life, and sometimes their death. You are their death and, despite yourself, sometimes their lives as well. We fight, we argue, we play out our games upon the board of their landscapes, yet can you truly say you do not love them, even as I do, even as you snap their weirds for ever?'

She was silent, and this time he knew that she was smiling, and that her smile was gentle. He had appealed to her vanity, to her sense of the purposes of fate, and to the woman's heart hidden deep within her ancient rags. It was there, still beating and, in its own quiet way, despite her words, still hoping.

Hather Lambisson or the Ynglings. If it came to that the

80

choice was no choice at all. Hather would have to die. But perhaps it wouldn't come to that at all.

'The rules are simple,' she said at length. 'You may not manifest to Hather. Not directly.'

'Indirectly?'

'Three times. No more, no less. Are these terms acceptable to you?'

'Do I have a choice, Mother Skuld?'

'You do. You know that I can destroy the Ynglings here and now.'

He didn't know, and he didn't entirely believe her either. If that had been the case then there would be no need for these negotiations, no need for the elaborate web she was weaving to catch Hather's weird. Yet the terms, as she proposed them, gave Hather some chance. Perhaps only one chance in a thousand of regaining his son, destroying the vargr and retaining his life, but that tiny chance for his chosen champion was a chance for the Ynglings as well. And that meant a chance for mankind to grow and strengthen and mature.

'I accept your terms,' Odin said.

'Then we are agreed?'

'We are agreed.'

'No direct intervention?'

'None.'

'So be it.'

He could be lying, she thought. If he is, though, he dooms both Hather Lambisson and all his hopes. If he truly wants to preserve the Ynglings a little longer he'll keep to the agreement.

Beyond them Atyl Skin and his rescuers were long gone. Behind them, in the palace compound, the first of many alarms was about to be sounded as the guards changed and discovered their fallen comrades, throats torn away, lying in their own blood at their stations. Soon the royal palace would be ablaze with light and the full realisation that the vargr had sent its men into Uppsala. That suited Mother Skuld particularly well.

Yet still she had her doubts. Allfather's agreement had

come too soon, too quickly. There was something he was hiding, some secret which he hoped might yet defeat her. He wouldn't risk the dynasty by cheating to save Hather. That much she knew. But he might know something that gave him an advantage.

For the first time in the millennia of her life Mother Skuld began to doubt her own strength. Each time she contested with Odin their battle of wits ended in compromise. It had to, to preserve the balance between them. This time, though, she had her doubts.

That he'd sacrifice Hather, and his son, if he had to, was beyond dispute. It would be a small price to pay if he really wanted, finally, to displace the balance of their contests and win. There was no point in her destroying the Ynglings. Both Odin and herself already knew that they were ultimately doomed, as even the gods and Norns themselves were.

She looked up through her veil to where the god leaned on his spear. He was smiling, and his smiling worried her. It had too much of the look of someone who knew what he was doing.

The veil has its purposes, she thought. At least he can't see my uncertainty.

Behind the smile, however, Allfather was hiding his own. Old One-Eye felt trapped by her restrictions, and by the probing of her questions. He had always managed to keep his hopes and ambitions hidden before. This time, though, she had tricked him, forced him, into an open admission.

One chance in a thousand, Hather, he thought. Without my help, without me breaking the rules and destroying us all, one chance in a thousand isn't going to be enough.

Still smiling he turned away so that Mother Skuld wouldn't see the tears which threatened in his single eye.

With odds like that how could he win? How could he even reach a compromise?

Old One-Eye
and the runes

CHAPTER ONE

The despair of the dwarf-king

ALVIS STRETCHED out his hand, noting the tremors which caused his taloned fingers to twitch and jerk. The heavy rings upon each finger blurred momentarily in sequence, becoming flashes of coloured fire and gleaming metal in the torchlight, sending their shivering echoes onto the dullness of the studded iron door. Only that part of the heavy door which bore the runes was bright. That shone as if inlaid with silver fire, winking its star-bright warning to whoever might seek to enter.

ᚺᚨᚲᚢᚦᚢᛉ

Hakuthuz, the bent one.

Had the dwarf-king been asked if there was any place, any remote depth, in his subterranean kingdom that he feared to enter he would have stridently denied that such a place existed. Yet he was here, drawn here, despite himself and because of his fears for himself, reaching out a trembling hand to turn the rust-brown handle and enter a realm not entirely his own, a realm which belonged to the Bent One himself, and no one else.

Not that anyone else would have tried to claim it, Alvis shuddered.

His talons clicked against the metal as he forced his unwilling hand to obey. Desperate times call for desperate remedies, he told himself. Of all my subjects there is now only one who can help me.

Kulubak Magri, the thin hunchback. The most powerful sorcerer in the whole of Trollheim. Probably the greatest wizard on the Midgard side of Odin.

The only thing in Trollheim that I actually fear.

For Alvis to admit fear, even in the privacy of his own thoughts, meant that the King of the Dwarfs was truly frightened. With an effort greater than he had needed to muster for years he reached inside the iron ring and closed his fingers over it. Turning the handle he pushed inwards, feeling the heavy grating of a door that hadn't been opened for decades, listening to the squeal of forgotten hinges echo beyond in the cavernous reaches of the sorcerer's domain.

Then the thought struck him like a well-aimed stone. No one had seen Kulubak Magri for almost as long as Alvis could remember. Supposing the wizard was dead? Supposing that all he found were the ashes of a fire and the lizard-shredded corpse, nothing more than a fearfully deformed skeleton?

Before the shuddering could resume he heaved the door ajar and strode inside with a boldness he found both apposite and incredible. Releasing his hold he heard the clang of the heavy portal as it swung back behind him, closing itself with an ease infinitely greater than it had opened. As the clanging reverberated, pealing through the immense cavern like a demented bell, Alvis struggled to take stock of his surroundings.

He'd been here once before, as a dwarfling, with his proud predecessor Dvalin. Here he had stood and watched as the fires roared, their flames sending flickering shadows high into the fearsome blackness of the stalactite-clustered vaulting above. Here Dvalin had smiled, covering his own unease, whilst Kulubak Magri forged and welded the young dwarf's fate into a glittering, slender object.

86

He stood high up, near the roof of the cave, where generations before the stalactites had been broken away to provide unrestricted access. Now they had begun to reform, the broken bases ringed with small, sharp limestone spikes, like erratic and inverted crowns. A few centuries more and they might once again approach their former majesty. And the sorcerer-dwarf might still be alive, engrossed, entombed by his failure to notice that the living stone was working to immure him in his haunt for ever.

It wouldn't matter, Alvis reflected. He never leaves here anyway. He lives on the blind-worms and scuttering reptiles which inhabit this chamber of forgotten arts.

From the jutting stone platform where he stood a staircase, winding and twisting to follow the natural walls of the cavern, had been hewn out of the stone. Here and there it glowed where some strangely phosphorescent substance had been smeared onto its walls, supplying a feeble light for those foolish enough to pass the iron, rune-warned door in search of the creature which shuffled within. Several hundred feet below the barely worn steps, slippery with lichens that grew white and leprous in the darkness, the cavern levelled out. There, beneath and distant, where tiny fire-lights winked in diminutive cressets, where the forge glowed red like a monster's eye, like its master's eyes, movements Alvis would have greatly preferred not to think about were weaving their web of enchantment and perversity.

Slowly, like the struggles of a fly trapped by a spider, the movements ceased. Then the booming began, the booming which made Alvis reach up and cover his ears against its force, the booming which set the stalactites reverberating and shivering with its fearsome magnitude. The booming which held a question in its depths.

'WHY HAVE YOU LEFT IT SO LATE, ALVIS?' the booming asked.

He tried to turn and run before his nerve gave completely. He wrestled with the heavy door, clawing at the plainness of its surface, his taloned fingers scrabbling desperately for a handle which wasn't there to find. Thwarted, his heart pumping furiously, he turned back to face the depths.

No way back, Alvis, came a mocking thought. Only a way down. A way down to Kulubak Magri. That's all there is.

Mechanically, striving more for calm than for motion, the dwarf-king began the long descent. As he neared the closest phosphorescent patch it seemed to him briefly that it was composed of a thousand tiny, reflective, reptilian eyes, each glassy but alive, each squamous and distinct. Then the image faded, leaving only an area of glistening, fire-bright rock.

He passed the brightness and continued through the darkness, feeling the lichens slide away beneath his feet, feeling the squashing of night-seeking worms beneath his soles, with the echoes of the booming still humming in his ears.

'COME DOWN, COME DOWN,' the booming resumed, almost causing him to stumble, forcing him to reach out for the slime-dewed wall to steady himself in his descent.

'YOU SHOULD HAVE COME TO ME BEFORE THIS, ALVIS. ONLY SORCERY CAN HELP YOU NOW.'

He tried to answer, his whispering voice hissing like a strangled serpent into the gloom. 'I . . . set my faith upon others, Kulubak Magri. I was . . . wrong. I need your help.'

A sigh roared up, heavy yet somehow almost forgiving. 'TOO WISE, ALVIS, PERHAPS TOO LATE. PERHAPS THERE IS NOTHING LEFT FOR ME TO DO.'

He continued down. His own voice, by comparison, had sounded so small, so drowned in the sorcerer's echoing tones, that he wondered how it could ever have been heard. And yet it had. There might be hope for his future after all.

'You . . . said that sorcery could help me . . .'

'AND SO I DID. WAS I LYING TO YOU, KING ALVIS?'

He glanced behind him. He was almost half-way down.

'I know the . . . power of Tyrfing, sorcerer,' he wheezed, trying desperately to regain that sinister, regal edge which his voice had possessed before he opened the rune-carved door. 'So do you. You forged it for Dvalin. Then, when the sword was done, he bade you impress it with my fate. My weird is in Tyrfing, Kulubak Magri.'

'INDEED IT IS.'

'Then help me get it back. I need that sword. It represents my power.'

'AND MORE, KING ALVIS. TYRFING REPRESENTS MUCH MORE THAN JUST YOUR POWER. IT REPRESENTS YOUR LIFE.'

'I know that. That's why I've come to you. Something is hiding Tyrfing from those I sent to seek it. That's why I need your help.'

He reached the bottom of the steps and stood upon the cavern floor. Stalagmites, like cone-helmed sentinels, rose all around him.

It was true. In his youth, in those distant, time-shrouded days when Dvalin had chosen Alvis as his successor, the rites confirming that succession had been performed. One of the most important rites, and certainly the most binding, was the creation of an object that both typified and enshrined the very essence of the successor. Usually it was something small that could be worn upon the person, something easily portable which might be kept safe against theft or loss. Yet Alvis in his youth and pride had selected something which he hoped would be significant also of his power in days to come, something too large for him to wear or carry. He had chosen the sword Tyrfing, three feet of glimmering-bright steel blade, a further eight inches of gold-wired and plated shimmering hilt. A sword only ten inches shorter than he was himself.

Then Tyrfing had been stolen.

In those days there had been greater commerce between men and the dwarfs. Svafrlami, a mortal king guesting with Dvalin, had coveted the sword and stolen it. The theft was relatively unimportant to Alvis' predecessor. After all, it was the young dwarf's weird which was forged into it, not Dvalin's. For the sake of form Dvalin laid a curse upon the stolen blade, that same curse which killed Svafrlami and eventually even Starkadder, but he made no efforts to retrieve it. Even when Hather and Starkadder brought Tyrfing back to Trollheim to strike their bargain with Dvalin the sword left with them, part of a plan of Dvalin's own, part of a destiny he shared with them. All that Alvis could do was send spies to keep track of the sword, spies that told him of the plan to bury it with Starkadder. Thus one of his first acts after Dvalin's demise had been to send two of his prisoners, Thrudnir and Illugi, under promise of a pardon, to retrieve Tyrfing from Starkadder's mound.

But they'd failed. And disappeared. Probably caught out in sunlight and turned to slabs of stone.

Picking his way between the stalagmites he made towards the circle of lights which burned in the centre of the cavern. Around him sounded the steady dripping of water from the roof. Beneath his feet it lay in shimmering puddles, forming a miniature landscape of lakes and rivers and valleys with the limestone encrustations and projections.

It glimmered. It whispered to him. No help here, Alvis. Only madness. Go back or go mad. Nothing else for you here but madness and slow death. And perhaps some knowledge of your weird, it added as an afterthought.

With determination warring against his fear he continued his groping way towards the lights. 'You can help me, Kulubak Magri. I am your king. You have to help me. Now.'

The laughter roared and thundered. As it began to die the voice boomed out: 'DO I NOW? WHY SHOULD I CARE FOR YOU? WHY SHOULD I USE MY POWERS TO KEEP YOU ALIVE, LITTLE KING ALVIS? WHAT ARE YOU TO ME?'

He had to get Tyrfing back. The sword was his. It held

his weird. More than that, though, it controlled his life. It was the secret of his power and the token of his longevity.

The royal line of Trollheim had interbred to such an extent that they now almost formed a separate species of dwarf from commoners such as Thrudnir and Illugi. Lesser dwarfs lived their lives, usually spanning about three hundred years, without the need of tokens or magic to preserve them. Royal dwarfs, however, had developed several distinguishing traits. One was the quietness of their voices. Another was the fineness of their hair in comparison to that of other dwarfs. Yet the most important trait to Alvis for most of his life was that which was usually counteracted by the rites of succession. Their life-span.

In order to control their subjects a method had been devised by which their lives could be protracted indefinitely. The weird, the fate and essence of the future monarch, was forged into an object which held it safe. But contact had to be made with that object once every hundred years if the king's life was to continue. Dvalin had lived for eighty-seven years after nominating his successor. With the passage of a further thirteen waiting for Thrudnir and Illugi to retrieve Tyrfing from the realms of man, Alvis' hundred years were almost over. Now mere days remained, and no successor had been chosen. With his death Trollheim would descend into ungoverned anarchy. Without Tyrfing it was the end of the kingdom of the dwarfs for ever.

Only sorcery remained. The sorcery of Kulubak Magri. That's why Alvis was here. That's why he had striven so hard to master the only thing of which he was afraid. That which lay behind the rune-marked door of iron.

'I am your future, sorcerer,' the king replied, stepping into the lit area at the cavern's heart.

'Perhaps.'

The voice was still strong, still that of a creature which had mastered its own destiny, but it no longer echoed and deafened as it had done before. Alvis realised that the difference in volume might possibly be connected with the way that the figure had stepped out from behind an iron cone, open at both ends, mounted upon a wooden-geared frame atop a plinth of rough-hewn stones. Beyond the plinth a chaos of half-finished stone walls, staircases and arches rose like some extravagant ruin from the floor of the cave. Most of the walls bore shelves piled high with objects foreign and mysterious even to the eyes of dwarfish craftsmen. Fires burned in pits and charcoal glowed in braziers. Strange vessels of glass fumed and bubbled with liquids that were at once extravagant and exotic. Fire came magically out of tubes beneath them and the cressets burned with controlled flames with odd hues at their centres.

To the yellow, sunken, smouldering eyes of the frightened Alvis it was a wonder-place. A temple to deities unknown. A grotesque, vile, terrifying sanctum of perversity. Yet it was the only place in Trollheim where he might find his salvation.

Of all the wonders, of all the frisson-spurring features clamouring for his attention in that place, the one which stepped out from behind the metal cone was the strangest of them all. It was a figure he had seen almost a hundred years before, a figure which had lived longer and more arcanely than anything alive in Trollheim. It was shorter than himself, though only by some freak of vicious nature.

Slightly over four feet high, Kulubak Magri had stopped growing upwards at shoulder-height and instead bent over, a deformity of his slender, bony spine forcing his head forwards at a level with his upper torso. He seemed to lean permanently backwards in an effort to keep his feet beneath his centre of gravity. When he walked he shuffled, struggling to keep his balance, striving to force his thin legs to perform.

'How nice of you to come and see me, Alvis,' he mocked, his lips thin, his mouth wide, his teeth long, pointed, vulpine. 'How long has it been?'

He knows, Alvis thought. He has to know. He's mocking me. And I dare not mock him back.

'You know how long it's been, Kulubak Magri.'

The worst thing about the freak was its eyes. They

burned with dwarf-fires, but not with dwarf colours. The yellows weren't yellow. They were red, a deep blood-crimson crimson–blood bloody red. The red of horror and dementia. The red of terror and distraction. The red of madness and mystery and magic. Evil red.

Last, lost, lusting, desperate hope red.

'A long time, Alvis. Almost a lifetime.'

The mouth crumpled into a forbidding smile. The grey beard and moustache, a dirty colour, not a decent dwarfish white, thrilled with the effort of the unaccustomed expression. They quivered, chuckling silently, almost blackened by the shadow of the wizard's projecting, trunk-like nose.

Or snout, Alvis decided. Almost a hog's snout. Not quite, though.

Kulubak Magri was dressed in a long, tattered robe which was as black as the darkness around his abode. Only heavy chains and ropes of silver jewellery, festooned with more charms than Alvis had ever seen, let alone could hope to identify, broke its sombre ebony.

'Do you remember me now, King Alvis?' Kulubak Magri asked. His voice had lightened to the tinkling of silver bells, a tinkling which would have been completely lost in its former booming magnitude.

The dwarf-king forced a reply. In what he hoped were something approaching regal tones he said: 'I remember you, Kulubak. You are the hardest of all my subjects to forget.'

It's only a hunchback, he told himself. Only a dark-dwelling cripple. Nothing to be afraid of. But immediately he knew it for the lie it was. Had it been otherwise he wouldn't have been here, prepared to plead for the creature's help in saving his life and reign.

The dwarf-wizard sighed. 'It's so hard to be remembered in such a way,' he muttered, the snout-like nose threatening to snuffle as he spoke. Then he turned away, beckoning over his shoulder for Alvis to follow him.

They threaded their way through the maze of walls towards a wooden structure towering in the centre of the illuminated area. Occasionally Kulubak Magri would pause long enough to scoop a worm or spider from the wall or floor and crunch it between his wolfish teeth. Alvis shuddered at each distraction, but didn't falter in his pursuit. There was too much at stake for him to be sickened by the wizard's diet.

'I . . . need your help,' Alvis admitted hesitantly, unwilling to commit his future to the hunchbacked sorcerer.

'I know,' came the weary reply. 'But it won't be easy. For either of us,' he added knowingly. 'What you require needs platform magic, King Alvis. That's the worst and hardest kind. But I'm ready for it. I knew that you'd be coming before you even knew yourself. Whatever else you are, Alvis, you're not completely stupid. You knew, in your despair, that I was your last chance of life, your last hope of getting Tyrfing back in time to save yourself. So, I prepared. It wasn't easy to work out the precise formulae and ritual equipment which would be involved, but I prepared. I knew your fear of me would keep you away until your despair controlled your reason and overcame your loathing. I know I'm shunned, that most prefer to forget me, that even those who remember do so only in their nightmares. So, I'm prepared. But are you?' he demanded, suddenly turning back, his red eyes blazing with the force behind his question.

They stood before a wooden scaffold which towered high towards the stalactited roofing of the cave. Ladders stretched down its sides from the dim shadows where torches struggled to burn in the mephitic atmosphere around the upper platform, where something flopped in futile protest and occasionally threw out hoarse, tired, pain-filled bellowings into the darkness.

'Shall we go up?' Kulubak Magri invited. 'There's nothing to be afraid of yet. Nothing alive up there in any realm save bats, and my crippled sacrifice. You don't need to know the problems I had raising it up there, but I think you'll appreciate the effort involved, King Alvis.'

He tested the nearest ladder carefully, standing gently

with one foot, then firmly with both, upon the lowest rung. When he knew that it would hold Alvis progressed to the second, then the third.

'They take my weight,' the sorcerer remarked. 'They'll take yours. Go on, King Alvis. Climb up to the platform where we shall perform our evocations.'

Shuddering at the words, the dwarf complied. Behind him, breath from his snout warming the leather of his boots, he felt the presence of the sinister hunchback who held his life in taloned hands.

For a moment, near the top, Alvis looked down. The distant, winking cressets about the tangled walls looked like tiny, distant stars beneath him. His hands gripped the ancient, slime-coated ladder firmly, the fingers wrapping around until the points of his talons stabbed the flesh of his palms. How could he climb so high and still be beneath the ground? It wasn't possible.

The whole mad, desperate venture wasn't possible, but without it King Alvis knew he had only a few nights left to live.

He'd sent out others through the years, looking for Tyrfing. Somehow, though, he'd trusted Thrudnir and Illugi. They had stood the best chance of success because of the fate that threatened them if they failed. Now there was only the dark, doubtful sorcery of Kulubak Magri left to save him.

He climbed on, carefully keeping his eyes on the rungs in front of them, occasionally venturing to focus them beyond, on the far side of the massive wooden scaffold, its tree-trunk legs spliced and bound and reinforced with spars of petrified timber. Then the thought came to him, the most dangerous of all his unasked questions, and he faltered in his climbing.

'Go on,' the hunchback snapped beneath him. 'What's the matter? We're nearly at the platform.'

A bat flitted past Alvis' head, a wing-tip brushing at his hair. He shuddered.

What price would he have to pay for Kulubak Magri's help?

'It's not important now!' the sorcerer snarled in answer to the unspoken question. 'Get to the platform!'

Still unsure, still hesitant, King Alvis obeyed.

Almost fifteen feet from the top, so high off the floor of the cave that it was hidden in shadows and invisible from below, a structure projected from one side of the scaffolding. It had the appearance of a gigantic bow formed of overlapping, tightly-bound layers of horn. It was held in a drawn position by a complicated series of springs and levers and set horizontally. Parallel to the bow, resting on a central, grooved support, was the most massive spear the dwarf-king had ever seen, its ancient bronze head, rune-inscribed, pointing directly at him. His yellow eyes widened in horror.

With an extra burst of speed, anxious to be out of range of the fearsome weapon, he clambered up the remaining rungs and grasped the guard-rails around the platform. As his eager feet, the soles aching from the hundreds of rungs that had pressed into them, rested on the solid planking, the strangest sight of all awaited him.

The hind legs had been carefully hamstrung and bound with dressings to render the enormous ure-ox incapable of standing. Its hindquarters were supported by a padded wooden cradle slung from one end of an outsize gallows. The forequarters, almost three feet across, were held immobile by a gibbet constructed of carved wood and thick leather joined by riveted metal plates, so that it stood upon its forelegs but couldn't move forwards, backwards or to either side. Around the massive neck was a noose made of rope thicker than a man's fore-arm and greased with bear's fat to run more easily.

The creature's huge brown eyes rolled with the pain of its restrictions and mutilations, the whites at the corners flashing in the dim light of a single flambeau. An occasional semi-strangled bellow struggled from its throat, and it twisted and rattled furiously in its harness as its tormentor climbed onto the platform behind King Alvis, the six-foot span of vicious horns describing short, thwarted arcs with their tips.

96

'The sacrifice,' Kulubak Magri announced proudly. 'It's been here, helpless, for three days now.'

His words bit home. Three days. How could he have known for so long that the dwarf-king would be coming? How could he know the answers to questions that hadn't yet been asked? And those red eyes, unlike those of any other dwarf, and stunted growth. He should have been man-sized, not a dwarf at all. Yet no man has eyes like that, either.

What are you, Kulubak Magri? Some creature out of the depths of Loki's blue-faced daughter's kingdom? Some monster out of Hel?

It didn't matter. Only the platform mattered, and the work to be done thereon. Only the finding of Tyrfing really mattered.

For the first time since completing his ascent Alvis was able to take stock of his surroundings. Kulubak Magri shuffled over to the flambeau and used it to ignite the cressets set around the guard-rail and attached to the out-size gallows. The gallows itself was built into the very structure of the scaffold and rose treble their height above them, almost to the tips of the stalactites crusted about the roof of the cavern, the uprights supported by diagonals which were themselves strutted for additional stability. They supported a beam almost two feet square and over thirty feet long to which the noose about the ure-ox was attached towards one end. The main area of the platform was covered in ure-ox hides, nine of them, cut square and stitched together to form one single enormous square covering. The centre one seemed to dip slightly, as if it covered some trap or depression in the floor. It was also fouled with the droppings of the trapped creature harnessed over it.

'Whatever you do,' Kulubak Magri commanded, 'stay on the hides. Don't venture near the edges. Do you understand me?'

Alvis nodded, his tongue mute in perplexity. How could the hunchback have built such a structure single-handed, let alone have hauled some nine hundred pounds' weight of ure-ox up there? Truly he was in the presence of sorcery.

From inside his silver-crusted black robes Kulubak Magri produced a carefully knapped flint knife, set in a handle of ruddy dwarf-gold. With an expression which was more a leer than a smile he asked: 'Shall we begin, King Alvis?'

He paced the edges of the ox-hides, describing symbols in the air with the ancient knife. 'Do you come from the earth?' he demanded, his voice echoing within the immensity of his surroundings. 'Do you come from the sky? Do you come from Trollheim? Do you come from Jotunheim? What are you, Herjan? What are you, helmeted one? Where are you, Grimnir, the masked one? Will you come to me?'

He paused against a windlass and pulled hard with his free hand on the lever controlling it. As the noose tightened a fraction the ure-ox bellowed with renewed fear and pain, its mouth slobbering with the intensity of its torment.

Alvis sensed, rather than felt, that a band of thin mist was beginning to form in the air beyond the platform. Slender white tendrils reached out for each other, forming a ring, slowly growing like the spun web of some invisible spider.

Kulubak Magri renewed his pacing, the pain-cries of the mutilated, imprisoned sacrifice the only sounds until he began his invocations once again.

'Are you coming to me, Sanngetall? Are you coming to me, right-guesser? Will you come to me, Sidskegg? Will you come to me, Long-beard? Bileyg, Baleyg. Sigfod, Allfod. Biflindi, Helblindi. Are you coming to me?'

His voice rose, almost reaching that booming pitch and intensity that Alvis had first heard upon passing through the rune-carved door. The mist thickened, strengthened, began to stretch out its tendrils towards the edges of the platform. Alvis felt his legs weaken beneath him and the sour, metallic taste of fear bite at the inner corners of his mouth.

'Are you there, Oski? Are you there, fulfiller of desire?'

Something was there, Alvis shuddered to himself. Something was out there, standing on nothing but the mist, and something, some things, black eyed, black bodied, black winged, were flapping between the stalactites stabbing down from overhead. There was something familiar, something terribly familiar, about the names which the sorcerer was howling into the darkness.

Kulubak Magri set his fingers to his mouth and whistled, short, sharp, shrieking whistles which hurled themselves against the distant stone, bouncing back, compounding their echoes, reaching an intensity which the dwarf-king felt would surely deafen him.

The whistling stopped, replaced by a low, muttering mumbling, a wordless mumbling which, though wordless, somehow had sense and meaning, a mumbling which grew louder, becoming a chant, becoming a tuneless, wordless song, each phrase of which was carefully orchestrated to form a descant with the echo of the phrase before. And in that tormented, echoing descant was a force which Alvis felt could bring the stalactites crashing down, impaling both themselves and the platform, tearing on down, carrying their stricken bodies with them, stabbing with shattering force at the floor of the cavern over a hundred feet below them.

'I call you, Vak. I call you, Thekk!

'I call you Glapsvid, Fjolsvid!

'I call you, Oski, Omi!'

The flapping overhead intensified.

In the mist, eyes of liquid amber began to prowl, eyes hidden in mist-grey bodies as yet little more than shapeless, stalking fears.

'It is I who call to you, Vak. It is Kulubak Magri who calls to the alert one. Will you answer me?'

The mist-grey bodies began to take on form. Their eyes burned. Their jaws slavered. Their feet dug claws into their formless floor.

Alvis felt the first of many tremors rack his limbs. There was another shape out there in the mist, a shape which grinned and waited, a shape as yet unformed that was waiting to test the sorcerer's full power rather than hesitating.

'I do not have to come to you,' a deep voice whispered. 'You have no real power over me, Kulubak Magri.'

Alvis dropped to his knees upon the ox-hides, his robe sticking to his scrawny body, wet-through with sweat and urine.

'Not him!' he whispered, urgently. 'Kulubak! Not HIM!'

'He is the only one who can help us now,' came the calm reply. 'Come, Ygg. Come, terrible one. We need you . . .'

The hunchback shambled across to a rope anchored in one of the outer squares, the polished, knapped edges of the flint knife winking in the light from the cressets.

'Come to us, Hangagud,' he howled, placing the knife against the rope. 'Come to us, God . . . of . . . the . . . Hanged!'

The strands of fibre parted. The ure-ox howled. Alvis hugged himself in terror.

Kulubak Magri grinned.

Then everything happened at once.

The hide-covered trap beneath the ure-ox fell away, plunging the strangling, crippled beast down through the very centre of the platform. As the thrashing creature reached the bottom of the drop the gallows-beam bowed with its weight. The noose tightened. The bow released, sending the bronze-headed spear deep into its heart, forcing a final, cacophonous bellow from its lips before blood jetted up through the throat and mouth to fountain briefly through the trap, to spray those above and the ground so far beneath, to splash the gallows and the rope and the dwarf-king where he swayed upon his knees and the hunchbacked sorcerer.

The mist solidified. The wolves howled with delight and prowled beyond the guard-rail. The ravens settled on the gallows. The one-eyed god leaned smiling against the spear called Gungnir.

100

'Welcome to my home, Allfather,' Kulubak Magri smiled in calm return.

In the ensuing silence, more dead with his fear than living with his hope, King Alvis clambered unsteadily to his feet.

Odin suppressed his desire to laugh. Instead he asked: 'An elaborate performance, dwarf. You must want something very badly.'

'You know very well what we want,' Kulubak Magri replied, showing no trace of the fear Odin's presence was causing Alvis. In the silence following his statement there came only the low growling of the pacing wolves and the distant dripping of shed blood from the scaffold down onto the ground beneath.

Eventually Odin nodded. 'You want Tyrfing back,' he smiled, though the merriment was gone from his expression, replaced with a grim acknowledgement of their shared awareness.

'No more, no less, Allfather. Will you tell me where the sword is?'

Odin shrugged. 'The vargr has it.'

For the first time, as the god spoke those words, a trace of something, perhaps doubt, perhaps even fear itself, crossed the dwarfish hunchback's features. 'There is a vargr?' he asked, his voice tainted with incredulity.

'There is.'

'But why should a vargr want Tyrfing? What use is the sword to such a one? It doesn't make any sense, Allfather.'

Alvis looked at the prowling wolves, then up at the ravens, one of which was preening its pinions with a midnight beak. At Odin, however, he wouldn't cast his eyes. Dwarfs didn't gaze upon the Allfather. Not even Kulubak Magri should be gazing upon the Allfather.

Let alone questioning him.

'For reasons of its own,' the god replied.

In the huddle of his dampened robes King Alvis tasted, at that moment, the nadir of despair.

CHAPTER TWO

The returning of Atyl Skin

IT COULD have been Sudrafell, but it wasn't.

The charred ruins of Hather's home lay four days to the south of Uppsala. This smoking, gutted ruin, huddled against a landscape dusted with the first flurries of winter snow, black upon a dirty white like the smudging of ink upon monkish vellum, lay two days to the west of Omund's capital. Here the ground wasn't falling gently away towards the sea. It was rising steadily, taking Hather and his companions up towards the distant misty mountains.

The place was called, or had been called, Vigaknoll. Looking down on the smoke-shrouded horror from a nearby ridge Hather Lambisson could only reflect that the name, which meant Killer's Hill, was sadly something more than just appropriate. For Vigaknoll the name had been prophetic.

Vermund Bjarnisson rubbed a gloved thumb across his single eye, seeking to wipe the dust of travel, the tiredness, the sadness out of it. He muttered an indistinct oath which revealed itself as steaming air in the chill of late afternoon.

It was almost sunset. Behind the distant peaks, their whiteness flecked and stained by the roseate splashes of advancing twilight, the sun was going down, throwing long, black shadows of night across their world. Above them the sky brooded grimly, heavy with the threat of coming snow.

Vermund hawked and spat to clear his throat. 'It's still smouldering,' he muttered. 'We're narrowing the gap, Hather. At most we can only be half a day behind them now.'

Thorvald Brotamad was on the far right of their little group as it was lined along the ridge, five mounted figures, each leading a pack-horse, each wrapped in winter furs and heavily armed against the ending of their pursuit. He drew his heavy cloak of bear's fur closer and eyed the greying clouds. Then he shook his head and glared across to where Hather sat his mount in their centre.

'It's not right,' he snapped. 'It's all too easy. They've left us a good trail to follow, and that means they're playing with us.'

Hather Lambisson scratched his beard. Around them the world was silent, anticipating the coming of night and an uncertain future. Slowly Hather nodded.

'Perhaps they are,' he said quietly, urging his horse forward, beginning a slow, careful, watchful approach to the place that had been the thriving town of Vigaknoll but a few brief hours before.

For a moment or so the other four watched him, then Leif Half-Foot, the reins of his pack-horse tied around a gloved wrist, began to follow. Horsetail and Vermund exchanged glances, then spurred down and out to either side. As Thorvald Brotamad shook his head doubtfully and joined them the five riders, still abreast of each other, steeled themselves to observe their quarry's latest savage handiwork.

Flanked by his companions, each of whom was keeping an alert watch for any sign of a waiting ambush, Hather thought back over the circumstances which had brought him to Vigaknoll. Less than a month before he had been happy in his own hall with his wife and child. Old Tisti and Thorkel Tongue, more friends from his childhood than old nurse and steward respectively, had been alive. Now disease had claimed the old Lappish woman at a time when Hather felt he could have used her advice most. The vargr had killed his wife Gudrun and Thorkel Tongue, and little Svipdag was a helpless prisoner, trapped in the insane hands of the creature which was leading them across Sweden in a desperate and ill-prepared pursuit.

Thorvald Brotamad was right, Hather thought. The vargr *was* playing with them. Even the freeing of Atyl Skin and the leaving of the trail they were following at present was a part of the vargr's dreadful game.

But why? Simply as a demonstration of its viciousness and cunning? Or was there something more, something that fed the nagging, undefined doubt at the back of Hather's mind?

Two mornings before, King Omund's face had been purple and suffused with barely suppressed rage. Its accustomed pallor was entirely absent, and the grey eyes had blazed with a demonic light. That the vargr's men should enter the palace complex undetected and unopposed was bad enough, but over and above that they had freed the king's prisoner, that Dane from whom sooner or later Omund's torturers would have extracted a confession of Danish complicity.

'They freed him!' Omund stormed. 'And probably with inside help. My palace has become a nest of viperous traitors, Hather. Well, you've got your trail to follow, now. I don't care how you do it, but find the vargr. I've already promised you all the help you need. Find it! When the king isn't safe within his own stockade the very foundations of the state are beginning to crumble. It's time this vargr and its Danish swine were taught a hard, bloody lesson!'

Hather had listened and nodded, keeping his own counsel. Perhaps he wasn't entirely convinced about the Danish involvement Omund regarded as irrefutable, but the surprising rescue of Atyl Skin went at least some way towards proving Omund's case, adding a dramatic weight to the evidence of the bloodstained coins that the king had produced the day before.

Yet why did the vargr want his son? As a means of

104

ensuring that Hather followed in pursuit? Why should that be so important?

The question remained unanswered as they drew closer to the broken gates of Vigaknoll. Outside the stockade the huddle of artisans' workshops and the homes of the poor stretched charred and shattered, small flakes of thinly-falling snow melting into hissing steam as they touched hot embers. Here and there a body sprawled, hacked and forgotten in its falling.

Death stank in the growing darkness, lit briefly from moment to moment by the moon, waning towards its last quarter, emerging spasmodically from behind the snow-laden clouds.

Slowly, slipping the keepers free of their sword-hilts and loosening them in their scabbards, the five travellers dismounted and tethered their beasts. With that highly refined, instinctive caution which came from long years of staying alive in a hostile environment, walking softly with drawn weapons and shields held ready, they made their way through the fallen gates, into the heart of the stench of burned wood and roasted flesh, into the thinning smoke and the steam from the thickening snow, into the occasional flame and dying red of twisted embers.

A child, perhaps eleven, perhaps twelve, lay fallen in their path, its wide eyes staring sightlessly into the falling whiteness, relaxed in death except for the left hand, frozen into a clutching clawing at the ground beside its body. In the dim light it wore two mouths, one above the chin, the other below it. Both gaped red with escaping blood.

Other bodies lay around it. Nearby a woman, perhaps the child's mother, was doubled over on her knees, grasping the wound in her chest with reddened hands. Even as they watched some stiffening or contracting of dead muscles pitched her over on her side, huddled in death like a foetus in a ravaged womb.

Expiring timbers cracked. Fires hissed. The thickening snow, unmindful, continued to fall.

And they saw him.

He sat in the shell of a fallen longhouse, head in naked,

cold-red hands, feeling the lump at his temple. He was armed with a sword, still in its scabbard, and a long knife lay in the ashes at his feet. He seemed completely oblivious of them until Hather's sword began its pricking at his throat.

'I think you have something to tell us, Atyl Skin,' Hather said harshly.

The Dane looked up, drawing himself carefully erect where he sat, his Lappish coat rustling slightly with the movement. Beneath his shaggy eyebrows his grey eyes showed pain and the lingering traces of a numb, excess-dulled sickness at the carnage which had taken place around him.

'There's nothing he can say to save himself,' Thorvald Brotamad spat. 'Only one of them would still be here, alive and armed.'

He raised his sword to strike at the Dane's neck, but Hather whipped his own weapon up to block the stroke. The two blades clashed as they met and Thorvald turned blazing, furious eyes upon his companion.

'We talk first,' Hather said quietly, his voice menacing. 'Then we do what we have to. Put your sword down.'

Hesitantly, reluctantly, the scar-faced mercenary complied. As he did so Hather kicked the long knife out of the Dane's reach and, with the edge of his weapon to Atyl Skin's throat, drew his sword and threw it after the knife.

'You must know I wasn't with them,' their prisoner began. 'They left me here on purpose.'

'Unwounded and fully armed?' Leif Half-Foot demanded.

Atyl laughed savagely and brushed back his hair to show the gash at his temple. 'You call this unwounded? They almost split my skull open.'

'You didn't try to resist, or your weapon wouldn't have still been in its scabbard, Dane.' It was Vermund Bjarnisson who spoke, his single eye catching the light of a nearby fire and glittering harshly.

Atyl Skin shrugged. 'They must have armed me after they knocked me out. I was their prisoner whilst they

sacked this place, helpless to do anything to stop them.'
He thrust out his bare hands, displaying the raw patches
about his wrists where he had struggled against the ropes
which held him. 'You think I'd let them murder children if
I could do anything about it?'

Hather lowered his sword and rubbed the side of his
nose with his free hand. It felt hot and uncomfortable
behind the long nose-guard on his iron-bound helmet of
tough black leather. For some moments there was only the
cracking of cooling timbers and the steam-hiss of snow-
smothered fires. Then he said: 'I have no reason to doubt
you, Atyl Skin.'

'But I do!' Thorvald snarled.

'Leave him!' Hather snapped back. 'I want to hear what
he has to say, Thorvald. He might have some news that
will be useful to us. Control your anger or I'll have to
control it for you.'

The big man muttered into his beard and lowered his
sword. Perhaps Hather was younger and less experienced in
duelling, but he'd acquitted himself well against Starkadder
during their duel before Dalalven, and Starkadder was
the only man that Thorvald would admit to himself he'd
feared.

Besides, he reasoned, we share a common goal. There's
no point in diminishing our numbers and our chances by
killing each other off.

'You know they freed me, Hather,' the Dane said slowly.
'But do you know why? I'll tell you. It was an excuse.
Nothing more. They needed a way of providing you with
a trail to follow, so they infiltrated the palace at Uppsala
and freed me.'

'And that's all?' Askel Horsetail asked incredulously.

'Something more, perhaps,' Atyl continued. 'My "rescue" helps to strengthen King Omund's belief that the
vargr is in league with the Dane-Lands against him. But
I give you my word it's not true, Hather. I know it isn't. I
didn't tell you before, but I'm on King Gorm's business.
For some time now he's been losing shipments of coin and
weapons destined for the Oslofjord rebels. The longship

107

fire-scuttled at Raven's Point was one of them. My job is to find out where the cargoes are really going.'

Vermund and Hather nodded. Thorvald scowled. Leif Half-Foot and Askel Horsetail, on the edges of the group, eyed their grim surroundings warily.

'We should get out of here, Hather,' Horsetail muttered, 'before the vargr doubles back to attack us.'

Atyl Skin shook his head. 'That won't happen,' he said. 'The vargr wants you to follow for a while longer. There won't be any ambushes from what I've heard. Not yet, anyway.'

Hather nodded and bowed his head. When he looked up his eyes were bright with impending tears. 'And . . . my son?' he asked hesitantly, almost afraid of the answer he might receive.

'The boy, Svipdag? Well and, so far as I can see, unharmed. But he's not going to stay that way indefinitely. The vargr intends to sacrifice him at the next new moon. It wants his heart. Don't ask me why because I just don't know.'

The words were spoken in a flat, drained, emotionless voice, but their very calmness created a brief instant of panic within Hather. Yet as quickly as the moment came he fought it down. Precious though his son was, his last reminder of that first marriage to poor, ill-fated Astrid, neither his anger nor his fear would help their quest. If the vargr wanted them to follow then it also wanted them to catch up. And if they were successful, if they tracked the vargr to its final lair, then there was at least a chance that little Svipdag could be saved.

With the desperation of a drowning man Hather clung fiercely to that chance, blotting from his mind any lingering turmoil or emotion which might jeopardise its achievement.

Vermund laid a hand gently upon Hather's shoulder. 'It won't work,' he said sadly. 'The snow will be covering their tracks. There's no way for us to know which way they're going now.'

'Yes, there is,' Atyl Skin smiled knowingly. 'That's

why they kept me alive. Hundermann wanted to give me to his dogs but the vargr . . .'

'Hundermann?' Thorvald Brotamad interrupted. 'Is he still alive?'

'Still alive,' came the reply, 'and as nasty as ever. You know him too?'

'He served Olaf of Trondheim for a while in my youth, almost thirty years ago. He still has his dogs, you say?'

The Dane nodded. 'Seven of them. But I doubt very much that they're the same ones. No hound lives that long.'

Hather looked from Atyl Skin to Thorvald. 'Who is this Hundermann?' he asked.

'A mercenary from the south,' Thorvald replied. 'Either a Frank or a Hun. I've never really known the difference between the two. He'll serve anyone, or any thing, if the price is right. A giant of a man, almost seven feet tall, with a way with animals you wouldn't believe unless you saw it. When I saw him he had a pack of the largest, most evil hounds you've ever seen. Crossed Dane-hounds and wolves from the look of them.'

Atyl Skin felt his mouth twitch into a nervous smile. 'That's what he has now. The same dogs your steward spoke of before he died,' he added, looking at Hather. 'Hel-hounds if ever I saw them.'

'And the vargr saved you from them,' Hather continued. 'An unusual act of kindness, Atyl.'

'Not really,' came the reply. 'As I said, it wants you to follow. I've been told where they're going next. That's why they left me here. They were keeping me along in case the snow blotted out their trail. As soon as it did they intended to leave me so that I could tell you how to continue your pursuit. There's a tributary of the Dalalven flows out of the mountains just over a day north of here. The river will be starting to ice over for the winter but there's a ferry-crossing slightly south-east. They intend to cross there.'

'And their eventual destination?' Hather asked.

Atyl Skin shook his head. 'I don't know, but they'll leave sufficient signs for you to follow. Some sort of fortress in the mountains, I think.'

'On the far side of the Dalalven?' Horsetail queried. 'To the west? There's hardly a hill worth the naming to the east. So it must be west . . .' His voice tailed off, adding to the uncertainty in his tones.

Hather studied his face, noting the doubt which was clouding the warrior's dark eyes. 'What is it, Askel?' he asked gently.

'You've never been up there or you'd know,' Horsetail answered. 'It's not good news, Hather. So far as I know there's only one place in that area they could be using as their base.'

'Can we take a short-cut?' Leif Half-Foot demanded. 'Surely if we know where they're going we can head them off? With a change of horse from a steading on the way one of us could be back in Uppsala in just over a day. If there's a short-cut we could meet them with Omund's army.'

Hather nodded. 'That makes sense. Is there a short-cut, Askel?'

The older man shook his head. 'Not that I know of. But it will only take them about four days to reach their stronghold. There's nine nights before the glimpses of the moon. That gives us four for the army to catch up.' He paused and stared at Hather through worried eyes. 'The part I don't like, if I'm right, is where they're going. It's not a good place, Hather. It's supposed to be an old, abandoned entrance to Trollheim, sealed-off now it's true, but still a haunt of dwarfs and sorcerers. I've never seen it, but they say it spans both sides of a chasm through which a river runs, and that the only way in or out is along that river. If they saw us coming they'd pick us off with arrows like ravens on a ure-ox's carcass.'

Leif Half-Foot rubbed his fleshy face. 'I've heard of it,' he said. 'They call it the Dark Stronghold where I come from, but its real name is Skroggrmagi. And in case you don't know, that means . . .'

110

'. . . the *monster's maw*,' Horsetail interrupted. 'Unscale-able cliffs to either side. Easily defended, even by the merest handful. If they reach Skroggrmagi, Hather, there's nothing we, or Omund's army, can do to get them out.'

With a scowl Hather Lambisson sheathed his sword and, muttering over his shoulder, turned and began striding back through the snow towards his horse.

Vermund Bjarnisson followed his vanishing figure with puzzled eyes. 'What was that last remark?' he asked his companions generally.

'He said that we'd better find a way to stop them before they get there,' Atyl Skin replied. 'Though how a mere handful, even a handful of Sweden's best, stops nearly forty riders, Hundermann's dogs *and* a vargr, is beyond my knowing.'

CHAPTER THREE

Saeunna

SHE HAD retreated from reality, away from a ghastly present into a strange, mysterious, recent past which offered in its dreams a sacred haven from her tormentors. Outside her the screaming and the burning had begun.

Within, wrapped safe from harm in the mantle of an old god's promise, she smiled with her memories, standing again beside that distant ice-palace, the frozen waterfall where no water fell except as sharded ice, that waterfall too cold, too deep in winter to exist in her homely landscape.

'I feel I should know you, sir,' she whispered. 'You have the look of one I ought to know.'

Less than an hour before she had carried the milk from the byre into the longhouse kitchen, where her father and his brother sat with their wives and children. She had supped simply off warm bread, salt herring brought up from the coast, and the fresh milk ladled from its wooden pitcher. Then, leaving the men over their ale, talking of others and their deeds, boasting of what they would have done themselves, she had gone with the other women and her younger sister, brother and cousins, to the area behind the partition where they slept communally upon beds of straw.

'What's it like to be a proper woman, Hildigerd? What's it like to be a *wife*?' she asked, so many times.

112

'You'll know one day,' came the answer. 'A man will come here to the ferry one day and make you his wife. Then you'll know. It's better to find out that way, Saeunna. . . . All men want the same thing, but not always in the same way. They're as different as their faces and their dress, and you can't judge their worth by either.'

So she went to sleep, upon the straw, and woke up with the one-eyed traveller beside the frozen waterfall.

'Perhaps you know me, child. Perhaps you don't. It doesn't matter. It doesn't matter at all.'

She looked up, her green eyes wide with wonder as the glittering, frozen cascade towered up towards the waning moon. The ice-palace winked and whispered its mysterious promises in the shifting light, sparkling and speaking with the voices of its vanished, flowing past.

'You don't need to know me, Saeunna. It's not important.'

'But I should know who's speaking to me, master. Otherwise I won't know how to address you properly.'

The stranger nodded, then he smiled. 'Address me as a friend,' he answered gently. 'Call me Harbard.'

It made sense. His beard was grizzled-grey, as was his moustache and the hair which escaped in wisps from beneath his iron-bound helmet. His face was kindly, though strong. It held no trace of weakness or despair, no echo of the frustrations he was feeling.

No echo of the pain she had to come.

Brown gloves covered the hands which held his light blue travelling cloak about him. Close by a pair of wolves, friendly as fear-trained hounds, lay with their lupine muzzles on folded paws.

Two ravens flitted and circled beneath the moon.

'Where am I, Harbard?' Saeunna asked.

His single eye burned brightly on her in the night, searing through her tattered, work-stained dress to the fresh young seventeen-year-old beneath.

'You'll be a prize for some man soon,' he said, ignoring her question, appraising red-gold hair and the scent of morning fields, fields dewed with love and hope for the

113

coming day. 'You shall know what it is to have a man, Saeunna.'

With an effort he looked away, raising and stretching out an arm, pointing away from the waterfall towards the dark, grim huddle straddling the frozen chasm downstream. There the ice-bound river vanished from sight, blotted out by jutting, twisted, asymmetric towers and pinnacles the like of which the girl had never seen.

'This is the gorge of Skroggrmagi, at the foot of the mountains,' Harbard told her. 'This is where your love may be returned with gratitude and hope.'

Her eyes widened and her tongue threatened to stick tight in her mouth. Yet she struggled to reply: 'But . . . this was never built by man . . . this . . . monster's maw . . .'

Harbard nodded slowly. 'It was built by a dwarf-king, many centuries ago in the days before man held dominion upon the face of this land. When they knew of his coming and dominion the dwarfs abandoned it, sealing off the undergound passages leading down into the depths of Trollheim. The men of these lands have yet to learn the art of building such things in stone. It will come to them, in future years, but for now there are only these mysterious and terrible reminders of an ebbing dwarfish power. Look hard,' he added. 'See there.'

From the depths of the structure shone a light, pallid and disturbing in the darkness of its bulk. It seeped out into the night from a stone-framed window to which shards of coloured glass yet clung, tainting and tinting its feeble rays.

'Someone lives there?' Saeunna asked, feeling her firm jaw drop open as her words escaped into the air on frosted breath.

Harbard shook his head. 'Not quite,' he said. 'Someone *waits* there.'

'But what's he waiting for, Harbard?'

The one-eyed god studied her questioning features. 'For many things,' came the eventual reply. 'For you, for others, for the opening of the passages to Trollheim, and for a creature sprung from myth that must not come to birth.'

114

It wasn't a nightmare. She knew from the shreds of gentleness which bound her in its depths that it wasn't a nightmare, but it had a power, a force, which threatened her even as she knew her body slept. She had never been to Skroggrmagi before. Indeed, she didn't even know of its existence, so she knew she must be dreaming and pinched her arm.

Saeunna felt nothing. Nor did she wake up.

'When you see Hather Lambisson,' Odin said, 'I want you to give him a message. Will you do that for me, child?'

'If you want me to. But who is Hather Lambisson?'

'That doesn't matter now. You'll know him when he comes. And he will know you by the fates of others.'

'You're speaking to me in riddles, Harbard.'

Odin smiled sadly. 'The price of plain-talk would be too great for me to pay, little Saeunna. Riddles are all I have left to me. Even my message is almost a riddle.

'Tell Hather to think upon the thirteenth heart. Do you hear that?'

Saeunna thought for a moment, then smiled, then bowed her head in assent.

'Repeat it back to me.'

'I am to tell Hather Lambisson to think upon the thirteenth heart. Is that correct, Harbard?'

'That will do very nicely, child. Believe me, I'm so sorry this has to happen to you.'

She studied his face, puzzled by his last remark. The single eye seemed sad and the corners of his mouth were turned down beneath the grey moustache. Then a movement at the corner of her eye caught her attention.

One of the wolves was rising to its feet. With a lazy yawn the other made ready to follow its mate. The ravens screamed and settled. The wolves cried out. Then they were gone, with Harbard, and Saeunna was at home at the ferry-crossing at the dawn, and a sword-point was pricking at her throat.

Following the persuasive promptings of her captors, at first not understanding if this was reality or merely a

115

further phase of her dreaming, the girl shook off her coverings and stepped outside into the chill red stainings of the morning. She stood in line with her family, men, women and children together, watching as her father showed the giant with the spiked black hair how the ferry-raft worked upon its guide-rope.

The river was crusted along its banks with thin ice, brittle ice that gave before a sword or war-axe. Whilst her father explained the crossing, a helpless prisoner between grinning guards, to Hundermann, others broke the raft free of its frozen moorings.

Saeunna's eyes widened and she rubbed the sleep from their crusted corners. Thirty, perhaps forty men were waiting to make the crossing with their pack-goods and animals. They were strong men, fierce men, but none that she would want for the Harbard-promised husband.

Four cossings. Certainly no less. Too many men and animals to cross in three, her father was explaining.

Saeunna's little sister clung to her waist with circling, stretching arms. Instinctively she reached a hand down to smooth the frightened youngster's hair in a reassuring gesture she was far from meaning.

So many men. So fierce. So weapon-clad. And, in their midst, its golden muzzle bright with crimson dawn, the wolf-clad figure with the strange, unhuman voice, its face expressionless behind the precious mask.

Saeunna shuddered as its eyes surveyed the prisoners briefly. They were dark eyes. Mad eyes. The eyes of terror and the eyes of death.

In Skroggrmagi someone waited for this gold-masked figure, for this creature sprung from myth.

'A were-killer,' Hildigerd muttered under her breath. 'A vargr.'

Between Hildigerd and Saeunna a little boy was trying not to cry, not to be afraid. Saeunna's little brother was trying desperately to face the end of his short life like the man he'd never be.

Led by a halter around his neck, stumbling and dirty behind the vargr, was a boy scarcely older than the

116

watching child. They could almost have played together, the differences in rank proclaimed by their clothing forgotten in the levelling games of childhood. Only Saeunna would ever know his name was Svipdag, and that he was the son of Hather Lambisson, and that his was to be the thirteenth heart.

The first group, including the vargr and the captive child, boarded the raft and crossed under her captive father's supervision. The giant, the one they called Hundermann, who spoke with a thick southern accent, controlled their progress with his straining muscles. The six, no, seven savage hounds, giant and fearsome like their master, waited with the others, so silent and unmoving they might have been carved from forest pine. Only when the now-empty ferry returned did one of them utter a bark of greeting.

His face expressionless, his eyes so blank as to be almost unseeing, Hundermann walked up to the animal and kicked it hard between the forelegs. Though it fell and rolled in agony for a moment the dog uttered no further sound.

The second party boarded the ferry as the sun climbed higher above the plains to the east. The longest shadows shifted slightly, shortening. Hundermann took them across. Saeunna's father, still under guard, was led towards the line of prisoners and pushed into place between Hildigerd and Saeunna's younger brother. His face was sorrowful and his eyes held waiting tears.

Oh, Mother Frigg, Saeunna thought. We're going to die. They're going to kill us and we're going to die. They're going to kill us all.

Hundermann came back. The third party went aboard. As the giant hauled them away from the bank some unspoken, unseen signal passed from ferry to shore. The one that dragged Saeunna, numbed, incapable of screaming, chilled by the horror of falling children and brutal, mindless rape about her, was handsome to the point of beauty on one side of his grinning face. It was only the other, eaten and pock-marked by some ravaging disease, that showed his nature as it should be seen.

117

Outside, her father tried to fight naked weapons with bare hands, hands that rapid slashes sent flopping uselessly into the boot-thawed slush, followed by his falling blood and silently-screaming severed head.

Saeunna's brother, roped and howling, was dragged towards the landing stage. Hildigerd died spraying blood-frothed words when the penis in her vagina was replaced by a shortsword.

But Saeunna didn't see that. Nor did she see the Danish coins Hildigerd's grinning murderer dabbed in red puddles and scattered across the ground. Saeunna had retreated into her dream, away from the stark reality of slaughter which had reddened her world more surely than the morning sun.

She was with Odin in the gorge at Skroggrmagi, beneath the ice-palace, staring down at the huddled bulk of the dwarfish stronghold which straddled the river with its terrifying blackness.

Half-face, showing yellowed teeth in his lecherous smile, tore off his black-iron helmet and pulled at his studded surcoat, ripping it open to reveal the hair-dark flesh beneath. He drew each of the three long knives which covered his crotch and stabbed them into the wooden bed-platform he'd tossed Saeunna onto. Then he removed the belt and dropped his breeches to his ankles.

Briefly she emerged from her dream and looked from the eaten face down the expanse of hairy flesh to his penis. It's small, she thought. I thought it would be bigger than that.

Is this the husband Harbard promised me? Is this all I have to enjoy before I die?

On the ferry, approaching the opposite bank, Hundermann heard the shouts and followed the pointing fingers with his eyes. Then he returned his mind and mighty strength to its task.

The vargr didn't want those distant riders killing yet.

Half-face filled her nostrils with the stench of his breath. Murder-hardened fingers tore her dress apart and dug into **the soft flesh of her young breasts.**

A head appeared around the door. 'Morg,' it called. 'Riders coming. Get your prick back in its house and stand ready.'

Morg giggled and began to grope Saeunna's vagina. Finding it near-dry he licked his fingers and began to probe again. 'My prick's standing ready for me,' he whispered. 'Isn't it, fuck-child?'

She wasn't listening. As he approached she missed the clashing of weapons outside and the shouting of battle-frightened men. She was with Odin at Skroggrmagi.

'Tell Hather Lambisson to think upon the thirteenth heart,' Odin said.

'The thirteenth heart,' she said aloud, unconscious of the horrible reality-drenching swords around her.

'I think you're ready for me, little girl,' the grinning half-face droned, its lips wet with anticipating spittle.

The last member of the third party scrambled ashore. His arms aching, his dogs upon the further bank, his small, dark eyes blazing with ferocity, Hundermann hauled upon the rope, striving to return for those who remained behind, those who were now fighting for their lives.

Harbard was right. It didn't matter. It didn't matter what they did with Saeunna any more.

Death comes when it's ready. It comes on shining steel. It comes with the warm rush of escaping blood, spraying naked breasts, soaking into the fabric of a ripped and tattered dress, staining the straw beneath a dream-mad half-woman half-child.

It comes with the arching, spraying, falling body of a half-faced aggressor. It comes upon the blade of Hather Lambisson.

Outside they hacked and hewed, parried and blocked, slashed and thrusted. Outside they howled and fell with shortening shadows. Inside Morg died without a word, the force of his falling almost wrenching Hather's sword out of his grip.

Hundermann reached the landing stage. Three anxious figures scrambled aboard the ferry, two bearing wounds, the third sprayed by his comrades' gore.

119

'Any more?' the giant snapped.

A wounded outlaw laughed hysterically. 'From those devils?' snarled the unwounded one. 'Dead or dying.'

'WILL YOU MOVE THIS THING?' howled the third. 'Where's Morg?'

'Forget Morg. His prick was bigger than his brain! If he's not dead already he will be soon!'

With a low growl, so low and bestial that it could almost have come from one of his hounds, Hundermann began to haul upon the rope again. He looked up as feet thudded hollowly upon the landing-stage. Howling wrath, blade bloody, Thorvald Brotamad leaped the ice-flecked watery gap towards them.

Onto a waiting sword.

His feet landed squarely, his knees bent, body leaning backwards. For a moment he stood upon the edge of the raft, his dark eyes studying the length of reddened steel projecting from his throat beneath his thick, black beard, a beard turning crimson with escaping blood. For a moment he stood there, twitching with horrified disbelief.

His weapon slipped from numbing fingers into the river beneath. As his killer released his grip upon the flesh-sheathed blade Thorvald Brotamad forced his mouth into a bubbling smile. Then he toppled backwards, arms out-stretched, into the rushing water beyond the ferry.

The rope whipped, smacking Hundermann across the shoulders as Atyl Skin slashed through it. The giant's knuckles were skinned against an upright timber guide but his grip held. Spitting oaths into the wind he struggled to bind the slack against the upright, to secure it so that the raft would drift down and across to the opposite bank.

The current flashed with brief red tendrils as it bore the body of Thorvald Brotamad down towards the distant sea.

Close by the landing stage a body moved, questing fingers seeking a pain-discarded sword. Askel Horsetail spiked it into the slush before it could rearm.

He looked around. 'Where's Hather?' he barked to

120

Vermund Bjarnisson, standing close beside the longhouse and nursing a rilling slash acoss his lower sword-arm.

Their horses wandered, untethered, amongst the dead.

Vermund tossed his head towards the longhouse. 'In there,' he called back. 'With a survivor. A girl they were trying to rape before they killed her.'

'A girl, you say?' Horsetail forced a grin. 'That sounds like young Hather Lambisson to me.' Then he turned and they both watched the corpse of Thorvald Brotamad float out of sight upon its final journey.

Vermund approached his old friend and laid his good arm around Horsetail's shoulders. On the distant bank Hundermann and the other three were scrambling to the safety of their waiting companions. Amidst the throng a wolf-like face shone with the morning sun's reflected splendour.

'No ifs or buts,' Vermund said gently. 'We had to send Leif back to Uppsala so that the army could meet us at Skroggrmagi. Thorvald took his chance with the rest of us. At least he died like the brave fighter he always was.'

Horsetail blinked and showed his teeth, the smile more ferocious than kind. 'It's what the Norns had written for him,' he mumbled. 'May Odin take him to Valhalla.'

Vermund laughed harshly through his scowl. 'He'll take us all before this jaunt is through,' he grunted, more to the rushing river than to his friend. 'But a death like Thorvald's is all a fighting man can ask.'

In the longhouse Hather had draped a blanket around Saeunna's nakedness. She studied his face with wide, green eyes, eyes that struggled to regain some expressive token of comprehension that her ordeal was over.

Beneath the landing stage, its body still tied, the lead-rope caught around a support so that the tiny corpse pulled and strained with the passing current like a human fish-float, the lifeless form of Saeunna's brother mocked the retreating vargr. As Vermund found it he cut the rope free, sending it down the river after the vanished Thorvald. Then he shed a tear.

'They wanted that child,' he said to Horsetail. 'That's

121

why they didn't gut it on the shore. But why, Askel? Why did they need a little prisoner like that?'

Saeunna managed a sad smile beneath Hather's comforting. Somehow, he thought, she looked like his first wife, though with red-gold hair. It was almost as if Astrid had been given back to him. He kissed her gently. Then she put her arms around his neck and wept. Her body shook with sobs as he stroked her blood-soiled hair.

'Are they . . . all . . . dead?' she asked, her voice a whisper under tears.

He gripped her shoulder firmly in reply. Then he asked: 'This is hard, but I want you to think for a moment. It's very important to me. I have to know if there was a little boy with them. A boy with dark hair and probably in good clothes. Can you remember him?'

She looked up with wet eyes and sniffed before she nodded. Her face glistened with spent crying and the flush of her despair. 'On a halter,' she replied. 'The one in the golden mask . . . was leading him. . . . Who is he?'

'He's my son,' came the reply.

She thought for a moment, staring up into the face of this fair-haired fighting man in costly armour. 'You're Hather,' she said. 'You're Hather Lambisson, aren't you?'

He held her at arms' length and stared at her. 'Do you know me, girl?' he asked.

Saeunna shook her head. 'A one-eyed man called Harbard told me to give you a message. He told me in a dream.'

Hather stiffened as she spoke, vague memories stirring. The name of Harbard was familiar, a name he'd heard so many years before. He released Saeunna and stood up, frowning. Then he remembered. For the first time since his quest for little Svipdag and the vargr had begun he remembered the man whose ghost still haunted his life, the man called Starkadder.

It was Harbard who had opened the gates of Trollheim. It was Harbard who had helped them on their way to meet King Dvalin in the castle at the centre of the burning lake.

Harbard. Greybeard. *Odin!*

122

'What's your name?' he asked her.

'Saeunna.'

'What's the message that Harbard gave you, Saeunna?'

'You are to think upon the thirteenth heart, Hather Lambisson.'

The thirteenth heart? As messages went that was worse than useless. Which thirteenth heart? The one the vargr was to eat? Whose heart? Little Svipdag's? Atyl Skin had told him that. He already knew that. And yet. . . . If Harbard *was* Odin the message must have some other significance.

She watched him with her large, green eyes, then reached up to smooth the frowning from his lips. 'Are all my family dead?' she asked, suddenly calm, almost peaceful.

He stared down at her. So like poor, lost Astrid. So friendless and alone. 'I think so,' he answered.

'Then I have business with this vargr, too,' she continued. 'That's why I'm going with you, Hather Lambisson. To Skroggrmagi.'

Her words shook him out of his perplexity, though adding to it in their way. 'How do you know about Skroggrmagi?' he demanded.

Saeunna smiled bitterly up at him. 'Harbard told me about it, Hather, in my dream, in the days when I was happy. And though he didn't say so in as many words he implied that, if I went with you to Skroggrmagi, I might find happiness there once again.'

CHAPTER FOUR

Death of a Christian

TOWARDS EVENING on the following day Saeunna led her rescuers across a ford higher up the river, where the twisting, turning land at the foot of the mountains slowed its otherwise rapid progress towards the sea. Behind them, as they rode, the gibbous crescent of the moon's last quarter was rising into a frost-bright sky.

They were three days at most from the gorge of Skroggrmagi.

By now, riding hard and fast, Leif Half-Foot should have returned to Uppsala to fetch the army Omund had been so busily assembling. Starting immediately, taking a direct route, mounted soldiers could reach the gorge and its mysterious fortress in a little over four days. That left two to find a way inside and rescue Svipdag, though Hather was slowly and painfully beginning to realise the impossibility of the task ahead.

Not only the vargr, but the sorcerer behind the vargr stood ready for them as well.

Saeunna surprised Hather and his companions by her determination and versatility. Taking dead Thorvald's place in their party came almost naturally to her. Though she wasn't particularly tall she had picked over the bodies of the seven outlaws they had slain until she found weapons and armour that suited her build. She rode well, her father having maintained a small stud-farm at the ferry-crossing as well as a dairy-farm to provide for their day-to-day needs. Travellers in that part of Sweden could be few and far between and the breeding of horses for sale supplemented their income.

Now there was nothing. The herds were slaughtered or scattered. The outbuildings lay in charred ruins. The longhouse was deserted and the ferry-raft, cut free by Hundermann after he had drifted downstream and ashore on the further bank, was lost and drifting down towards the distant waters of the Baltic Sea.

For a little while, as she dressed the bodies for their graves, she had cried over her slaughtered family. Her tears for her little brother, though, were mingled with relief at the fate he had escaped. From what her new friends told her of the vargr it became obvious that the boy was being taken prisoner only to have his heart torn living from his body on this very night.

Briefly, this gave them hope. If the sequence of bloody sacrifices could be broken there was every chance that the vargr's plans could be frustrated. Yet they knew, even as they voiced the possibility, that the hope was false. Somewhere, somehow, a heart would be found for the creature to consume beneath the waning moon.

Nothing was going to stop the vargr, Saeunna thought. Not even an army from Uppsala. Nothing could stop a beast that had murdered its way across the Swedish mainland.

Not even Harbard, or Odin, or Allfather, or whatever the one-eyed god's name really was.

Yet those doubts were not shared by Leif Half-Foot. As the warrior rode his final, failing horse towards Uppsala he could only wonder at the fires which ringed the city round, fires that flickered against the supplies assembled for the biggest army he had ever seen. The silhouettes of heavily-armed men patrolled between the flames, watching and talking, waiting for the time when their orders would come, listening to the spreading rumour that they were to be led by no less a person than the king himself.

125

Gloved hands caught Leif, breaking his fall as the horse stumbled before the palace gates. Through hazy eyes he saw a face peer into his own, then a voice was calling: 'Open the gates. It's Leif Half-Foot!'

They supported him until the cramps left his legs and he could walk on his own once again. Standing unaided, swaying slightly, his hands numb with cold and his toes aching for some warmth, grimed with dried mud and slush from his desperate ride, he waved them away.

'Take me to King Omund,' he said, his voice hoarse with the urgings he had bestowed upon successive horses. 'I have to see the king.'

A sentry led him stumbling, resisting and resenting proffered help, towards the royal apartments. As they drew closer members of Omund's personal guard took over the duty until he stood before a closed door in the vestibule of the king's longhouse. A guard rapped upon the exquisitely-carved planking with the pommel of his sword, and a muffled voice from within called for them to enter.

The guard opened the door and ushered Leif inside. Omund was sitting nonchalantly in an armed chair. Across the trestle-table from him, also seated, was a brown-robed figure with a heavy gold amulet of the White Christ upon his breast, a figure that turned questioning green eyes upon him before rising to support the weakened fighter.

As Omund watched, one corner of his mouth twitching beneath his straggly moustache, Brother Gerard led Leif to the vacant chair and sat him down. Then he poured a goblet of wine and held it to the soldier's lips. As the force of the liquid began to warm his body with its strength a little colour returned to Leif's face. He struggled to rise.

'I must stand before my king,' he grunted.

'That's not necessary, Leif,' Omund responded. 'You've obviously ridden hard and long to bring us news.' The voice held a trace of amusement which Half-Foot failed to notice, but which caused Gerard's eyes to narrow slightly as he replaced the goblet upon the trestle table.

'Shall I leave you, sir?' the missionary asked.

Omund pursed his thin lips and waved a hand

dismissively. 'That's hardly necessary, Brother Gerard. You've been a good friend to my reign in the past. Stay and hear what Leif has to say. It may have some bearing upon your movements.'

The monk shook his head. 'That's hardly likely, sir. This land isn't ready to accept the Gospel of Jesus Christ yet. Either that or my poor efforts are too insignificant to make much impression. Yet I believe that the teachings of the one you call *Hvitakrist* can be of benefit to Sweden. That's why I must return to England for a while, to raise a new mission to your shores, with your permission, King Omund.'

'You must do what you think is right,' the king replied, his smile persisting.

There was an irony in those words. Perhaps Omund didn't yet understand the part that Brother Gerard had played in the downfall of King Oli, albeit accidental. Gerard had come to Sweden some thirteen, perhaps fourteen, years before as a young missionary full of hope and ambitions for his faith. His companion, Brother Hugo, had been released from a lingering death by the merciful spear of an old Norwegian mercenary named Starkadder. Seeing in this legendary figure the embodiment of the pagan spirit, Gerard had sought Starkadder's death, even betraying the old man and his young companion, Hather Lambisson, to Oli's madness. In his youth and folly the missionary saw the king's gratitude bestowing upon him the first bishopric of Sweden, and an unobstructed spreading of the new faith he carried with him.

But the betrayals weren't over. Starkadder, freed by Vermund Bjarnisson, had killed Oli and spared Gerard's life. Whilst Starkadder was dead, had been for thirteen years, Hather Lambisson had grown in position and respect. Yet he had never alluded to Gerard's betrayal of him, even extending a friendly hand in his pagan way. And the missionary recognised a debt, owed to Hather and his dead companion in that grim adventure, which he had yet to find some effective method of repaying.

Do what I think is right, Gerard echoed in his mind. **What I think is right is to repay Hather Lambisson.**

127

Perhaps bringing him to Christ will be payment enough in its way. That's why I have to return to England for a while.

'Now, Leif,' King Omund grinned wolfishly. 'What have you ridden so hard to tell me?'

In a far corner of Gerard's mind a tocsin rang. Omund had been so concerned about the vargr before. He'd spent a small fortune raising an army to pursue it. Now, with one of the vargr-hunters before him to report, he displayed a casual unconcern.

'Have you found the vargr?' Gerard asked.

Leif shook his head. 'No, not yet. But we know where it's heading for. It's taking its men into a trap.'

Omund thumped down onto the table with a jewelled hand. 'Excellent,' he beamed. 'Then we have it. Where is it going, Leif?'

'The old dwarfish fortress at Skroggrmagi.'

The king's grey eyes widened in surprise. 'Up into the mountains? Can my army reach it in time to prevent it gaining its full powers?'

Leif nodded. 'Four days of hard riding should do it. That leaves three before the glimpses of the moon.'

Omund stood up, smiling broadly. 'This is splendid news,' he responded. 'For tonight, Leif, you must rest here, in my quarters. Tomorrow, with fresh horses and supplies, you will return to your companions with this message. You will tell Hather that the army is less than a day behind you, and that I shall lead it against this Danish menace myself.'

With a half-sigh, half-laugh of relief, Leif Half-Foot struggled to his feet and bowed slowly to his king. 'I shall tell Hather that, sir,' he said. 'And I thank you for the honour of your hospitality.'

'You are indeed a generous ruler, King Omund,' Gerard added. 'Leif's news, and your response, fills me with hope for this land's future. Now, though, I must formally request your permission to withdraw from the court.'

In the pause that followed he wondered if his words had sounded too hollow, too unconvincing. The warning-bell was still ringing its alarm, tolling steadily and loudly for an ill-defined suspicion. Something was terribly wrong,

128

and the sooner he got back to England the better it would be for him.

'I shall miss you, Brother Gerard,' Omund said gently, almost with a trace of sadness in his voice. 'You have our permission to withdraw, and may your White Christ go with you.'

Was that irony? As he bowed and withdrew the monk felt his uncertainties deepen. Yet even if his suspicions could be defined they were probably unfounded. The fear which had gripped Omund's court with the coming of the vargr had promoted many such ill-formed urgings amongst Omund's retainers.

Outside the royal apartments the night was as clear and frosty as it was for Hather and his group. The crescent moon leered down upon Uppsala, mocking the army with its distance, laughing at Brother Gerard and his worries as he walked across the compound towards the stables along the perimeter wall.

His pack-mule was loaded and waiting, and a chestnut mare had been tethered beside it. Two guards squatted under cover nearby throwing bone-dice and betting their pay upon their falling. One of them looked up and grinned at Gerard as he passed. He glanced down, his green eyes taking in the cloth spread for their game and the coins, some of them gold, scattered upon it.

And the monk's suspicions gathered form. And the shadows became alive with watching eyes.

Returning the grin with a forced smile, Gerard un-tethered both animals. Holding the reins of the pack-mule in his right hand he mounted the mare and started towards the palace gates. Pausing before them he nodded to the sentries on the inner side, then glanced backwards as the gates swung inwards to permit his departure.

The complex lay quietly sleeping in the night, frosted and unsuspecting beneath a waning moon. He rode through, winding his path out of the clustered dwellings before the gates and down between the camp-fires on the plain. This was a good night to be leaving Uppsala.

As he reached the edge of the camp he urged his mare

129

west before he fully realised what he was doing. His thoughts were occupied with the fragments of a puzzle that had yet to yield its sense to his struggling brain.

Leif Half-Foot guesting in the king's apartments. Why? As a mark of appreciation and respect? Leif was a good fighter, one of Omund's most responsible commanders. They all were. Hather had proven his valour and ability several times. Vermund Bjarnisson was the king's marshal. Horsetail and Thorvald Brotamad had both commanded long and well. They were the best King Omund had. The most loyal to their country. The most responsible . . .

Why had Omund let his best commanders form the group which hunted down the vargr? Wouldn't it have been better to send out scouts and keep Hather and the others to lead the army which destroyed it?

And why were those two guards back in the stables betting Danish gold?

He should have turned east and ridden towards the Baltic coast. From there he could have taken ship to England. To ride west across a wild, troubled land would both delay him and expose him to the possibility of unknown dangers.

Setting his heels to the mare's flanks he swung from west to north, unknowingly heading towards Dalalven. Riding harder, faster, so fast that an unknowing watcher would have thought he feared pursuit.

And in those moments, as the mare responded to his tugging at the bridle, Brother Gerard knew what he had to do. His return to England could do nothing to repay the debt he owed to Hather Lambisson. There was only one sure and certain way of doing that. Perhaps he didn't have all the pieces of the puzzle, but he had enough. That was why he was riding towards Dalalven and, eventually, Skroggrmagi. To repay Hather for his life. To show him the fragments of suspicion.

Whilst Leif Half-Foot slept the sleep of the exhausted, Omund received the report with blazing fury in his huge grey eyes. A gesture was sufficient to convey understanding. In the stables, in anticipation of the royal commands,

130

two guards soon lay dead and a night-dark stallion stood saddled and champing for its rider.

As the rider sped through the open palace gates, as Omund cursed beneath his breath and filled a goblet with Rhenish wine, as hoofbeats shattered the quiet of the army encamped before Uppsala, pursuing hoofbeats, the drumming of a loyal assassin, Gerard continued his desperate ride towards Dalalven, the pack-mule now freed of its burden in case the mare should falter in its strength.

With the coming of dawn Leif was roused and bathed by the king's attendants. After a good meal of salt fish, bread, cheese and ale he appeared before Omund long enough for the message of the previous night to be repeated and confirmed. Then he was led to the stables and given a mount, a spare, and a pack-horse laden with supplies. By midmorning he was riding towards Dalalven, unconsciously following in the tracks of Gerard and his murderous pursuer.

With the experience of a seasoned fighter, Leif broke his ride to change mounts every few hours, saving the energy of the individual horses in case some effort should be needed later, unknowingly making better progress than either Gerard or his pursuer.

Ahead of him, now aware of being followed, the monk rode hard, the pieces beginning to fit together in his mind. Somehow he had to reach Skroggrmagi. Somehow he had to warn Hather of the danger which lay ahead of him, a danger compounded by betrayal and its accompanying despair.

And behind him, riding steadily despite the tiring of the fierce black stallion, the killer gained by painful lengths.

As the occasional backward sight of his pursuer became a drumming in his ears, less intense than that of his own mount but steadily gaining in intensity, Brother Gerard decided upon a desperate gamble. Reining in he slowed his failing mare, then turned to face the oncoming rider, his right hand raised, holding the cross-amulet of the White Christ high above his head.

Once he knew that the pursuer was within range he

called: 'Turn back, soldier. Turn back from here, lest the curse of Jesus Christ descend to blight your days and those of the ones you love!'

He saw the face behind the heavy nose-guard, a face strained with its efforts yet grinning in malicious anticipation. One of Omund's household guards.

And then there was a dark speck upon the horizon, a speck which resolved with the passing, fearful moments into a rider with two spare horses. As Gerard's heart pounded with his fear, as his eyes widened in terror as his pursuer slowed the stallion to a walk, the sound of distant hoofbeats drummed into the chill-soft air.

'You see?' the missionary called. 'You are yourself pursued. There comes one with new orders, or your death. Christ is ever merciful.'

The rider came closer, reined in alongside the mounted monk, a drawn sword in his right hand, its shining blade winking in the mid-day sun.

The pain was over almost before it began. With the thrust came a rapid, blinding agony which closed Gerard's eyes against the snow-white landscape. Then they opened once again as the numbness stole from his extremities into his body, then to his whirling, spinning brain. As he slipped from the saddle to the death-white ground, away from the life-reddened weapon in his killer's hand, there was only peace, and the consciousness of a debt remaining unrepaid.

Then the assassin turned and charged Leif Half-Foot, drops of Gerard's blood flying in its wake as the weapon whirled above his head. Leif rode low, sword drawn. As the riders passed the killer slashed wildly, missing the warrior's back by inches. Wrenching on the reins, slowing and turning with the effort, Leif rode in pursuit, coming upon the guard before he had properly turned his stallion, his clean sword slicing through the side of the killer's neck, sending him pitching over and off, reddening the ground with the force of his deathly falling.

His brows furrowed with the effort of unwilling understanding, Leif Half-Foot dismounted and turned the corpse of Omund's guard with his boot. Then he walked back along the deep-dug tracks of their conflict to where Brother Gerard, his robe darkening with escaping blood, lay dying in the snow.

The monk was clawing for his fallen cross. Leif placed it in his hands and watched in silence as Gerard raised it to his reddened lips and kissed it in token of approaching death. Then he stared up at the help which had come too late.

Bewildered, his sword stabbed into the ground beside him, Leif could only frame his question. His tongue stuck to the roof of his mouth as his lips moved with the single word, breathing steam into the coldness of the day.

'Why?'

Gerard smiled calmly. He no longer felt pain or coldness. He no longer cared about his debt to Hather. At last, if Christ would give him time to help a follower of Odin, there was a way it might still be repaid.

He spoke calmly, unafraid of his approaching death. ' "*Verumtamen ecce manus tradentis me, mecum est in mensa.*" '

'I don't understand your Christ-speech, monk. My own tongue. Say it in my own tongue.'

Gerard's eyes closed in assent. Without opening them again he said: ' "But yet, behold, the hand of him that betrayeth me is with me upon this table." Can't you guess, Leif? Tell Hather . . . that I loved him . . . in my way . . .'

He took no breath once the words had left his mouth. The man who had once dreamed of being the first-ever Bishop of Sweden lay dead upon the land he'd come to save.

Leif gathered the scattered horses. In the dead guard's pouch he found some coins of Danish gold. As he rode on towards Dalalven and Skroggrmagi he turned the monk's last words in his mind, trying to make some sense of them, of Gerard's death, of the traitor from King Omund's household guards who had done the killing, the traitor who had taken Danish gold to betray his king. Above him, as he rode, two ravens circled in the snow-grey skies.

He never saw the one-eyed watcher with the wolves.

CHAPTER FIVE

In the vargr's camp

HUNDERMANN, REACHING out a giant hand and pulling scraps of meat from the spit-roasting lamb with his horny nails, scraps that he tossed for his waiting beasts to fall upon and squabble over, was scowling into the flames. Elsewhere the bulk of the vargr's company sat huddled around two other fires, each of which was cooking a stolen animal. Around the perimeter of the camp no fewer than eight sentinels were watching for signs of pursuit in the freezing darkness, wrapped in fur cloaks that gave scant protection from the deepening winter.

'We could have stopped them then and there, at the ferry,' he growled. 'That would have been the thing to do. As it is, we've lost men, and they're still following. It's not what I would have expected of you, master.'

Across the yellow glare, so small in comparison to the southerner's giant frame, sat the wolf-skinned figure of their demented leader, the lower part of the golden mask hinged down to reveal a shadowed mouth in which viciously-white teeth glistened from moment to moment with the shifting, twisting flames. Even the massive hound-master had never seen the vargr's face, nor any part of its body beneath the skins it wore. The hands that reached out to cut strips of meticulously-carved meat from the roasting lamb were sheathed in gloves of fur that gave the impression of paws rather than human hands.

The vargr ate in silence, inserting strips of meat into the opening in the mask and drinking from a long-necked leather flask. When its meal was over the mask hinged back into place, renewing the impression that Hundermann sat before some gold-faced werewolf. The only concession to humanity made by the mask was around the eyes, which were set more closely together above the muzzle than an animal's would have been, their colour behind the golden skin masked by pieces of fine-cut polished glass, reflecting the firelight back, making them seem to blaze with an inner, less-hallowed light of their own.

'You've already been told, Hundermann,' it replied. 'Hather Lambisson follows us to Skroggrmagi. That is the way it has to be.'

That voice always worried the giant. There was something unreal about it, something that added to the overall impression of a being at once human and inhuman, a true were-creature. Of course, anyone who spoke from behind a mask would have a muffled voice, yet in the tones of the vargr there was also a power, a deepening resonance, almost a metallic quality which rendered a disturbing unreality.

There was one other thing the giant had noticed as well. The creature never spoke when the mask was open.

He shook his head and looked away. Though he was the vargr's lieutenant, the closest any of its band had come to being a trusted servant, for none would ever want to be its friend, he couldn't understand the reasons behind their campaign of terror and violence. They raided, they murdered, they took weapons and gold and left them in pre-arranged places along their route. True, each of them was well-paid, amassing a personal fortune which would make them rich enough never to need to kill or fight again. Hundermann himself could return to his homeland on the banks of the Rhine and live like a king. They feared nothing. They were strong enough to defeat anything

135

short of an army. Yet at the ferry they had run from six men.

The vargr laughed at the big man's perplexity. Even in its strangeness it seemed imbued with a natural humour, though not a humour which was totally sane. 'You worry too much, my friend,' the creature began. 'There's nothing to concern yourself with. Hather shall die, as his brat of a son shall die, when the time is right. And that won't be too long now. Tomorrow we reach the gorge at Skroggrmagi. Hather is at least two, perhaps three days behind us. We have plenty of time to prepare for his coming. Atyl Skin served us better than he served his friends when he cut the ferry-rope. It's a pity, though,' it continued with a deep, disturbing sigh, 'that we lost the boy Graff took. I needed him.' The mask tilted upwards, as if the wearer was peering through the glass-covered eyes at the pallid crescent of the moon above them.

Elsewhere Hather's company was camped close to the place where Saeunna had shown them the ford. Leif Half-Foot was still in Uppsala, sleeping the sleep of the exhausted in King Omund's royal apartments.

'How is Graff?' the were-killer asked. It was a simple enquiry, no trace of concern for the wounded man's condition sounding in its voice.

'Not good, master,' Hundermann replied. 'He'll probably be dead before we reach Skroggrmagi.'

He felt the dread begin to rise from his bowels towards his throat. He knew what was coming, and it was butcher's work. With the boy they had captured at the ferry lost, the vargr needed another heart, a fresh-ripped heart. And it needed the heart that night.

Behind the mask eyes narrowed in appreciation of Hundermann's distaste. A paw lifted to point at a distant peak outlined against the cloudless blueness of the night sky.

'Bring me his heart when the moon passes behind that peak,' the vargr commanded.

Hundermann struggled with the threatening shudder, finally managing to suppress it before it could be brought

136

to birth. Butcher's work, and on one of their own as well.

It was no way for a fighter to die. Graff had been with them since the beginning, when the vargr's company was first assembled from picked men bought at extravagant prices. He'd done his share and more, and it had been his effort on the ferry-raft, though badly wounded, which had killed Thorvald Brotamad.

It wasn't right. It wasn't fitting for him to be butchered like that, no matter what power his master might ultimately derive from it at Skroggrmagi, with the coming of the glimpses of the vargr-moon.

Even so, he sighed inwardly, shrugging to himself. I've done everything else the vargr wants. And there has to be an end to all this bloody bestiality soon.

He'd thought of betrayal. Whilst he was hardly squeamish and took pride in the silent efficiency with which his dogs killed, Hundermann had himself been occasionally revolted by the brutality of their raids. Yet betrayal would serve nothing. All it would do was get his death. The only course of action was forward with the vargr, even if he didn't fully understand what they were aiming for.

'Yet what if King Omund sends an army in pursuit?' he'd asked his master. 'We can stand against small townships, and Hather's friends are hardly enough to feed my dogs with. But Omund's no fool, even if he is a weakling. He won't stand for us gutting his good people for ever.'

'Omund will have other things to worry about,' came the vargr's reply. 'He'll forget us when the war with the Dane-Lands starts. We might even prove of some benefit to his enemies. The one who will give me my full power has no love for puny Omund or the Ynglings.'

It was as much of an answer as the giant southerner could expect. There was no point in asking further questions, in trying to fathom the identity of the sorcerer who stood behind the vargr. That some unholy alliance between naked power and insane will had been forged was all too apparent. To attempt to question it could only end in frustration.

In reality Hundermann didn't want to know. It was enough that some magical power lay behind the vargr's actions, a power which had so far led them virtually unscathed in their carefully-charted route across Sweden.

'Does it have to be Graff's heart, master?' he ventured. 'One of our own men's? Why not use the boy's now? His father will still follow us, if only for revenge. Then you can take his for the thirteenth heart at Skroggrmagi . . .'

His voice tailed off. A warning hiss issued from the mask across the fire from him that made him falter into silence.

Why was he so afraid of the small figure that he'd never seen without its wolf-guise? What made him so reluctant to challenge a creature that he could have snapped in two without straining a muscle in his mighty frame? Perhaps he'd know when they reached their destination. Perhaps he'd know a lot of things then.

Meanwhile he would do what he had been doing. He would swallow his bile and obey. He would wait, secretly afraid, until he saw the one behind the vargr, until he saw the one who waited to give it powers beyond his dreaming.

'When you bring me the heart,' the vargr ordered, 'bring me the sword as well.'

'As you desire,' he said with unaccustomed meekness.

The were-killer stood up and drew a cape of wolfskins about its shoulders. Then it turned and strode off into the darkness beyond the circle of firelight.

Hundermann sat alone, except for the dogs which lay in silent dreams or sleepy wakefulness around the half-stripped carcass of his meal above the fire. With a muffled curse he reached out and snatched the spit from its supports.

'Come on, my children,' he growled. 'There's no man-flesh for you yet, so make your meal of this.'

With an effortless swing of his mighty arm he hurled the spit away, hot fat and the odour of charring meat tailing behind it. As one the dogs, suddenly alert, sprang to their feet and pursued their unexpected feast.

The giant stood up and flicked his eyes towards the waning moon. It stood a fraction from the designated peak. Swallowing hard, Hundermann moved around the fire until he came to the vargr's pack, where it rested on wolf-fur on the ground. Beside it, wrapped in earth-stained sacking, a long, slender, sword-shaped object waited. Picking it up he moved slowly, head bowed, to where Graff struggled with impending death at a little distance from one of the other fires.

Dark, pain-filled eyes flickered up at Hundermann's own as the giant approached. His bare head, the black hair hanging in sweat-matted plaits, rose slightly from the makeshift pillow beneath it. Pale, blood-drained lips wrinkled into a smile in the depths of a tangled black beard.

'So . . . it's sent you . . . for my heart?' Graff asked in a muttering whisper. 'Don't lie to me, Hundermann. . . . You have the sword there . . . in your hand. . . .'

'It's not my work,' came the gruff reply. 'If only you'd kept hold of that brat on the landing stage. But you have to know this, Graff, you're dying anyway.'

Graff tried to laugh, but only bubbled blood. 'Do what you have to,' he grunted. 'I'm not fit . . . to stop you. But tell me something first. Am I right that only you . . . and it . . . have seen that sword?'

Hundermann nodded. 'It's the vargr's. It's had this sword since before we formed. And you're right. Only the master and I have ever seen it unwrapped.'

'Then I'll tell you something . . . Hundermann. The blade is long and straight, with two keen edges . . . and it carries no runecharm. The hilt is . . . wrapped with gold wire. The guard and pommel carry plates of gold stamped . . . with scenes of legend. . . . And its name is Tyrfing. . . .'

The giant felt his small eyes narrow in their deep sockets. There was no way Graff could ever have seen that sword since the vargr's company was formed, yet he had described it perfectly.

'How can you know such things?' Hundermann demanded, his voice an urgent whisper.

'Come . . . closer,' the dying man hissed. 'Take my heart, Hundermann. I can't . . . prevent you. . . . But listen to my story first. . . .'

Above them the crescent moon touched the brooding blackness of the peak. For some moments more there were only the noises of the camp, the crackling of failing fires in the night, the low-voiced talk of companions in the darkening circles, the snoring of those who had passed into uneasy sleep, and a whispering that none but Hundermann could hear.

Then the wrappings fell free of the sword Tyrfing, the gold-hilted sword with the runeless blade, the blade of legend. The blade that killed Starkadder.

One of Hundermann's massive fists crashed against Graff's jaw with brain-jarring force, rendering the final mercy of unconsciousness. Seconds later Tyrfing had done its bloody work.

He took the sword and the dripping heart to the waiting vargr. He left it using Tyrfing's edge to slice the raw muscle into strips that could be fed through the mask. The sounds of those choking, gurgling swallowings nearly turned his already weakened stomach.

If ever a creature was pure evil, then the vargr was that creature. If ever a weapon had evil forged into its very metal, then that weapon was Tyrfing.

Had Graff told the truth in those dying whispers? Once long ago, Hundermann knew, his dead comrade had been a seaman, even owning his own vessel, bought for him by an unnamed patron, at one time. His story was unusual, almost incredible, but it could be true. Certainly only one who had seen Tyrfing before could describe the sword so accurately.

But was it true? Could it really be as Graff had said? Could anyone, any thing, contemplate the horror that the dead man had described?

The giant ordered two of the sentries to bury their slaughtered companion, more out of respect for the words he'd been entrusted with than through any spirit of friendship or concern. Then, with the guard changed in the

140

small hours of the morning, he lay down to attempt a short and fitful period of sleep. His dreams were wild and he awoke sweating more than once, despite the stark white coldness of the landscape beyond the failing fires. With the coming of dawn he cast off his skin blankets and wrapped his sweat-chilled body in a fur cloak.

About him as he stood, watching the sun rise over the eastern plains, the vargr's camp came slowly back to life. So dark, he thought, standing alone in the grey-pink dawning of a day that threatened snow, his hounds licking the sweat from the massive hands hanging at his sides. Everywhere else the day will be light, but here there can only be darkness.

Shortly before noon they reached the frozen river, its icy length winding up through the foothills of the winter mountains. They followed along its banks for as far as they could, a train of dark, huddled, mounted figures against a world of whitened anguish. As the banks on both sides began to narrow and steepen the vargr spurred its horse out onto the ice, careless of harm, secure in some obscure, pervasive belief in its own invulnerability. They followed, hesitantly, but the river was frozen solid and easily took the weight of men and animals. Ahead of them the sides of the gorge twisted to the right, rising in walls of primeval, ice-scourged rock.

Hundermann increased his pace until his mount drew alongside that of the vargr. 'This looks a good place to set a trap for Hather Lambisson,' he advised.

The smiling in the vargr's metallic voice could only have been matched by one beneath the golden wolf-mask. 'There's no need to, my friend,' came the reply. 'The fortress itself is trap enough. We have three days to pre- pare for Hather's coming, and a further three before he watches me tear the thirteenth heart from his own son's living body.

'Watch now,' it continued. 'As we round this turning you will see the fortress of Skroggrmagi. I warn you, Hundermann, you have never seen a sight such as this in all your life.'

141

The creature was right.

As they followed the course of the river around the bend in the gorge the dwarfish citadel came into sight. Towering above and behind it, increasing its bulk and density by darkening its details into silhouette, the ice-palace of the frozen waterfall shimmered and dazzled in the mid-day sun. Light seemed to cascade instead of water, blinding and terrifying with its intensity, rendering the huge, river-spanning archway beneath the fortress a gigantic, blazing maw as of some arcane, gigantic, time-forgotten monster.

Skroggrmagi. The monster's maw.

Horses towards the rear of the column shied, their riders struggling to control them, as one of the company, terror-stricken by the unearthly, brooding presence of the place, howled with pure terror and tried to gallop back along their frozen path. The horse went down in a shower of ice-chips, skidding along the surface with legs flailing, throwing its panic-stricken rider further down the icy slope. Still screaming, now with pain to frame his horror, he clambered to unsteady feet and half-ran, half-slid, stumbling and cursing from their sight. Hundermann's hand tightened upon his bridle but the vargr laid a restraining hand upon his arm.

'Let him go,' it said. 'Such a niddering is of no use to us. If he lives that long he'll run into Hather and his death.'

Reluctantly Hundermann complied. It had not been reprisal that threatened to motivate his pursuit. The fleeing man was Thorfinn, the surviving friend, since Morg's death at the ferry, who had helped with the freeing of Atyl Skin from Omund's dungeon at Uppsala.

The giant shrugged and resumed his ride. If Thorfinn managed to escape he was well out of it. Perhaps such flight would be the wisest thing for them all.

They maintained their pace, riding steadily nearer to the fortress, though a nervous silence, punctuated only by the neighing of the stricken horse upon the ice behind them, had descended upon the column. Briefly Hundermann considered the possibility that there was some force opposing them that was beyond the limited powers of

142

simple humanity. Their number had diminished to thirty or so. They had, one way or another, lost a full quarter of their number whilst their pursuers had only lost one man so far.

It wasn't right. Yet so many things about this desperate, enriching venture weren't quite right.

His dogs, heavy-clawed, were coping with the frozen surface well, though all this running over ice and frozen ground was bound to have some effect upon their stamina. Occasionally, as they loped beside the horses, they looked up at him with grinning jaws, though their eyes proclaimed the discomfort underfoot. Soon now, he thought. Soon you'll be able to rest and warm yourselves. But from the look of that place up ahead there won't be much comfort for the rest of us.

As they drew closer the dazzling effect of the sun upon the frozen waterfall diminished, enabling them to pick out features of the dwarfish fortress which spanned the gorge. Clusters of towers rose from the stone-built structure, towers covered with the writhing, grotesque figures which so resembled nightmare carvings, yet were actually the bodies of dwarfish malefactors petrified by exposure to sunlight. In form the fortress of Skroggrmagi resembled an enormous bridge upon which some demented monarch had decreed a town should be built. Holed and broken roofs, the missing pinnacles of turrets, the ruinous walls and sharded windows, windows that would be shunned in daytime, shuttered from the inside against the destructive presence of the sun, leered down at them with the tatters of their former glory.

It was a place of majesty and wonder, a place of mysteries older than even the accursed Yngling dynasty itself. It was also a place of fear, and it was fear that clutched at Hundermann's heart as they rode into the deep shadows of its central archway.

The vargr had come to Skroggrmagi, as Hather would. And of the two only one might leave that place of wonders, that dwarfish outpost in a shunned, forgotten gorge, alive.

143

CHAPTER SIX

Crasyllus

SHE WAS so like his poor, vanished Astrid.

Had she looked, Saeunna would have seen only the determined mask which Hather Lambisson's face had become. Behind them, equally grim and resolute, rode Horsetail, Vermund Bjarnisson and Atyl Skin. Less than three days ahead of them, now approaching the fortress at Skroggrmagi, the vargr and its company rode along the surface of the frozen river.

So like Astrid, Hather thought. Even our meetings for the first time have been similar. Both dressed in rags, both threatened with rape. Only the colour of their hair and eyes is different.

He'd loved his second wife, the vargr-murdered Gudrun, as well as he could. She'd never been the great, heartbreaking love that Astrid had been, nor could she, if she'd lived, ever have become. There was about Astrid that wonder of first, youthful love, a wonder that remains always, deluding, undiminished, to create a memory which is never quite true. There was no way in which Gudrun could have fought and defeated that memory, and she didn't try. In her own quiet way she had been content to be the wife of the master of Sudrafell and the surrogate mother of his child. And it was all that Hather asked of her, unconsciously relegating her to the roles of servant and ornament.

144

Beneath them the moving hoofs of their horses measured out the frozen miles of their pursuit. In their minds and hearts dwelt a fear of what they might encounter at its conclusion, but it was a fear that none would admit or deign to be weak enough to show. That's why their faces were so grim, so determined, so set in masks which betrayed the true nature of their haunted thoughts.

She rode with the same apparent determination as the others. To begin with it had been necessary to fight them every inch of the way for the right to ride with them after the vargr. Whilst woman might be almost man's equal in many ways in their world she wasn't regarded as a suitable companion for adventure, let alone danger. Yet Hather was puzzled by the message she had given him from one he believed to be the Allfather, and it was his curiosity which had tipped the scales of argument in her favour, that and her manifest determination to follow behind them whatever happened.

And without Saeunna's knowledge of the river they would be even further behind their quarry. Without her showing them the ford, which had seemed almost impossibly difficult until they actually attempted it, spurred on by her example, the vargr's lead of two and a half days would have lengthened and strengthened into an almost insurmountable obstacle to little Svipdag's rescue.

When they made camp that night Hather found himself avoiding their new companion, taking the first watch to avoid having to speak to Saeunna whilst she prepared a meal from their supplies. That she possessed a certain beauty was indubitably true, but it was a beauty which disturbed Hather, stirring feelings within him which he had believed lost for ever with Astrid's disappearance.

It wasn't right, not with Gudrun so recently dead and little Svipdag still a prisoner in the hands of a murdering maniac. He shouldn't be starting to feel this way. Not so soon. And not with the grim pursuit of the vargr yet to draw to whatever dreadful, dangerous climax lay ahead of them.

Yet her eyes were green and her hair was red-gold. Her

145

skin was white and her breasts were firm, and Hather, despite himself, found that he wanted her and fought the harder against his wanting because he knew that it was there.

He stood alone upon the frosted landscape, away from the cheerful warmth of the fire, away from Askel and Vermund and Atyl Skin, and Saeunna, listening to the night-wrapped sounds, the distant howling of the wolves, the crying of the midnight ravens. He set his mind firmly to unravelling the riddle which Harbard had spoken to Saeunna, who had told him to think upon the thirteenth heart.

It had to be Svipdag's. It had to be his son's. There was no other reason why the vargr should keep its little captive alive. Anyone else it had encountered had been murdered, except little Svipdag and Saeunna. . . .

Her name again. She was a human ghost, haunting him, creeping unbidden into his most secret thoughts.

He had known, even as he stood before King Omund at Uppsala and heard the vargr mentioned for the first time, that he had heard the legend of the vargr before. Only one person might have told him of such a creature. Old Tisti. It had to be the old Lappish woman, the old, devoted nurse who had left him all she owned in her age-browned oaken chest. Now all that remained was the ring, still wrapped in its shred of goatskin in the pouch at his belt. He felt it through the leather layers of pouch and glove which separated it from his hand. Still there, still heavy and solid and mysterious.

Slowly, carefully, he opened the pouch and took it out. Unwrapping it, he replaced the goatskin and slipped the ring over his gloved finger, holding it up to the fitful light of the gibbous moon to study again the rayed design it bore. Some Lappish charm, no doubt. Perhaps one day he would find out what it meant.

The other things, Hather felt, were gone for ever. The chest and its contents, the strange box of bronze with its dark, granular powder and oddly-woven rope, the powders in their leather bags, were things that he would never see again.

Tisti, why did you have to die? I need you, Tisti. I need you now.

Is there nothing left but needs and hopes that can never again be fulfilled?

The thirteenth heart preyed upon his mind. He lowered the hand which wore the ring and stared into the darkness, listening once again to the calling of the wolves and ravens. If Tisti had told him the legend of the vargr she would also have told him about the hearts. He knew she had. He remembered the telling. But they had been words spoken to a boy impatient to be away, a boy who thought that his practice with the little javelin and wooden sword would teach him more than the mysterious, arcane ramblings of an ancient Lappish woman.

He scoured his memory. There had to be thirteen hearts. He remembered that much. Yet there was something special, something peculiarly dreadful, about the thirteenth, something that, if he could only remember it, would solve so many riddles in his life.

Where are you, Tisti? Valhalla or Hel? Where are you, now I need you more than ever?

Hather covered his tired eyes with the hand which wore the ring. No secret message, no special intuition, flashed into his thoughts. If help came at all it wasn't going to be that easy.

He looked back towards the camp. Saeunna was smiling as she scooped stew from a pan with a wooden ladle and offered it to Atyl Skin. In that moment he abandoned his quest for answers and gave way to simple, yet barely understood, jealousy. It wasn't right. She shouldn't be smiling at the Dane like that. Or at Vermund or Horsetail. Why had he taken such trouble to exile himself to the edge of their camp? It should be Hather Lambisson, the man who'd saved her from rape and death, who took that smile to warm his frozen limbs.

It wasn't right. It wasn't just.

Neither is life, came a voice from the deeper recesses of his brain. That's why Svipdag's in the hands of the **vargr. That's why Gudrun's dead. And Astrid. That's**

147

why you're standing alone in the snow whilst the others are laughing before the fire. Justice, true justice, is a luxury, Hather Lambisson. It doesn't come from King Omund or Odin or the Norns. It comes from a source which is older, wiser and more secret than any one of them. It doesn't cheat like men or lie like gods. It doesn't bluff and hide like Norns. It simply is, and the man who finds justice finds a treasure beyond his power to price, and a prize beyond his power to measure.

With the ending of his watch, after an immeasurable period of waiting and tormented thought, Vermund strode out to relieve him. The older man smiled and nodded as he took his post, and as he walked back towards the fire Hather sought some meaning in the greeting which had not been there to find. When he sat down he was sullen and broody, forcing Saeunna to restrain any smile she might have bestowed upon him in deference to his apparent mood.

And that bit home as well.

He slept badly, when he eventually gave over his brooding and sought the coverings of his bed-skins on the snow. The cold didn't worry him, though his steaming breath condensed into freezing droplets on his beard and moustache. He dreamed of his son, his chest ripped open, and a gold-masked horror raising a straining, pumping, dripping, living bloody muscle to its muzzle. The gold mask, gory from its feast, turned to smile at him, to congratulate him on the flavour of his son's flesh, to bait him with the lesser terror of his own approaching death. Then a crystal waterfall fell apart in deadly, frozen shards, and Hather Lambisson awoke to the dawning, drenched in frozen sweat.

Beside him, her eyes ringed with black tiredness, her hands soft, her voice caressing, Saeunna wiped his brow.

'Just a bad dream,' she whispered. 'Nothing more. No prophecy, no vision of the future. Just a bad dream.' Then she kissed him lightly on the lips and was gone, like the dreaming, in the dawn.

He pulled his aching body, shivering, to its feet. She

was squatting on her haunches, renewing the failing fire with fresh-found wood, cooking salt herring and gently warming beer for their breakfast. In the distance, where Hather had stood and brooded so many hours before, Atyl Skin leaned on a spear, the roseate rising sun on his back, staring in solitary vigil towards Skroggrmagi, waiting a day and a half beyond them.

Beside him Horsetail was snoring softly. At his side, still fast asleep, Vermund Bjarnisson opened and closed his mouth in dream like a dying fish.

He walked over and stood beside her where she worked above the warming fire. She looked up, smiling, as he approached. For the first time in his life Hather wanted to boast, to tell a deliberate lie, to impress her with the knowledge that he was the man who'd killed Starkadder, to make her want him with his greatness and his legend. Yet he held his tongue.

'You were dreaming,' she said in a whisper, unwilling to raise her voice and wake the two exhausted warriors who still slept beside Hather's bedding. 'You were awake before I touched you. I hope you didn't mind.'

He didn't mind. How could he mind? But Astrid and Gudrun, his two dead wives, rose up to haunt him as he began consciously, for the first time, to think about a third.

What was there about this woman? What was there about this green-eyed, red-gold-haired beauty, bred from a ferryman and his wife, that made him want her so? It couldn't have been the things she'd been or done. Perhaps it was what she yet might do, and the way she somehow knew that she would do them.

Where are you Harbard, Odin, Allfather. I heard your wolves and ravens in the night. I heard them. I know you're here somewhere. Won't you show yourself to me? Won't you tell me what I have to do to save my son, to save Saeunna, and myself?

They broke camp and rode on, only Hather aware of the distant, unseen, one-eyed watcher who stood alone save for his pacing wolves and circling ravens. If Saeunna knew of her part in the game they played, the game which might

149

save Hather's son from death and his land from the savage horrors of war with Denmark, she gave no sign. Towards noon the skies darkened and they felt a heavy warmth pervade the air about them. The noontide darkened and became oppressive, threatening a storm with flashing lightnings and the rolling of powerful thunder overhead. As they picked a path for their ponies through a straggling copse of pines there came a vicious flash which seared the base of a tree ahead of them. The horses reared in fright and became difficult to control. The air grew thick with the stench of heat-charred wood.

Then, for a moment or so, there was a stillness such as they had never known, a stillness so signal that they became afraid of it.

Saeunna eased her mount forward towards the lightning-blasted tree. Her tired green eyes struggled to make out the symbols which had appeared upon its tortured bole.

'Hather,' she called. 'There are runes here. Perhaps you can read them.'

He rode towards her, his eyes following the line of her pointing finger. As he drew level he saw the cuts in the bark near the base of the pine, saw them and read a word which stirred vague memories within his troubled mind.

ᚲᚱᚨᛋᛃᛚᛚᚢᛊ

Crasyllus. That's what the runes said. Crasyllus.

It meant something. He knew it meant something. He had seen that word before, though written in symbols very different from the runescript of his native land. When last he saw them they were in monkalpha, in Latin . . .

But where had he seen them? Crasyllus. A name? Not Norse, not Swedish. Yet somehow he knew it was a name, and a name that might yet have some relevance, some effect upon his future.

'Is this your doing, Allfather?' he called.

The world grew still, terribly still, about him. Whatever answer he had expected to his cry, this wasn't it. This

150

stillness, this deathly silence, a silence so heavy that it masked the hoofbeats of his approaching companions, was as much a threat as the overt violence of naked weapons at his throat could ever be.

Living or dead, famous or forgotten, who was Crasyllus?

The one-eyed god furrowed his distant brow. That's all, Hather, he thought. I've helped you twice, now, and this time I came close to breaking the rules which prevent me from becoming directly involved in your struggle. If you don't know, don't remember, don't understand, there's no more that I can do for you.

The two wolves, Geri and Freki, prowled the hem of the god's cloak. His hands reached down to fondle shaggy grey ears, to stroke their necks and sooth their blood-lust. At the uppermost branches of the mutilated pine twin ravens perched for a moment. Then, sharing their master's foreknowledge, they rose flapping into the air, cawing stridently.

There is one thing left that I can do for you, Hather. One thing and one thing only. Saeunna's dream was the first. These few runes are the second. When I help you again, indirectly, for the third time, I shall be stretching my agreement with Mother Skuld to its limit.

If only I could reach out and pluck the vargr from your life I would. But I dare not intervene directly. I have to work in riddles, in symbols, for the sake of a destiny which goes beyond your own. I dare not help you any more. Not yet.

Saeunna's horse reared, throwing her, as the second bolt struck, the lightning bolt which shattered the base of the ancient pine destroying the runes of Odin for ever, sending its splintered, ancient length crashing earthwards with a shuddering, juddering roar of fragmented timber. Within seconds Hather had dismounted and was beside her fallen form, an arm cradling her head, his eyes peering urgently into hers, seeking hidden pain, seeking the brief, consuming terror which must have engulfed her in that fall.

'Are you hurt?' he asked, his voice shaking with emotion. 'Are you all right, Saeunna?'

It was something in the way he spoke her name that told her how he really felt. But it was too soon, too early. It was impossible that he could be returning her own feelings that soon. She didn't yet know herself what she felt for him, whether there was anything beyond the power of gratitude, beyond the knowledge that he had saved her from rape and death at the ferry, that might in their wildest imaginings bear the immortal name of love.

Too soon, but too strong. It was there, unspoken, struggling to remain unacknowledged until a time might come when it could truly be named as love, or lust, or longing.

She allowed him to help her to her feet, struggling to ignore the nagging pain at the base of her spine. 'Nothing broken,' she replied, masking the discomfort behind a forced smile. There was no time for her to be hurt, to slow them down. Whether or not the pain eventually disappeared was immaterial. For Hather's benefit it had to be gone now, otherwise he would have no choice but to leave her behind.

And she had Harbard's word that there would be work for her to do at Skroggrmagi.

The reverberating echoes of the pine's falling were silenced beneath a rain of large, heavy droplets that thudded through the pine-needles overhead, dripping down into the snow at their feet to make holes like elf-shot in the whitened ground.

He helped her to remount before they rode around the base of the pine, its length now blocking their original path. His eyes sought the runes again to confirm what he'd read, but they were lost beneath the blackened, splintered bark about the base.

Crasyllus.

I know that name. I know I've heard that name. Or seen it. It sounds a name Old Tisti would have known.

They rode on, through the chilling rain. The spattering, pattering droplets drowned out thought and washed away the shards of a memory that wasn't ready yet to be recalled. Some days had yet to pass before, in a single, terrible moment of realisation he would recall a day almost twenty years before when a little boy sat in the hut of his ancient Lappish nurse and stared into the open chest, his blue eyes wide with wonder and childish curiosity.

'What's that, Tisti?' he asked in his unbroken voice. 'And that? And that?' He pointed as he spoke.

'Just herbs and powders, little Hather. Things I make my cures with. Things I use to remember the dark gods of my homeland.'

'And this box, Tisti? What's in here?'

She frowned for a moment, then shrugged and smiled. Why shouldn't her little boy know? One day he might need to know about her greatest treasure. One day he might need to remember what it was for. After all, she'd probably never have a reason to use it, but when Hather Lambisson grew to manhood it might one day save his life.

'That's the powder of Crasyllus, little Hather. There's nothing like it in the north. Perhaps there's nothing like it in the whole wide world any more.'

He placed his small hands on the edge of the chest and peered down past the raised lid. There was a small hole in the top of the ornate bronze box, though the light in the old woman's hut was too dim for him to make out the nature of the contents within.

He looked up at her, standing bent above him. 'Who was Crasyllus?' he asked.

Wide-eyed with wonder, little Hather? Very well, I'll tell you about Crasyllus, and his powerful powder.

'Come and sit down over here, by the fire. That's it. Now, little Hather, you want me to tell you about Crasyllus? Very well, if you really want me to. It's a sad story. The ending isn't happy, so you must promise me you'll try not to cry. Will you promise me that, little Hather?'

He tried to summon a disdainful sneer onto his childish lips. 'Men don't cry, Tisti,' he admonished her. 'Not grown warriors, anyway.'

Her wrinkled lips puckered in an effort to suppress a hurtful smile. 'Of course they don't. Now then, try to

153

imagine a time almost two hundred years ago. That's over twenty times as long as you've lived so far, little Hather. You remember I've told you before about that wonderful city to the south, where the White Christ's emperor sits upon a golden throne? The metal-domed, beautiful city with walls of coloured glass that men have named Byzantium? Well, in those distant days, before even the famous Varangian Guard was formed, an emperor ruled in Byzantium who was a good man, a man who loved peace for both himself and his people. His court was rich and famous, and he spent his money gathering the greatest scholars in the world about him and letting them study and work.

'Some of these men were what are called monks. That means that they gave their lives to the White Christ. . . .'

'In the same way that a warrior gives his life to Odin, Tisti?'

'Very nearly. These monks were skilled in things that people here in the north know little of. They were the inheritors of a great deal of ancient knowledge, such as the applications of the strange herbs of the southern lands for healing, and for making men unconscious so that they didn't feel pain when a growth needed to be cut out. Some say that they could even cure madness by taking off the top of the skull and replacing it without killing the person they were trying to help.'

'But how did they know how to do these things?'

'Oh, from ancient writings, marks made with a dark liquid upon vellum or plaited, dried leaves called papyrus, and from traditions handed down from lost and legendary lands with names like Thule and Aegypticus and Graecus. And the Emperor of Byzantium encouraged them all to come and make his court a centre of learning that would be renowned throughout the world.'

'And one of them was Crasyllus?'

The old Lapp nodded. 'He was amongst them. Crasyllus was a monk of the White Christ. He was famed for being what they called an alchymical magister, a worker with strange metals and compounds and substances from the earth. He knew how to work with the strong waters

154

which will dissolve even the hardest metals. But the thing he knew about best and worked hardest on was the thing they called Greek Fire.'

Hather's young brows knitted together. For a moment there was silence in the circular hut. Then he finally asked: 'What's Greek Fire?'

'Something that they used in wars in the earlier days. The secret is lost now, but it was a compound that they would rub on the enemy's weapons in the night. Then, when the sun came up, the weapons would burst into flames and be destroyed.'

'Did you ever see it work, Tisti?'

She shook her ancient head. 'No, little Hather. I know about it only from what Crasyllus told my grandfather before he died in frozen exile. You see, the things Crasyllus did were too warlike for the emperor. The monk found ways to make Greek Fire last longer and work faster. And he discovered other things as well.'

'Like what?'

'Like his powder. He was a great and clever man, was Crasyllus. Perhaps he was too clever for the man he served and the time in which he lived. He found a way to take some of the ingredients of Greek Fire and make them stable, so that they would keep longer. Eventually he learned how to make a powder that burned more quickly, more fiercely, than Greek Fire, which would keep for hundreds of years.

'One day he took the emperor out onto a distant plain and showed him how it worked. It burned so hard and so fast that it dug an enormous hole in the plain in the merest winking of an eye, roaring like a fire-giant and showering the ground with the earth it had ripped out and hurled into the air.'

She paused and studied the boy's face. He was watching her with wide-eyed wonder.

'Crasyllus expected the emperor to praise him,' Tisti continued, 'but that great lord just turned and walked away, scowling. Crasyllus rode back to the city behind him and went straight to his workshop. He knew that he had lost the emperor's favour instead of pleasing him, so

155

he packed a mule with whatever money and clothes he had, and what remained of his terrible powder, and left Byzantium before the emperor's soldiers could arrest him.

'He was only just in time. The soldiers came and found him gone, so they set fire to his workshop. There was a terrible roaring and the place where Crasyllus had been working blew apart with the force of a thousand tempests, killing most of the soldiers and destroying many houses. When the emperor was told he knew that Crasyllus had discovered a secret that was far too dangerous, so he sent men after the monk to catch up with him and kill him, to prevent him from telling how the powder was made to anyone else.'

'But they didn't catch him, did they, Tisti?'

'No, little Hather. They didn't catch him, though they pursued him north across the world until they lost his trail in the snowy wastes of my homeland. There he died, in exile, in my grandmother's tent of reindeer-skins, a saddened man. And all that there is for anyone to remember him by today is in that box of bronze.

'The powder of Crasyllus.'

The powder of Crasyllus.

Crasyllus. The name had to mean something. Yet the rain was washing away his efforts to remember, beating down in chill, slanting shafts that stung as they struck against bare flesh, soaking Saeunna and the men and horses that made their slow, painful way towards the vargr's stronghold.

Hather and Saeunna still rode together, an unspoken agreement dictating their positions in the column. The pain from her fall was fading and the discomfort had left her eyes, softening them once again. Rain streaked her face like tears, blurring her features, though Hather tried not to look across at her, afraid of what he might see, afraid of what he might dare to hope for.

I didn't love Gudrun, he thought. Not as I should have done. I loved Astrid, but the hurt came with that loving. She hurt me, hardened me. She made me close in upon myself. I'm sorry, Gudrun. I should have loved you better. I should have loved you as I love my son.

His features hardened beneath the trickling, running drops that fell upon it, chilling his cheeks and turning his beard into a sodden, icy wrapping. Suddenly he felt lost and defeated, for a brief moment permitting himself the luxury of despair, the relief of relaxing his tenuous hold upon the hoped-for future. Little Svipdag was going to die, and there was nothing he could do about it. All he was capable of achieving was to follow, and watch, and die himself. And those who rode with him were doomed also, as was his homeland and the Yngling dynasty itself.

Nothing left to do but die.

Then he stiffened, drawing up his unconsciously slumped shoulders, regaining his grip upon an unknown destiny, clutching it with the reins of his horse in a crushing determination which pushed his fingernails into the leather of his gloves until they cut it.

It's not the dying that's important. That comes to everyone, sooner or later. What matters is the manner of that dying. I know that. We all know that. I'm as much a pawn in an unknown game now as ever I was when I followed Starkadder to Dalalven.

But Leif will be back in a day or so. And Omund's army won't be far behind him. Then we'll storm the fortress at Skroggrmagi. Then we'll rescue my son and there'll be time to live again, and think about the better times to come.

Beside him, as they rode on, Saeunna felt the change, the renewal of that precious thing called hope. As she turned her head beneath the hood of her travelling cloak she saw that Hather was looking at her and smiling. Even if only for a few brief, precious days, there was a future to be shared.

Behind their trailing pack-animals Vermund and Horsetail exchanged glances and grinned. They might be damp and weary, but there was a warmth in their expressions that spoke of sharing their leader's hope.

Only Atyl Skin, riding on his own behind the others, remembered in his frowning at that moment that the clouds of war were gathering to unleash a greater storm than that they rode through.

CHAPTER SEVEN

The sorcerer at Skroggrmagi

'ARE YOU there?'

The vargr's strange, metallic voice echoed in the vastness of the columned, high-vaulted inner chamber, its walls devoid of windows and its distant corners badly lit from the fitful lights which burned in forged-iron cressets.

'Can you hear me? Are you there?' Its words echoed, reverberated, then faded into the heavy folds of the encroaching silence.

Perhaps they were too early. Perhaps its master would only manifest with the coming of the glimpses of the moon. Perhaps the dwarfs had lied when they had brought it here to make the pact, to make the arrangements which governed the unusual trade they had decided.

Whilst Thorfinn fled back along the frozen river on foot, back towards whatever fate awaited him along their travelled trail, they had pushed on towards the dwarf-forged fortress. Beneath its river-spanning arch the vargr's men had, for the first time, seen the broad stone ramp which led up to a doorless entrance. The stones of the ramp were worn, but enough of their oddly-grooved surface remained for their mounts to find footholds. The vargr had ridden in first, its men, afraid of the sheer strangeness of their surroundings, unaccustomed to and frightened of stone-built structures, hanging back to watch its ascent. Only when it had gained the entrance and turned its mount to face them, safe and unharmed, did they begin to contemplate following.

Hundermann followed first, stopping and calling to his reluctant hounds, urging them to obedience by the growling strength of his voice, a strength reflected and magnified by the soaring bulk of the towering fortress above them. As they obeyed, as he joined his master at the top of the ramp, the others exchanged glances and nervously began the climb from the frozen river to the yawning, monstrous entrance to the stronghold.

Inside they found stabling for the horses and, close by, along a low, wide corridor, a room where the vargr's child prisoner, Hather's son, could be confined until the time came for his bloody death.

A single torch burned in a bracket on the wall, betokening the habitation, by something or someone, of the fortress. Hundermann, his animals whining and cowering at his feet, took it in his hand and walked ahead, igniting the ready cressets as he passed, stooping to save his head from scraping on the low ceilings of the passages, kicking open doors as he passed them, wrestling with the thickened, age-woven cobwebs which festooned and shrouded the upper areas of the corridor-walls.

Behind the giant and his dogs strode the gold-masked vargr, incautious, unafraid, unlike the men that followed, mouthing their fear-brought oaths in urgent whisperings, occasionally laughing nervously until they heard the continuing echoes join together in a humming which returned to haunt them into silence.

Eventually they came to a high hall, its floor littered with fresh rushes over the imperfectly swept glass of the high, sharded windows, making the flagged floor beneath crunch and rustle under their booted feet in a way that did nothing to allay their growing terror.

On long trestle tables set together stood fresh food and ale. Lamps burned dimly in the stale air of the hall's lower

159

reaches, shedding their yellow light onto the waiting provender, tainting it with strange shadows. High up, where the afternoon sun streamed in on shimmering beams, piercing the cobweb-banners that flapped in despairing tatters from the roof-beams, the air played cold and curious games with the tracery of dust and neglect.

'The food is good,' the vargr announced with careless unconcern. 'Sit and eat. There's nothing you need do now but wait.'

They hesitated, some staring up to the light-prisoned dust-motes near the roof, others shuffling their feet upon the flags and rush-strewn shards of dwarfish windows. The place didn't feel right. It was so silent, so forgotten. Like a tomb.

Hundermann strode forward, a long knife in his hand, and cut strips of beef from a cooling haunch which he threw to his dogs. To begin with they sniffed the meat warily, then settled down to hold the strips between their paws as they chewed and ate in silence. With a grin the giant carved a strip for himself and sheathed his knife. Then he swilled wine from a silver pitcher into a glass goblet and drained it down. Encouraged by his example the others began to follow suit, the luxurious food, after their journey with its meagre rations, loosening tongues and dispelling fears as they consumed it readily.

'Keep them here,' the vargr muttered to its lieutenant. 'Nobody is to follow me, Hundermann. Not even you.'

He nodded, forcing more food into his mouth. He'd learned a long time ago that you did what your master told you and asked no questions, especially if the master paid as well as the vargr and could provide food like this after a long, hard ride. Even the fires that burned in the broad hearths to either side of the hall were welcome to chilled bones and cold-cramped fingers, albeit their light was strangely blue in the old, tired air of the ancient fortress.

Hundermann permitted himself the curiosity of turning to follow the vargr with his eyes as it strode away towards the low door in a shadowed corner. For a brief period, as the door creaked open, he saw the torchlit passageway beyond and glimpsed the steps at its end, steps that spiralled upwards out of sight. Then the door slammed shut and his master was gone from sight, vanished into the inner, mysterious depths of the stronghold at Skroggrmagi.

'Have you brought the things we need?'

The voice seemed to roar out of the very walls of that inner, windowless chamber. It came from everywhere, almost deafening and frightening even the hardened were-killer the vargr had become with its force and violence.

'I . . . have.' The vargr's voice was weak and hesitant by comparison to those strident tones. Its eyes peered through the mask, seeking the origin of that sound, finding nothing.

'The sword Tyrfing? You have Tyrfing, as we agreed?'

'I have Tyrfing.' It stepped further into the chamber, turning and peering at the emptiness, seeking in its corbel-crusted heights some sign of sorcerous habitation, some trace of life behind the disembodied calling of its mentor.

'And the boy, Hather's son. Is he alive and unharmed?'

'He is, and he shall remain so until the glimpses of the moon.'

The voice laughed coarsely, its laughter drowning out all other sounds, including the harsh, fearful, mask-rasped breathing of its servant. 'That's good,' the sorcerer continued. 'Very good. And Hather Lambisson is following to save the boy?'

'He is, though I shall gut the brat and eat its heart in front of him when the vargr-moon is come. But you, do you remember our arrangement?' Still the vargr turned, staring up, searching for the sorcerer in the shadowed heights.

'How could I forget? Since first you came to me and proposed our bargain I've thought of little else. We play our own games, you and I. You want the powers of the vargr, to transcend the vulnerable state of your mortality and wreak your vengeance as you will. The only thing that might have prevented you, apart from your own fear and distaste, has been counteracted by your bringing of Svipdag Hathersson to provide you with the thirteenth heart. The only thing which might have stopped me would have been your failure to deliver Tyrfing as we agreed. Now all that remains is for us to await the glimpses of the moon. Then both our schemes will come to their fruition.'

The silence returned, heavy and menacing. Then the sorcerer asked: 'Will you show me Tyrfing?'

'I have it,' the vargr replied. 'Will you show me yourself? I've never seen you. It's not right that we should deal with each other thus. We should meet face to face.'

The laughter resumed. 'You shall see my face when I see yours again, when you take off that mask I made for you to eat the thirteenth heart. The others didn't matter. Oh, they had some importance, they were a discipline, a training for what is yet to come, but the last is the one that works the trick, that takes you beyond any surviving vestige of your humanity into the realms you've sought to make your own. That's the one which will enable you to complete your vengeance in all its bloody, warmongering terror. . . . But how do I know that you have Tyrfing?'

'You'll see it, at the vargr-moon. When I've cut Svipdag Hathersson's heart from his body I shall bury its length in his father's body and leave it there for you. It will have no other work to do for me when those two are dead. The other can die by other hands, doomed by his greed, betrayed by his own betrayals of his bravest friends. . . . Only then, when I am truly vargr at last, shall Tyrfing be yours, my unseen friend.'

A sigh whispered about the chamber. 'Then so it must be,' the sorcerer responded. 'Look to your right.'

Peering hard through its mask the vargr made out, in the shadows between the flickering cressets, a doorway in the wall with a slumped, whitened, tangled shape beside it. Walking slowly, carefully, eyes alternately raised to the vaulted roof and flickering towards the doorway, it approached the brooding quietude of the inner chamber. Slowly the tangle of ivory fragments resolved into a dwarfish skeleton, the flesh long gone, eaten away by the tiny, nibbling teeth of rats and mice and the mandibled jaws of the spiders which even now inhabited the hollowed skull. Beside it the doorway was webbed over by

162

fat, dark, watching shapes that scuttled on arachnid legs before the paw-gloved hand that swept their homes away.

'None gave him permission to leave his post when the fortress was abandoned and sealed off from the rest of Trollheim,' the sorcerer explained. 'The obedience of the true dwarf is total. Until an order is revoked it remains an order, and no dwarf will disobey. Now, open the door.'

The brazen handle turned beneath the pressure of the paw. Slowly, with the screeching creak of dust-dried, tortured timber, the door swung inwards upon a scene that was terrible in its implications.

Inside was a large, circular chamber, its arched roof ruined at the apex, admitting strong shafts of afternoon sunlight. Beneath, supported by four petrified dwarfs, their faces now stone masks of frozen, final agony, a heavy slab of southern marble, its veined whiteness powdered grey with age-old dust, stood table-like, awaiting the sacrifice of a little child that would stain its purity with the completion of the vargr's design.

'Up there,' the unseen sorcerer continued, knowing that at its words the vargr would raise its eyes to the roof, 'the vargr-moon will stare down in its darkness on your work. It is to this place that you will bring your surviving prisoners to witness the deed. It is here that you will leave Tyrfing for me when our bargain reaches its fulfilment. Through that broken dome the glimpses of the moon will bring us both what we desire.'

The vargr nodded. The time was coming. Mere days remained until the mask could be removed. And then, with its victims secured and its vengeance prepared, with Svipdag Hathersson helpless upon the dwarf-held marble and his father watching helplessly in bonds, with the bestiality and brutality of its initiation gone for good, it could settle, throughout the centuries of power remaining, to the full and skilful realisation of its grim ambitions for the north.

'And you will come to me, then? I shall see your face?'

'Is it so important to you to know who I am? Yet I forget, you are still, to some extent, a human, and as such you have a human curiosity for inessentials. Yes, you shall see me then. I shall reveal myself, as you shall reveal yourself, as you shall have to reveal yourself so that Hather and his son may know their slayer before they vanish into death for ever more.

'Simply ritual, my little vargr. Nothing more than ritual. A plot, a plan, an entertainment staged by masters for their victims and themselves. You seek a revenge which, by your scheming, even now is gathering momentum to itself. With Hather's death there will be nothing to prevent it coming to fruition. Nothing at all.'

The vargr nodded, reassured. The months, the years of brooding and planning, were coming to their grim fruition at last. Soon, so soon there would be fresh blood on that marble slab. The first heart had been tough, revolting. Hot and wet and salt-sweet in its dripping, staining redness. The second had been almost as bad. But they had become easier to consume, easier to see and touch and raise to fearful lips to eat. Now at last there was only one of those pulsing, blood-leaking lumps of muscle to swallow. It would be young and tender, not old and fibrous like Graff's had been the night before. Now there were only six days and seven nights to wait, and on midnight at the seventh night little Svipdag would die, mere moments before the killing of his horror-sickened father.

You're going to watch, Hather Lambisson. You're going to be here to see me take the sword you laid in old Starkadder's grave-mound and cut your son's heart from his body with it. You're going to watch and spew with impotent terror. You're going to know what it feels like to face a vargr's wrath and vengeance. And then, when you and your little brat are dead and gone, when there's none of your hateful tribe left to know how weak you were, to realise the reason for my fury and revenge, I'll destroy the one you serve. Though the machine of his destruction is already in motion.

He's deader than you are, Hather, though he'll keep his life a little longer. Nothing can save him, and nothing can save you or your son. No gods, no Norns can hide you from a vargr's vengeance. You'll find no help this side of the grave.

164

'You should return to your men,' the sorcerer urged. 'They are already frightened at the strangeness of this place. They will have noticed your absence and become even more worried, little vargr. Go back to them. Reassure them. They must wait out the days for you, with you, but there will be work for them and their swords and weapons afterwards, when the waiting is finally over. Even Hundermann's dogs will have their chance to feast on frightened flesh eventually.

'When Hather's men catch up you must keep them at the entrance to the gorge. Prevent them from coming closer until the night of the vargr-moon. I have my reasons for saying this. You must wait, but I still have preparations to make. Only when the moon is dark, on the last night, must they be able to approach and enter this place. They will come, have no doubt of that. But they must not see the ice-palace beyond this fortress, nor the fortress itself, until they approach upon the dark of the final night.

'And if you hear strange noises, if you glimpse odd shadows on the walls, say nothing, do nothing. It will be none of your concern. I am here, though you cannot see me. I am here and so are some of mine. They will be doing my work, preparing for those moments when Svipdag is ready to yield up his childish heart to you, those moments when our fears are the greater in case some unforeseen circumstance should thwart our machinations.'

The vargr nodded slowly, the muzzle of the wolf-mask catching the shafts of afternoon sunlight and glimmering brightly in the dancing dust-motes trapped within them.

Six days and it would all be over. Six days and Hather Lambisson and his son would lie dead in this chamber. Then everything else could follow, would follow, inescapably.

If the foundations of the House of Yngling had begun to crumble with the reign of Oli the Great, they would crack apart and shatter for ever under Omund Olisson. And with the coming of the vargr the days of the Yngling dynasty were numbered. Mere days. Perhaps a week or so. No more.

CHAPTER EIGHT

The approach to
the monster's maw

THEY KNEW that sleep was out of the question in that rain, so they rode on until it began to freeze into hail and finally into a thick and gentle snow before they camped. Atyl Skin unwrapped dry tinder and kindling and cleared a space upon the frozen ground whilst the others sought for firewood and Askel Horsetail watched the route they still had left to follow. Once the fire was alight Saeunna saw to the duties she had taken upon herself, the preparation of hot food and something warm to drink against the chilling weather. As dawn broke on the last day of their journey, the morning after the vargr and its unknown mentor had spoken together in the depths of the dwarfish stronghold ahead of them, they fell into fitful sleep around the smoking, snow-steamed fire.

'Until the sun is overhead at noon,' Hather determined. 'Then we break camp and continue. No more than that. By sunset we should be at Skroggrmagi. That leaves us tonight and five more to find a way inside and kill the vargr.'

It wasn't a thought to induce easy dreams. They had all seen sufficient of the vargr's handiwork of butchery and terror along their route to know that the days ahead would

166

be fraught with fear and danger. Even a seasoned commander like Vermund Bjarnisson had sense enough to be respectfully afraid of what still lay ahead of them.

Yet they slept, and dreamed, each woken only by the need to stand a watch. They'd ridden hard and long and painfully to make up the time they had lost finding a ford across the river. Now they snatched what rest they could, each eager for the surcease which came with sleep, each wrapped in furs against the deepening winter, each hoping for a future that might not come.

The army would be here soon, they thought. Leif Half-Foot must have delivered his message and be well on his way back from Uppsala by now. Omund's army would be close behind him, ready to storm the vargr's stronghold and slaughter the monstrous outlaw who ruled within. After all, that was what Omund had raised the army for. To kill the vargr.

Beside the fire Saeunna watched as they fell asleep, one by one. Horsetail stood beside the tethered horses, watching by the picket-line, seeking some sign of returning ambush along the trail the vargr's company must have travelled. Yet when he was relieved by Atyl Skin he had seen nothing, and the Dane took over the vigil in the falling, whispering snow.

Leif can't be too far away. A day's ride. Perhaps two. Certainly no more.

Atyl Skin stood alone with his thoughts, not noticing when Saeunna heaped the last of the firewood onto the fire and curled up in her skin blankets for the night. He had begun to form his suspicions some time before, to realise the complexity of the conspiracy about them. When Leif Half-Foot returned he would have news from Uppsala, and between the lines of his message the Danish agent might be able to read the confirmation or denial of his fears.

His loyalties were divided between the friends he had come to know as he rode with them and the duty which his loyalty to King Gorm might require him to perform. He was still a Dane, and his first obligation was to his

167

country. Much as he might want to stay with Hather there could be another, even more hazardous, kind of work for him to do.

If he was right. And, if he was, he would be doing the vargr's work as surely as if he rode with Hundermann and the others.

When he felt the eyes boring into his back he turned in sudden alarm, his weapons challenging and his senses alert. Yet there was nothing there for him to see, only the sleeping camp and the fire which threw a fitful light into the snow-spattered darkness. Nervously he sheathed his sword and relaxed his stance, still conscious of the watchers though somehow convinced that his instincts, for once, had betrayed him.

Close by, in the shadows of another world, the one-eyed figure peered at Mother Skuld and smiled.

'Will he do your work, do you think?' Odin asked her.

The old woman shrugged beneath her wadmal veil. 'Who knows?' she muttered. 'You should know. You've sat upon your high seat since last we met, my Allfather. You've looked out across the world from your high seat and seen what is to be.'

He shook his head. 'Not all of it, Mother. You and your sisterhood have veiled some of the future from me. You've shrouded it in your mists and hidden both hopes and fears from my divinations. You know that I have to save the Ynglings from destruction for a while, yet you still place your obstacles in my path, binding me about with your threats and rules. You don't make it easy for me, you know.'

He felt, rather than heard, her laughter. 'Is a victory that comes easily worth the winning?' she asked him. 'A thing worked for is a thing that is treasured, Odin. As the Allfather you must know that already.'

'Yet the rules you make me play by are hard, Mother. Indirect intervention on three occasions will not be enough. You know that. I can never save both Hather and Omund unless I cheat, and if I cheat you've threatened to end the game, and the Yngling dynasty, for ever. What am I to do about that, can you tell me?'

'Have you thought that there might be others with a stake in our playing, Odin?' she asked. 'There are so many pieces on the tafl-board, and tafl can only be won when the king is free, or surrounded by at least three pieces from the enemy ranks. If others join the game, then the rules might have to change.'

He felt his ancient heart leap up behind his mail. She knows, he thought. She knows that there is another upon the scent of its own ambitions. She knows that I've made a bargain somewhere else. She could void the game, here and now.

'I've played by your rules,' he said determinedly, though not entirely truthfully. 'I've restricted myself to aiding Hather indirectly twice, so far. And I don't think you can say Saeunna's dreams or some runes upon a tree-trunk amounted to more than the most meagre of hints to help his memory. Not with the old Lapp woman dead before this all began. You snapped her life-thread before she could really be of service to her foster-son. Now he's on his own.'

'If Hather Lambisson is truly your champion, Allfather, if he's the true protector of the Yngling line, he'll find a way to save Omund, or you'll find a way for him. If he's not, then his life has no further purpose and he might as well lose it at Skroggrmagi as anywhere else.'

Odin looked down the length of the spear Gungnir upon which he leaned. He knew that Mother Skuld was right, that she could on rare occasions even show mercy for the sake of a greater purpose. He couldn't count on her doing so, though, and that meant that he would have to try all the harder to force an acceptable stalemate.

Her rules permitted him to intervene indirectly once more. How or when that intervention came was up to him, but he knew the effort, the vital effort, would be wasted if it came before Hather and his companions had reached the dwarfish citadel. Around their camp the falling snow was blotting out the dawn, making the day almost as

169

dark as the night had been. Their sleep wouldn't offer too much refreshment in such circumstances, and when they approached Skroggrmagi the following night they would be just as tired and vulnerable.

'If it can be done, Mother Skuld,' Odin announced, 'I shall save both Hather and his son from the vargr. But I won't do it at the expense of the Yngling dynasty. If it comes down to a choice between Hather's life and Omund's I shall save Omund. I have no choice.'

Only a desperate gamble, he added inwardly.

Her veil nodded in appreciation of his words, though he could never be sure to what extent she saw into his heart and read his secret thoughts. As he turned and walked away, back to where his wolves and ravens played their games of tag in the thickening snow, he felt her hidden eyes upon his blue-cloaked back.

Well, the bargain's struck, I shall keep my side of it. I only hope my treacherous partner in this work will keep to his.

Shortly before noon Hather's party broke camp. The snow had stopped, permitting flashes of orange-gold sunlight to break through the clouds and stain the landscape as they travelled. In the distance loomed the foothills of the mountains and the shimmering ribbon of the frozen river that wound into Skroggrmagi.

They would soon be there.

Horsetail saw the shape first. It was grey and patchy, covered with badly cleared snowflakes where the frozen fingers had ceased to do their work. The hair was rimed and the eyes stared painfully up from a badly frostbitten face. The figure was still moving, if the painful, sinew-cracking convulsions of half-frozen limbs could be called movement. Hather dismounted and trudged through the ankle-deep snow towards the dying man, kneeling beside him, restraining his agony with a hand upon his shoulder.

'There's a little wine left in that skin,' he called, gesturing towards one of the pack-horses.

Atyl Skin urged his mount level with the beast and

took the goatskin flask in his free hand. Then he rode across to where Hather knelt beside the figure and peered down.

'It's Thorfinn Helgisson,' he muttered, his breath steaming in the sunlight. 'He was riding with the vargr.'

He tossed the wineskin to Hather and watched as it was lifted to Thorfinn's chapped and blistered lips. He saw the eyes blink painfully in acknowledgement of the kindness and the throat move as the wine was swallowed, allowing a brief, comforting warmth to flood the dying man's body and limbs.

'You're . . . Hather Lambisson,' Thorfinn croaked. 'You have . . . no reason . . . to help me. . . .'

Hather smiled grimly. 'There's little enough I can do for you now, Thorfinn Helgisson. You can't be too far from your dying.'

'I know,' the outlaw replied, wearily. 'But I thank . . . you . . . for your kindness.'

He blinked hard, obviously suppressing pain, his body heaving with some hidden spasm. Then he said: 'Don't go there . . . Hather. Don't go to Skroggrmagi. . . .'

'Is my son still alive? Is Svipdag safe?'

'He is . . . and will be until the . . . glimpses of the moon. But you can't . . . save him now. Not now they're there . . . in that place . . . of horrors. There are . . . a thousand places . . . they can ambush you, Hather. Even an army . . . would be cut to pieces before it could storm . . . the fortress.'

Hather nodded. 'Even so, we have to try, Thorfinn. There's more at stake than just rescuing my son, though the boy's life is very precious to me. Your master, the vargr, has to be killed. You've done its work. You must know that it's the very embodiment of all that's evil. . . .'

His voice trailed away into silence. Thorfinn's eyes were still open, but the emptiness of death was all that stared up into Hather's face.

They left Thorfinn Helgisson there and continued towards the distant hills, weighed down and silent by the number of the tasks ahead of them. Hather's head was bowed as he listed them to himself, hoping for some opportunity to discover an easier path.

Rescue my son. Kill the vargr. Destroy the sorcerer behind the vargr's power. It's all so much easier to say than it will be to do.

Odin, help me?

But he has helped you, Hather. He's sent you Saeunna and the riddle of the thirteenth heart. He's cut runes upon the pine and reminded you of the name Crasyllus. Think, Hather. Think hard. Think of Omund and the blood-stained Danish gold. Think of Atyl Skin and the massacre at Raven's Point.

Think of the way that the vargr has been leading you here, forcing you to follow behind your captive son. They could have waited at the ferry. They could have waited and killed you there, but they didn't. Either the vargr, or the sorcerer, wants you to follow all the way to Skroggrmagi. There must be something for you to do there, something only you can do, or see, or suffer.

'It's time the vargr and its Danish swine were taught a hard, bloody lesson,' King Omund snarled. But Hundermann is a southerner, not a Dane. Thorfinn Helgisson was as Swedish as I am.

You're wrong, Omund. They're not Danes. The gold comes from the *Bright Eagle*. Somewhere there's treachery buried in all this.

And the vargr is only part of some dreadful conspiracy, only a fragment of the hidden whole. It may be my fragment, but there's more to this than the vargr and its sorcerer. If I can find the whole I'll know where my own fragments fit. Then perhaps I'll stand some chance of understanding them.

Saeunna hung back, leaving him alone with the puzzle of his thoughts. Behind her Atyl Skin struggled with his own beliefs and theories. Vermund nursed his wounded arm, the gash stinging with the cold of their journey, worrying the aged warrior with its persistence. Horsetail scowled down at the reins in his hand, used, like the others, to living on his instincts, concerned like them that

172

he was riding towards a fate that he didn't, that he might never, understand.

Vargrs and sorcerers. Sorcerers and vargrs. Things they had thought were gone from the north for ever. Things that shouldn't exist in the first place, let alone persist into the world they knew and loved. Yet in five nights the vargr-moon would rise into the sky and, one way or another, the end would come.

Perhaps for all of them.

Shortly after dark they reached the place where the sides of the gorge began to rise, leaving only the frozen river for their path. There they made their camp, deeming it safer to leave their entry into the monster's maw until daylight. If Thorfinn had been right then there would be an ambush waiting.

Hather tossed beneath his bedding. That didn't make sense either. Why should their enemies have continued to lead them to this place only to kill them from ambush? They could have done that at the ferry, if they'd chosen. What purpose could an ambush serve at Skroggrmagi?

With the dawn they rose and ate. Leaving the horses tethered they stepped out upon the frozen river, following the chipped, grooved path cut by the vargr's horses. They found Thorfinn's mount quickly, two of its legs broken, cold and stiff and silent on the ice. Ahead of them the high walls of the gorge twisted to the right.

Hather glared at Saeunna where she walked beside him. She smiled defiantly back, every inch a valkyrie with a beard-axe in one hand and a short-sword in the other. His efforts to persuade her to stay with the horses had been vain and he'd abandoned the attempt. Even so, he was unwilling to expose her to the danger that must lie ahead.

'We should spread out,' Vermund grunted. 'If there is an ambush ahead we present too tidy a target bunched together like this.'

Hather nodded his agreement. 'A line across the gorge, then,' he said.

They spaced apart, Hather and Saeunna in the middle with Atyl Skin to their right and Vermund on the outside.

173

Horsetail took the far left, sword in hand, peering through snow-tired eyes towards the twist in the gorge ahead.

Was there movement?

Vermund's eyes narrowed suspiciously. This was the ideal place for the defenders to spring any surprise they had in mind. Saeunna felt the fine hairs at the back of her neck begin to rise.

Atyl Skin looked across to Hather and nodded. It was too quiet, too easy.

As they reached the bend and caught their first brief impression of the gorge-spanning fortress and the glittering ice-packed waterfall behind, the hissing began. Hather leaped sideways, grabbed Saeunna and threw her back along the frozen river in a tangle of flailing limbs and weapons. Then he dived for the cover of the rock-wall to his right. Atyl Skin darted back, losing his balance on the ice as feathered shafts clipped and skidded off the surface between his feet. One arrow, aimed higher than the others, glanced from his Lappish coat, its trajectory almost spent.

Only Askel Horsetail, on the further side of the gorge, remained where he was, swaying slightly on his shuddering legs, the fingers about his sword-hilt weakening, releasing, permitting the weapon to clatter to the ice beneath.

Two arrows had found his throat.

THE THIRD PART

Of killings and the glimpses of the moon

CHAPTER ONE

Thoughts of betrayal

THEY MADE three attempts that day to rescue Horsetail's body from where it had fallen. Each time warning arrows fell close by, biting at the ice, some even stabbing into the warrior's corpse. Eventually they withdrew to the entrance to the gorge in a black mood of despair and desolation.

Saeunna, little more than her pride hurt by her slide along the ice, resumed her by now accustomed duties and prepared a meal towards evening. By this time they were beginning to run short of supplies so Atyl Skin took her beard-axe and went out onto the river to cut a haunch from the dead horse. He returned wearily with the dusk, dragging the dead meat, trailing sluggish, blackened blood in his wake.

Water was no problem, providing they could keep the fire alight to melt the snow. There was also an urgent need to put some heat back into their badly-chilled limbs, so they ranged as far as they had to before the gorge to find firewood and dig down through the snow for any grasses beneath that could be dried for tinder.

As night fell they sat huddled in their furs, making the most of their provisions and the carefully husbanded heat, supplies of fresh wood drying in the circle of its warmth, to some extent shielding those who needed its comfort against its power to help them.

Hather sat alone, his face grim, his bearing defeated. Saeunna took him a horn of luke-warm water and a bowl of boiled horse-meat and held them out. He looked up, blankly, unseeing, his hands remaining folded beneath his bearded chin. Sensing his greater need for solitude she set them down in the snow beside him and returned to the others.

'We've lost a good friend today,' Vermund explained gently. 'Hather and I have known old Horsetail for years. I fought beside him many times. So did Hather, in more recent times. He met us both when Horsetail and I were charged with guarding Omund at Dalalven. That was when he was with Starkadder, just before the death of King Oli.

'You know, girl, it's not right to leave old Horsetail out there on the river. We didn't have time to get Thorvald's body back and raise a mound above it, but I'd like to think there'll be a monument for Horsetail.'

He stared at her, permitting her to see the tears that clouded his single eye in the firelight. She reached out her arm, placing it about his shoulders, drawing his head down onto her bosom.

'I'm too old for this,' he whispered. 'I don't know what use I'll be to Hather now.'

He pulled away and sat up, wiping his eye with the back of a gloved hand. 'They could hold us back for ever, you know,' he continued. 'Unless they want us to, we four are not going to get through that gorge. My guess is that's what Hather's brooding about. And he's right. It's stupid. They lead us here, deliberately, then keep back. I don't understand it at all.'

'It will all come right,' Saeunna assured him. 'Your friend Leif should be back from Uppsala any time now. He'll bring King Omund's army. They'll help to storm the gorge and get us inside.'

Vermund nodded. If it can be done, he thought, then that force can do it. I helped to assemble it. The best fighting men in the whole of Sweden. Not even a vargr could stand against it. Well-trained and well-equipped. And they'll be here soon. They'll help.

178

Unless Omund doesn't want the vargr destroyed.

The thought crept upon him unexpectedly and chilled him more surely than the snow about them could have done. How could he even contemplate such a thing? That was why Omund had raised the force. To kill the vargr. What other reason could he possibly have?

Mantled with furs and his own thoughts, Atyl Skin sat in silence. He had come a long way from Jelling in the Dane-Lands, where his master, King Gorm, held court. From there to Raven's Point to Sudrafell, where the vargr had delayed its killing long enough to deliberately leave Thorkel Tongue alive to give Hather its message. Then to Uppsala, where King Omund immediately accused him of being a Danish spy, which in a sense, though a very different sense, he was.

A brief period of imprisonment followed before his rescue, his easy rescue, by Morg and Thorfinn and Hundermann. Then they had taken him unchallenged, unobstructed, through the gathering lines of Omund's army to meet the vargr itself.

Why had Omund sent his best men in pursuit of the wolf-clad outlaw? They would have been more use to him in Uppsala, unless . . .

At first his ears failed to identify the distant hoofbeats for what they were. Only as they began to break in upon his musings did he spring to his feet, with Hather and the others, and take up his weapons to challenge the approaching rider.

'In the camp,' called a voice. 'Who do you serve?'

Hather sheathed his sword and turned to grin at his companions. Saeunna sighed and relaxed when she saw the expression. His black mood had passed, replaced by a renewed hope for their future.

He cupped his hands to his mouth and called: 'It's all right, Leif. Ride in and welcome.'

'Hather? Is that you? Thank Odin you're all still well and alive.'

Leif Half-Foot's rotund figure rode into the circle of the flickering firelight. Despite the cold his horse was flecked

179

with foam and he was sweating beneath his war-clothes from the journey. As he dismounted and handed the reins of his horse to Atyl Skin he surveyed the four grimy, weary figures.

'Where's Askel Horsetail?' he asked. 'If he's on watch he must have fallen asleep to let me get this close unchallenged.'

'Up there,' Vermund gestured, sweeping an arm towards the point where the ice-bound river vanished into the gorge. 'He's dead, Leif. They've killed him.'

The newcomer wrapped Vermund Bjarnisson in a close embrace. 'I'm sorry, my friend,' he said gently. 'I ought to be more careful with my tongue.'

They parted and Leif clasped wrists with Hather and Atyl Skin. Taking off his helmet he approached the fire and squatted before it on his haunches, the helmet discarded, his gloved hands stretched out towards its warmth.

'I've another death to tell you of, Hather,' he said, looking up. 'I can't make any sense of it, but perhaps you can. When I was riding back towards Dalalven I was moments too late to prevent one of Omund's personal guards from killing an old friend of yours. That Christian monk, Brother Gerard.'

Hather's eyes narrowed. 'Gerard's dead?'

Leif Half-Foot nodded. 'When I reached Uppsala the night before, he was with the king, asking Omund's permission to return to England. The king gave him leave and he set off that night. I'd have thought he'd have made for the Baltic coast to take ship, not ride for Dalalven. That's a long way from the nearest port and well out of his way.

'Anyway, about midway from Uppsala I saw one of Omund's guards strike him from his horse. I killed the traitor, then went to see if I could help the monk. I was too late, though. He was already dying.'

Atyl Skin listened in silence with lowered brows. Something was tugging at the scar beside his eye. Something was beginning to fit into place.

'He spoke to me before he died,' Leif continued. 'At first he mumbled in that church-speech of his and I couldn't understand it. Then he said the same thing in our own tongue.

180

'He said: "But yet, behold, the hand of him that betrayeth me is with me upon the table." Then he said something else. He told me to tell you that he had loved you in his own way. Now, can you make head or tail of this fish?'

Hather rubbed at his beard. He knew Gerard as well as anyone had done. The man's different faith, and his seemingly endless desire to inflict it upon others in a most un-Norse way, had made him difficult to understand. In addition Hather had forgiven, but never forgotten, Gerard's betrayal of Starkadder and himself when they had tried to rescue Omund from the fortress at Dalalven.

He loved me in his way, Hather thought. Is that why he was riding the wrong way? To tell me something? Could that be why he was killed? And why would one of Omund's guards be doing the killing?

He shook his head. 'You're right, Leif,' he replied. 'It's hardly the plainest set of facts I've ever had to deal with. But there again, this whole venture is something of a riddle.'

Atyl Skin said nothing. His suspicions were beginning to clarify, to form into a solution to the puzzle. It was too soon to tell the others, though. Better to wait a little longer. Then he asked: 'Is Omund's army coming, Leif?'

Their companion grinned and stood up in front of the fire. 'I have the king's promise that the army will be less than a day behind me, though I've probably travelled harder and faster than they can, so that day might stretch into two. I've rather lost track of time with all this travelling. Will that be soon enough?'

'That should give us a day to spare,' Vermund nodded. 'After tonight there are three clear days. The glimpses of the moon don't come until the third night. Even if they're crawling Omund's men should have arrived by then.'

Atyl turned his face away into the shadows so that they wouldn't see his doubting expression. In that moment he knew that he would soon be facing a painful choice between helping his friends and performing that duty which King Gorm would expect of him.

Saeunna scraped Hather's cold stew back into the pot which boiled above the fire and served him fresh when she saw to Leif's hunger as well. This time Hather ate readily, his hope renewed.

In two days at the most Omund's army would come. Then they would storm the gorge and the dwarfish fortress which spanned it and rescue his son. Killing the vargr could come later. Omund would doubtless appreciate its return to Uppsala for an exemplary execution, its power upon their futures broken for ever with its death.

He slept more peacefully that night, his fears diminished with Leif's news. Vermund took the first watch and Saeunna the second. When she roused Atyl Skin to stand vigil until dawn he was already awake. As he rose he gave her a singularly sad smile, but said nothing.

He stood alone in the vanishing night, leaning on a spear and staring at their world of ice and snow and mountains. Serve Hather or serve King Gorm. It was less of a choice than a personal agony to be faced up to and surmounted. Besides, he reasoned, even if he stayed there was no guarantee that he wouldn't die uselessly like Askel Horsetail, stiff and lonely on the ice beyond their sight. That would serve neither Hather's purposes nor the needs of his royal master.

When dawn came he had faced his choice and made it. Yet he could wait a little while longer. Until Omund's army came. That, after all, would be the deciding factor, the final proof he needed before he set out upon a final mission as desperate as Hather Lambisson's pursuit of his kidnapped son.

Two more dawns after this, he thought. Two more dawns and then we'll know, one way or the other. Then, in the space of a single day, Hather and his friends will have freed little Svipdag and taken the vargr, or be dead themselves.

That's why I smiled at you like that, Saeunna. You'll make Hather a good wife, if you live. But I don't think any of you are going to live much longer, and I'm sorry.

Tell Hather, in my way, I loved him. The Dane nodded. You loved him all right, dead Christian. That's why you set out upon a last, desperate venture to warn him of your suspicions. You died, Gerard, but Leif brought your message to Hather. He doesn't understand it. Not yet. And when he does it will probably be too late to do him any good. I can't tell him. He won't believe me. He'll continue to hope until the last. And then he'll die uselessly here in the gorge at Skroggrmagi.

Dear Odin, help my friends. You must know by now that I cannot.

That morning they made another attempt to recover Horsetail's body, but the showering arrows beat them back again. As they retired to their camp beyond the gorge Hather's eyes were blazing with fury and frustration. Saeunna laid a hand upon his arm in a gentle, soothing gesture.

'Wait for the king's army,' she comforted. 'Then there'll be enough men to erect a shield-roof above us when we go through the gorge. Isn't that more sensible than trying to go through now? If we can't even get Askel's body back, how do you expect to reach the fortress?'

He smiled faintly and laid his hand over her own. He knew she was right, that it made more sense to wait. Yet somehow he knew at the back of his mind that sense had little to do with this whole venture, that there was a deeper conspiracy than that which wrapped him round, that he was once again nothing more than a tafl-piece upon a board controlled by others.

He wanted to lean over and kiss her, but the riddles were keeping them apart, standing between a brief, urgent happiness that might well be the last that either of them ever knew.

The riddles persisted. That name cut in runes. Crasyllus. Her dream and its message from Harbard. The thirteenth heart was vital to the making of a vargr. He knew that. But why was it to be young Svipdag's?

'What's a vargr, Tisti?'

Her deep, dark eyes burned into those of the little boy beside her. 'You ask so many questions these days, little Hather,' she replied.

Was it before or after she had told him about Crasyllus? And what had she told him about Crasyllus?

183

'But what is it?'

'Something that was once a human being. Something that chose to make itself a monster for reasons of its own.'

'How did it make itself into a monster?'

'So many questions, little Hather. If I tell you that you'll have bad dreams for a week or more. Let it suffice that a vargr does very unpleasant things.'

'Like what? What does it do?'

She sighed. She never lied to her little boy, her foster-son. It would serve neither of them if she ever lied to him. Most of the time she put up with his questions readily, gladdened by his love, proud of his affection in her self-sought loneliness.

Children know how to love without betraying. When they grow up they forget the magic of that childish love. They recapture it only in fleeting, precious moments.

I love you, little Hather. I shall always love you. You will always be the tiny, pissing bundle I first held. Because I love you I can make something that will keep away the dreams. Because I won't lie to you I shall tell you how the vargr is made.

'It eats hearts, little Hather. To become a vargr it has to eat human hearts. It begins with the first heart in the glimpses of the moon. It eats the second when the moon is at first quarter, the third at full, the fourth at the waning quarter, and so on until it has eaten thirteen hearts. It begins in the dark of the moon because that is the time when works of darkness are best undertaken. It ends in the dark of the moon because that is when works of evil are best completed. And the vargr is evil, little Hather. It has to be evil to undertake such a thing in the first place. The hearts it eats must be raw and living. They cannot be taken from the dead or the preparations are for nothing. Thirteen living hearts, ripped from living bodies and eaten raw. Have you ever eaten raw meat, little Hather?'

The boy shuddered and closed his eyes. 'I tried it once, Tisti,' he said in a whisper. 'It wasn't very nice. It's much better cooked.'

She smiled. He didn't really understand the horror of

184

it all yet. He was too young and, in his childish way, too good. She'd seen so many dark and terrible things in her long life. She'd come to terms with horrors that her little foster-son was still capable of shutting out.

He wouldn't need her draught. He'd forget and sleep without bad dreams. And then she chilled.

I have to tell him, she thought. He has to know. I have to make him understand. He's been given to me for a purpose. I have to teach him everything I can. Whatever weaves our weird, whatever power the Norns and gods may have upon our destinies, I know that mine is to teach this boy.

'Listen to me, little Hather. Think back to that raw meat you tried. Was it bloody?'

He shook his young head violently. 'Ugh, no,' he said.

'Well now, think of the vargr eating raw hearts. Think of that raw, bloody meat. And think of where it comes from, little Hather. Ripped out of there,' she continued, jabbing him hard upon the chest with a horn-nailed finger. 'Torn out and eaten bloody and raw.'

He tried not to cry. Instead he flung his arms around her neck and buried his face in her shoulder. 'Don't eat my heart, Tisti!' he begged. 'I love you. Don't eat my heart!'

'That wouldn't stop the vargr,' she replied. 'But I'm not the vargr. I love you too, little Hather. I won't eat your heart. The vargr will eat any hearts. Young, old, man, woman, just so long as they come from a living victim. Any hearts at all, for the first twelve. . . .'

And then comes the returning dark phase of the moon, and the time to eat that last, special thirteenth heart.

Children could never become vargrs. That was another reason why she loved him so. He could never become a vargr. Not until he grew up. That was why she was telling him, so that if ever a sorcerer offered to make him a vargr he would be too revolted, too repelled by her words to accept, to become the monstrous, almost-immortal were-killer that the sorcerer would use for purposes of its own.

'The thirteenth heart is special, little Hather. Only one already a monster could even think of eating that special, thirteenth heart.'

185

He eased his face away from her shoulder and peered up through misted eyes at her wrinkled, hair-fringed mouth with its tired, discoloured teeth.

'What makes it so special, Tisti?' he asked, afraid of the question even as it left his lips.

And then she told him. And he gasped. And then he cried. And then she made the draught to help him sleep.

He sat there, his hand still covering Saeunna's, his thoughts so far away, so unconscious of the pressure responding to his own. She studied his unfocused eyes, reading sudden terror in their depths.

That couldn't be the answer. He'd remembered wrongly. He must have remembered wrongly. No one, no thing, could do anything that monstrous. Besides, it was impossible. Impossible.

'What is it, Hather? What's the matter?' she asked.

He forced a smile and banished the memory from his mind as best he could. He was wrong. It couldn't possibly be that.

'I'm afraid,' he said softly. 'That's all.'

'Shall I tell you a secret?' she said, almost laughing at him. 'So am I, Hather. I'm frightened too.'

He slid his arm about her shoulders and pressed her head to his chest. Her hair smelled of sweat and fire-smoke and her flesh was cold. He felt weary to the depths of his being. His fear for his son was tightening, knotting his stomach, fighting its own struggle with the grimly terrifying memory that would stay with him until their fight was over, until he lay dead beside his butchered son or rode out of the gorge at Skroggrmagi in his triumph.

The day passed into night. King Omund's army didn't come. The next day passed slowly, their ears straining through the seconds for the sound of the approaching forces, the sound they didn't hear.

'It's late,' Vermund grunted irritably as they sat about the fire. 'A day behind you, you said?' he asked Leif Half-Foot. 'Then it should be here by now.'

'It will be,' Leif replied, struggling to believe that he was

186

right, though the waiting had strained his credulity as well. 'King Omund said he'd lead it himself.'

Atyl Skin frowned into the fire. 'But did he tell you where he was leading it?' he asked. 'Did he say in so many words that he would lead it here to Skroggrmagi?'

Leif shrugged. 'Not in so many words, no. But the king assembled the force to trap the vargr. We all know that.'

'Let's hope King Omund knows it as well,' the Dane snapped.

Half-Foot jumped to his feet and glared down at Atyl Skin. 'He'll come. He'll be here tomorrow.' He turned to face Hather. 'He'll be here,' he repeated. 'You know that, Hather, don't you?'

'King Omund will lead his army against his enemies,' Hather responded without looking up. In his heart he knew what Atyl Skin was trying to say. 'Tomorrow we'll all do what we have to.'

He looked across at the Dane, his eyes bright in the firelight. Atyl Skin read the look and nodded slightly. Hather was making it easy for him. Live or die, succeed or fail, he would remember this man for the rest of whatever life remained to him.

The wrong man's on the throne of Sweden, Hather. It should be you. We've not spoken of it, but you already know almost all of it. I hope you succeed tomorrow. I hope that you can find and save your son. The vargr doesn't matter. It's a symptom, not a cause. Sweden is diseased.

They settled down for an uneasy night. Atyl Skin offered to take the last watch, into dawn, and Hather agreed with a curt nod.

'We'll all do what we have to,' he repeated.

I ought to stop him, Hather thought. He's fighting on the other side, though he doesn't know it. If he succeeds the Yngling dynasty will fall. Bad as it may be Odin wants it to last a little longer. Starkadder taught me that, in his way.

Goodbye, Atyl Skin. I know you'll be gone in the morning. If the gods are kind, if the Norns have written it, we'll meet again. Though the chances are we won't.

187

CHAPTER TWO

The ice-palace

THE LAST dawn came.

In the camp before the gorge at Skroggrmagi, Hather, Saeunna, Leif Half-Foot and Vermund Bjarnisson awoke to the sound of receding hoofbeats as Atyl Skin rode from the camp.

'Let him go,' Hather said simply. 'He's doing what he has to do.'

They didn't, couldn't, understand him, so they simply obeyed.

By mid-morning there was no sign of the expected army. 'Something must have slowed them up,' Vermund said quietly, struggling to keep any trace of the despair he felt from creeping into his voice. In his heart, though, he was beginning to suspect the truth, to know that the promised forces wouldn't be coming.

The ageing marshal wasn't sure whether he felt this or the Dane's departure to be the greater betrayal, though he kept his own counsel.

'It wasn't Atyl Skin's fight,' Hather muttered. 'His duty, as he sees it, lies elsewhere. I can't blame any man for doing what he feels he has to do.

'How about the rest of you?' he demanded, looking around him at the three survivors of his company. 'If anyone wants to ride away I'll hold no blame to him. Or her,' he added, staring at Saeunna.

188

'I've work to do here,' she replied gently. 'Harbard told me that. Wherever you go today, Hather, I'm going with you.'

Leif Half-Foot smiled at the girl. She might be slight beneath that dead-robbed armour, but she was strong beyond her build and her years. Then he looked back at Hather Lambisson.

'I've come this far,' he began. 'If you think I'll let you walk up that gorge alone you're mistaken. I'm with you, Hather. I'll stand beside you. I'll even die beside you, if I have to.'

'And you, Vermund?' Hather asked. 'I know your arm's still troubling you. It would be better if you stayed here with the horses.'

'So *you* say,' came the brusque reply. 'If you think you can keep me out of this you can go bugger a ure-ox. I've scores of my own to settle now. I want blood in payment for Horsetail and Thorvald, Hather. This vargr won't know what fighting is until it's seen me reddening my blade on its hirelings.'

Hather Lambisson grinned, the expression forcing the threatening tears back from his eyes. He had good friends to fight beside him. If he failed, then it would be because of betrayals he hadn't foreseen, not because of his choice of who would accompany him in this desperate venture. He could ask no more of any of them than they had offered already. If there was dying to be done before the next day's dawn they wouldn't flinch from it.

'There're weapons to be sharpened,' he said at length. 'Has anyone remembered to bring a whetstone?'

Four against thirty. Odds that meant certain death. And no way that any of them could see to even up those odds.

They waited until noon, then lay down to snatch whatever rest their anxious, expectant hearts would let them in the comparative warmth of the afternoon. Even Leif Half-Foot had accepted that the promised army wasn't coming. His mind remained active, struggling to work out what had gone wrong to prevent the assistance King Omund had promised.

189

Even if they come now they'll be too tired from the journey to fight, he thought. Odin help us. We're on our own. There's no one here to help us fight this thing, this vargr.

In the caves and corridors of Trollheim there were others who shared their concern about the actions of the vargr, though neither Hather nor any of his friends knew of their interest. The dwarf-king, Alvis, shrunken with fear within the depths of his purple robe, paced Kulubak Magri's cavernous home almost unceasingly.

The dwarfish sorcerer was taking too long. There had to be some news of Tyrfing within the next few hours or he was a dead dwarf. And by all the armies of Trollheim he'd take Kulubak Magri with him.

He looked up at the slowly decomposing body of the sacrificed ure-ox. How anyone could live with that stench, with the burrowing maggots that fell from the scaffold to the cavern floor, together with fragments from the carcass, was beyond him. Whatever that trunk-like nose of the sorcerer's was for it seemed to be deficient when it came to having a sense of smell.

Since the sacrifice, days before, he'd not lived in the tower at the centre of the acid lake. He'd stayed here, slowly beginning to master his fear of the sorcerer with the familiarity of his occasional presence. True, Kulubak Magri had spent hours, sometimes days, away from the cavern, vanishing unpredictably through the honeycomb of tunnels that led from it to the outer reaches of Alvis' kingdom.

At this particular moment, whilst the light of the afternoon sun would have been destroying any dwarf unfortunate enough to be above ground, Alvis was pacing alone. Kulubak Magri had vanished again, promising before he went that this absence would be the last. There was still something about the dwarfish sorcerer, bent over and red-eyed, that his king didn't trust, something that threatened devious betrayal at the last. Yet he had no choice. He had delayed coming here until it had been absolutely necessary. He had ascended the scaffold and huddled on the squared platform at the top, shitting himself

190

with fear, whilst his mentor used whatever power he possessed to summon the greatest of the gods, the Allfather, Odin, into Trollheim for a consultation which might save his life. Now all that remained was to pace and wait, to remain in whatever security the sorcerer's hands provided whilst whatever scheming was going on came to fruition.

Kulubak Magri would not betray him. He was Alvis, King of Trollheim. No single one of his subjects would dare to betray the King of Trollheim.

So he waited, fearful and nervous, and alone.

What's holding the freak up? Why isn't he back? He should be here by now, bearing Tyrfing in a taloned hand. He should be back with the sword by now. If he doesn't come, I'm dead.

Then, as his feet tired with the pacing, as fear clawed at his tiny heart and threatened his bursting, dwarfish bladder, Kulubak Magri returned.

Alvis rushed over to him. 'You have the sword?' he demanded. 'You have Tyrfing?'

Empty-handed, holding his taloned fingers out for Alvis to see that they held nothing, the sorcerer shook his head. 'But I know where it is,' he grinned, wolfishly. 'I know who has it. Will you come with me to find Tyrfing, King Alvis?'

The dwarf's heart leaped, then steadied. Just try to keep me away, he thought, though he answered simply: 'I shall come with you, Kulubak Magri. And this had better be the truth you're telling me.'

The sorcerer bowed low before him. 'Would I betray my king?' he asked, his face mock-serious in the phosphorescent glimmerings which lit the enormous cavern.

He lit a torch at one of the ember-strewn fires and led the way towards the tunnels. His eyes darting from side to side, half-fearing an ambush which he knew would be too clumsy a device to come, King Alvis followed him.

'Where are we going?' Alvis demanded imperiously as he tried to avoid stooping to enter a side-chamber from which several corridors opened out.

'To Skroggrmagi, great king,' came the reply. 'That's

191

where Tyrfing is. And there are two old friends of yours there as well. Thrudnir and Illugi.'

Alvis stiffened, then bent again to avoid bumping his head against the low roof. 'The two I sent out first?' he asked incredulously. 'I thought they were dead. And I thought Skroggrmagi had been sealed off from the rest of Trollheim.'

Kulubak Magri shrugged, the torch wavering uncertainly in his hand, its smoke stinging the following dwarf-king's nostrils. 'I found a way through,' he replied. 'That's how I found Thrudnir and Illugi hiding there and pressed them back into your service.'

'Pressed them back? I'll give them desert me when I need them. I'll . . . I'll implement the original sentence. I'll have them die from slow exposure. I'll teach them to desert their king. . . .'

'Not if you want to see Tyrfing again,' Kulubak Magri interrupted, grinning broadly where he led Alvis along the tunnels towards the abandoned dwarfish fortress.

The king fell silent. Until that moment he had refused to realise how completely in his sorcerer's hands he was.

The minutes lengthened into hours. Outside, in the daylight, the afternoon grew late.

They continued along the tunnels, their progress lit only by Kulubak Magri's dwindling torch.

'Will we reach there in time?' Alvis demanded.

'In time to take Tyrfing from the one who has it,' the sorcerer replied. 'We shall be in time, King Alvis. You will hold Tyrfing before it causes you to die,' he added, ambiguously.

Reassured, the dwarf-king followed on.

The afternoon above them faded towards sunset.

'Not far now, my king. We'll be at Skroggrmagi soon. Then you'll hold Tyrfing once again. You have my word that you shall, and only a fool would doubt the word of Kulubak Magri.'

They continued their progress through rock corridors that were low even by dwarfish standards. Eventually they came to a place where their path narrowed even further,

192

causing them to crawl through the narrow opening in the sharded stones of the walls.

'This is where the fortress was sealed off,' the sorcerer explained. 'Just beyond this point is Skroggrmagi, the monster's maw.'

Not the most comforting of appellations, Alvis thought.

They crawled on, tearing the cloth about their knees and elbows, until the passage opened out and the distant light of burning cressets could be seen ahead of them.

Soon be over now, thought Alvis.

Soon be some dying to be done, thought Kulubak Magri.

The sorcerer stopped and turned towards the following dwarf-king. 'Your word, now, King Alvis. You will do nothing to hurt either Thrudnir or Illugi. We still need the help of both of them to secure Tyrfing and your fate.'

Alvis nodded reluctantly. 'You have my word,' he answered. Until this is over, he reserved mentally. Then I shall have you all killed. If you had any sense you'd know that already. And then, my friend, we'll see which one of us has won.

Kulubak Magri stood up, crouching less and less as the roof of the tunnel grew higher above him. They were nearing their destination, nearing the fearsome, deserted citadel which the vargr had made its resting place until, finally, triumphantly, it consumed the thirteenth heart.

'I thought you were dead,' Alvis grunted as twin shapes detached themselves from the widening walls and stood before him.

'It's not been easy staying alive through all these years, sir,' Illugi replied.

'But I understand you've found Tyrfing. Take me to it.'

'We've found it, yes,' Thrudnir said. 'But we don't have it. It's still in the hands of another.'

'For a little while longer,' Kulubak Magri added quickly. 'It won't be long before you hold Tyrfing again, great king. Not long at all.'

The two dwarfs led the sorcerer and their king to the place where the tunnel ended in a heavy oaken door.

193

Straining against its dust-locked, cobwebbed hinges they forced it open and led Kulubak Magri and Alvis into a small, stone-walled room cluttered with an assemblage of metal piping and outsize, funnel-shaped objects. The king immediately recognised an apparatus similar to that which had frightened him during his first descent into the sorcerer's cavern.

'I had to deal with a human,' Kulubak Magri explained. 'Do you think it would have promised to yield Tyrfing to a mere dwarf? It needed a little impressing before I could deal with it. That's what all this is for,' he explained with a sweep of his hand.

'I had to promise a great deal before it would agree to part with Tyrfing,' he added. 'And I may still have to keep some of those promises.' As far as my pact with Odin will let me, he thought to himself. And as far as the Norns beyond Odin permit Odin to let me.

'And the sword,' Alvis demanded. 'Is it here? Is it here, sorcerer?'

Kulubak Magri nodded. 'It's here, King Alvis. We shall soon have it now. All we have to do is wait for the dark of the moon to rise in the heavens.'

'Why can't we go and take it, sorcerer?'

'Four dwarfs against thirty humans?' the creature asked, mock surprise clouding its voice. 'Not even King Alvis and his sorcerer could hope to succeed against those sorts of odds. Let us be practical for a little while longer. Besides, I have something that is guaranteed to persuade Tyrfing's possessor to part with the blade, even if it should prove initially unwilling to do so.'

Alvis suppressed a sneer. 'And what could do that much?' he asked.

'That could,' Kulubak Magri responded, gesturing towards an ornate bronze box which stood on the floor beneath the mouthpiece which connected to the system of pipes and funnels.

'So that's why you had us take that chest from Sudrafell before the vargr burned it,' Thrudnir mused. 'Will you tell us what it is now?'

194

The dwarf shrugged. 'I can, but you won't be any the nearer understanding its importance if I do,' he replied. 'Have any of you ever heard of the powder of Crasyllus?'

He looked around at the blank, struggling faces.

'I thought not,' Kulubak Magri continued. 'Now, before the sun sets outside and night is here, and even after sunset, there is work that must be done. This will be a busy night for all of us.'

More than that, he thought, it will be the coming to fruition of all my schemes and ambitions. After this there will be few left who can deny me anything. After tonight I shall be the most powerful dwarf in the entire nighted history of Trollheim.

I shall also be the only one of us four who is still alive, thanks to Odin. However, at present that's neither here nor there.

Outside the fortress, beyond the gorge, as the last sun for so many began to sink towards the mountains in the west, Hather and his friends stood ready to enter the gorge at Skroggrmagi. On the other side of the inner chamber, beyond the circular room with the marble slab, now prematurely stained red with the rays of the sinking sun, in the main hall of the bridge-built fortress, Hundermann sat with his dogs, watching the anxious pacing of the wolf-skinned figure in the golden mask.

'Soon now,' said the vargr. 'Very soon. Prepare to order the men back from the gorge.'

'And the boy?' Hundermann asked. 'Does he really have to die?'

'To doubt that is to doubt me,' the vargr snapped. 'Svipdag Hathersson will die tonight, and his father with him.'

Back beside the passage, in the darkened room lit only by his torch and flickering cressets, Kulubak Magri was examining the way that the oddly-plaited rope projected through the hole in the lid of the brazen box.

'That will serve,' he grinned. 'Now, you two,' he said to Thrudnir and Illugi, 'you have tinder and flint? You'll never be able to manage a torch up there as well as the

195

powder of Crasyllus. That's why you need some way to strike fire. The powder will do nothing unless you set some fire to it. Are you prepared for that?'

Illugi nodded. 'What will it do after that?' he asked.

'Nothing that you need have the slightest concern about,' the sorcerer smiled. 'It will work a powerful magic, if the tales I've heard of it are true. It will bring all of us the destinies we so richly deserve. Stay there, in the ice-palace, and watch it work, Illugi. And you, Thrudnir, stay there and watch it bring your destiny to fruition. It will offer you the most impressive sight that you will ever see.' And certainly the last, he added silently, grinning broadly.

'You remember the signal?' he questioned. 'You know when you have to set some fire to the rope projecting from the box of bronze?'

'We do,' Thrudnir replied. With a sigh he repeated the words learned by repetition. 'We see through the roof Tyrfing raised and gleaming. Then we light the rope and learn the truth.'

'Excellent,' Kulubak Magri grinned. 'Simply excellent.'

'And whilst these two are falling about a frozen water-fall with burning ropes,' Alvis sneered, 'what are we doing, sorcerer?'

'We're taking the sword you want, O king,' Kulubak Magri replied. 'There will be a short delay before the magic of the powder works. That will be enough for us to snatch the sword and retire into the tunnels. Do you think I would risk your life, or my own, for longer than I had to?

'Now,' he demanded of Thrudnir and Illugi. 'Have you removed your petrified brothers, as I instructed you?'

'In the dark last night,' Illugi answered him. 'At alternate corners.'

'Without damaging the marble?'

'Not enough for anyone to notice.'

'Then we will be ready with the sunset. Do you have the ropes and irons for your climb?'

'We have done, and taken possession of, everything that

we are even slightly likely to need,' Thrudnir replied wearily. This ceaseless drill was beginning to get on his nerves.

'This all seems terribly complicated,' Alvis snapped. 'Isn't there an easier way to get my hands on Tyrfing?'

Kulubak Magri sighed. There were some things the doomed dwarf-king didn't understand that he ought to, by now.

'If you hadn't shat yourself and passed out whilst I was conversing with Odin,' he reproached Alvis, 'you'd know that this was the best I could arrange. It has to be this complicated, King Alvis. Do you really think that Odin would help us if we weren't a part of a greater game he's playing on his own? That's why we have to rub ourselves with earth-colours and hide beneath the marble table. That's why these two have to take the powder of Crasyllus up into the waterfall. If you ever want to hold Tyrfing again you'll do what I'm asking. Is that perfectly, totally, for once in your lifetime, clear, my king?'

Alvis could only assent. Yet something felt wrong. Something in all these elaborate preparations wasn't right. Somewhere there was treachery afoot. He might not know the secret of the powder of Crasyllus, but somehow he knew that Thrudnir and Illugi would be climbing the frozen waterfall to their deaths. That, in itself, didn't matter. They were due to die anyway, as soon as his own survival was ensured.

What did matter was that he should regain Tyrfing in time to save himself from his weird. He already knew that the first thing he did would be to bury the sword's glittering length in the deformed body of Kulubak Magri.

Then he'd be safe. Then the rest of them could meet whatever fates had been assigned to them. Then they could live or die as their gods decided.

For all Alvis cared, for all he was truly worried about vargrs and sorcerers and kidnapped children and their fathers, the ice-palace could shatter itself into a million flying, splintering, death-blood-shearing shards.

Just so long as he held Tyrfing in his hands.

CHAPTER THREE

Sacrifices towards
a greater Sweden

UPPSALA HAD fallen into twilight. The sun had ended its
decline behind the mountains in the far west, leaving the
palace, the town, and the mighty army camped before it,
to whatever light the fires, torches and lamps might give.

Standing upon the palisade wall, surveying the host, the
largest force of armed men ever assembled within man's
memory, King Omund was smiling softly to himself. The
same plan that had trapped, and was about to destroy,
Hather Lambisson, had worked against him also, albeit
only temporarily.

It would have been a good night to start south for
the border with Skane. No moon. No falling snow. At
present the night was clear, with frost-bright stars winking in the moonless sky. But the dark period, the glimpses
of the moon, would work against his enterprise in the
minds of his superstitious soldiery, weakening their care-
fully-nurtured belief in their own invincibility.

The king shrugged. So they waited a little while. He
could afford to. By the Yule feast they'd have taken and
occupied Skane, driving the unprotected and unprepared
Danes back into the tangle of islands that bestrewed the
southern Baltic and the Kattegat. Then it would be a

simple task to raise fresh levies and use his new-won territories to build up a fleet of longships that could range between the islands of the Dane-Lands, ferrying his armies to fresh victories, reinforcing replacement garrisons, strengthening the grip of the new, greater Sweden and its ruling Yngling dynasty, upon both the north and history.

With the coming dawn the difficult part of his plan would be gone for ever, vanished and banished by the deaths of Hather Lambisson and his companions. In many ways it was a pity that he had to lose the best of his commanders, but they would have questioned his judgement and done all in their power to prevent the invasion he intended to launch. They didn't understand, as Omund did, that a contented, peaceful country is a weak country, that only by the demands of war and battle can a people, any people, be trained and brought to their highest pitch of civilisation.

War is the key to a good reign, he thought. War strengthens. It burns out weakness. It brings prosperity to the victor and a thousand welcomed sacrifices before the altars of the gods.

And with his death it will take from the people's minds all memory of the man who killed Starkadder. I shall be their new hero. Omund Olisson, master of a new and greater land. The mightiest king in the entire north.

He looked up at the sky. Soon now, over Skroggrmagi, the vargr-moon would be rising. With its coming his secret ally would remove the troublesome thorns of Lambi Nef's surviving kin from his flesh for ever. All those who mattered of the ones that had witnessed his captivity at Dalalven would never again be able to remind him of his former weakness by their presence. Thorvald Brotamad he knew, from Leif's report, to be dead already. That was good. The traitorous leader of his father's guard, who had stood aside whilst Starkadder committed his father's murder, was dead. Vengeance for one.

And then there was Brother Gerard. He'd never completely understood that monk who'd tried to bring his strange southern faith to the north. He too had stood aside and permitted the murder of King Oli. More importantly, though, Gerard had somehow learned the truth, or enough of the truth, about the army Omund was raising to seek to warn Hather of the king's intended betrayal. Well, he was dead too, now. A patrol had found his body and that of his assassin on the plains. That was vengeance for two.

That left Vermund Bjarnisson and Askel Horsetail, two more who had intrigued with Starkadder to procure his father's death, daring to take the life of a great and respected Yngling king. They would die at Skroggrmagi. So would Hather Lambisson and his son Svipdag.

All dead. All gone. Nothing to stand between Omund and his royal destiny. No shapes from the past to rise and stir memories of a best-forgotten truth, the truth that King Oli had been mad, that he had ordered his son Omund's death, that they had conspired against Oli to save Sweden from civil war and to rescue the broken, imprisoned Omund from his death-dungeon.

For Omund that had never been the truth. With the rising of the vargr-moon and the coming of their deaths it never would be true again.

Goodbye, Hather Lambisson, King Omund smiled into the night.

His real stroke of genius, however, the inspiration for his vengeance and the means of luring those who would have thwarted his plans to their destruction, had been to enter into the offered conspiracy with the vargr. It had come to him one day, whilst he was hunting upon the plains and his men were far behind, and offered an alliance for reasons of its own. He had immediately recognised the use that such a creature could have in dispiriting his enemies by its savage and barbarous tactics. The vargr could go on before his armies and ruin the morale of any who opposed him, killing and destroying in a way his armies, constrained to move to strategic destinations, impeded by their reliance upon supply columns for fresh arms and provisions, never could. The vargr would serve him well. This scheme he had devised to test it, a scheme which also forced Hather Lambisson to follow it to his death, was truly brilliant. Omund would never admit that the vargr was his own creature, initially pillaging his own people, as well as the Danes, to raise gold and arms for his growing forces. He never could. The atrocities which had been scattered in its wake were too fresh, too bloody in the minds of the subjects whose loyalty King Omund commanded. Well, when it began to raid the Danes, as it already had done with the massacre at Raven's Point, it would be serving both his own purposes and whatever bloodthirsty destiny it intended for itself.

A useful, secret ally.

The only doubt that remained to the king was the purpose behind the alliance. That it had been freely offered and was proving effective was beyond dispute, but Omund was aware that he had no real idea of the vargr's motives for helping him. Still, if by any chance it became disloyal, he could always turn his army to its original purpose and destroy it with force of arms.

Providing that army's not already committed in the Dane-Lands, King Omund.

His eyes narrowed at the thought, which he dismissed with the rationalisation that the creature had proved its loyalty so far. If there should be any betrayal at Skroggrmagi, if Hather escaped or the vargr should move against Uppsala, the army was ready to destroy it for him. And it wouldn't be committed to fighting in Skane until the vargr had ridden south and begun its raids ahead of him.

The plan was foolproof. One way or the other, with the coming of the dawn, Omund would know what he had to do. And sooner or later his men would begin the thrust south, the thrust that would take Sweden and Denmark into a war from which Omund would emerge the mighty victor.

CHAPTER FOUR

The sign of Ginnir

THE SUN had set. The vargr-moon was rising.

Hather looked at his three companions, armed and ready. His heart was pounding and his stomach felt sick. He'd eaten little that day, worried more by his growing fears for his son's safety than by any thought of the physical danger he faced himself. It was a concern they had all shared, comforted only by the words Harbard had spoken to Saeunna in her dream.

'This is where your love may be returned, with gratitude and hope.'

That was all, but it was the most reassuring fragment of the future that they had.

'Time to go,' Hather said grimly.

Vermund nodded. 'And if they're still out there, waiting in the gorge?' He drew a gloved finger across his throat in a cutting motion in answer to his own question.

'We fight our way through them or die,' Saeunna replied with a courage she was far from feeling. 'Hather has his son to save. I have my family to avenge. And we all have a vargr to destroy.'

Hather looked across at her, inwardly marvelling at the strength she exuded, a strength that prepared them for the coming conflict better than any food could have done. He wanted to smile and thank her, but the time for words and waiting had passed with the setting sun. Now there was only a time for doing, a time for facing their weirds in the gorge at Skroggrmagi.

With his sword clasped in his right hand and a bronze-bound wooden shield slung on his left arm, Hather Lambisson stepped out onto the frozen river.

Vermund followed him, the pain still nagging in his sword-arm. With a rapid exchange of glances Leif Half-Foot and Saeunna stepped out too. This time there could be no turning back if the arrows began to rain. This time there could only be a last, desperate gesture, and the hope that one of them might get through to accomplish their purpose against desperate odds.

They passed the horse where it lay, walking with careful, determined steps. To either side the walls of the gorge rose black against the narrow strip of sky. Ahead they began to bend in that dreadful, familiar turning to the right. From the darkness of the night behind them a wind began to blow, gentle at first, then strengthening into a current that clutched and caught at their cloaks, pressing them to the backs of their legs, moulding them to their bodies and whipping the corners forward to tangle against hands and weapons.

Vermund grunted with forced mirth. 'At least the weather's on our side,' he grinned beneath his lowered nose-guard. 'You'll never loose an accurate arrow in this wind.'

It grew stronger, almost pushing them before it, howling about their ears in a nerve-tingling parody of a hundred beasts in pain. In its depths, occasionally, Hather wondered if he could detect other sounds than wind tearing itself apart upon the rocky walls. From time to time there came the muted howling of something that wasn't just the air-currents in the gorge, something that might have been called from living, shaggy throats.

When it came they all heard it. Starting low, rising to a higher note, then falling to a third, protracted calling mid-way in pitch between the first and second, it seemed to come from above, from high up on the towering rocks.

From the other side of the gorge came the answering call. Before them, frozen to the ice, twin shafts still jutting upwards, Askel Horsetail's body waited.

Odin's with us, Hather thought. For whatever good that will do us, Odin's abroad on this night. But I know he'll only save us if there's other work to do for him beyond this place. Even in Valhalla.

Without breaking their stride, spread in a thin line across the ice, the four companions passed the fallen Horsetail and rounded the bend in the gorge.

No arrows fell. Ahead of them, a black, majestic, sinister silhouette rose against the glittering facets of the frozen waterfall. Beneath the arch they could see where the falls, frozen almost into a crystalline cascade of motionless spray, joined the river-bed. Then, for the briefest moment, their straining eyes caught a patch of darkness against the shimmering ice. A patch of darkness that moved, sweeping a spear-holding hand upwards as if it pointed to the face of the ice-palace.

Within feet of the archway, the dwarfish citadel rearing above them, in a place both terrible and compelling, they stopped and followed with their eyes the sweep of that pointing spear. As the figure faded and was gone, as the wind continued to howl about them, as the distant wolves proclaimed their affinity with its voiceless calling, they saw the sign which shimmered in the ice.

Hather felt the sharp intake of breath strain his lungs against his hammering heart. With an instinctive gesture he raised his sword-hand to look at the ring he had slipped over a gloved finger. Old Tisti's ring.

It had to be an illusion. Nothing could have made water, falling straight down even as it froze, form that pattern of rayed lines spreading outwards from a centre. No power on earth, he thought, could make water freeze in a pattern such as this. But a power out of Asgard, a power of gods and Norns, perhaps.

Leif Half-Foot felt his mouth drop open. 'The sign of Ginnir,' he muttered, his awed tones almost lost beneath the wind.

'You know this sign?' Hather demanded, thrusting the ring before his face. 'You've seen it before?'

Leif nodded. 'I was in the far north, in Bjarmaland, some years ago. It's a symbol used by Lappish wizards. They call it the sign of Ginnir.'

'But what is it?' Saeunna asked. 'What does it mean?'

'It means a meeting of good and evil,' came the reply. 'A meeting of the divine and the demonic. The Lapps set it upon the tents where they celebrate their mysteries, where their wizards conjure gods and darker forces.'

Saeunna looked back towards the ice-palace beyond the fortress. The sudden darkness of small black shapes, darting and swooping against its glittering surface caught her eyes.

'Look there,' she whispered, pointing with the beard-axe. 'Ravens. Two ravens. And they seem to be attacking something.'

'Or someone. I may only have one eye left,' Vermund added, 'but it's a good one. There's two figures climbing up through that treacherous mass of icicles and crevices. Carrying something, I think.'

Hather strained to make out the distant details. Two figures, yes. But they were too short to be men. Children? Unlikely. Beneath the arch of that gargoyle-crusted fortress built of stone, built with skills unknown in the north by an odd race he had encountered only once before, they must be dwarfs. Dwarfs carrying something. A large box. Heavy. Perhaps bronze. . . .

The memory never formed itself into words. There wasn't time for words. Instead it revealed itself as a series of flashing, fleeting mental images. A little boy listening at an old Lapp's knee. A burning hut at Sudrafell. A heavy oak chest and its bags of herbs and powders. And a strange bronze box with a vellum page written in monkalpha lying atop its contents.

The powder of Crasyllus.

The sign of Ginnir.

A meeting of gods and mortals and dwarfs. A meeting of the divine and the demonic, the living and the long-dead. Vargr and Hundermann and dwarfs and Saeunna

205

and Crasyllus. And wolves and ravens and a one-eyed god.

Thrudnir lashed out at the nearest raven with a paw-like hand. The bird screamed, flapped back, then darted forward and stabbed at his wrist with its beak, drawing a thin trickle of blood. Its mate clawed for one of Illugi's eyes. As the dwarf beat it off, the bronze box, slung from a length of rope between them, slipped from its precarious balance on an ice-ledge and threatened to drag them down from their perch. He reached out with the same hand and grabbed at an overhanging icicle. It cracked noisily and began to splinter, but it held.

Then the ravens, as suddenly as they had appeared, were gone.

The dwarfs sat down to get their wind, the box now secured between their seated figures on the ledge.

'As soon as we've lit the rope I'm heading for the nearest tunnel back to Trollheim,' Thrudnir announced. 'I'll take my chances with Alvis and Kulubak Magri. I've had enough of this hiding from sunlight and lugging strange chests about to last me a lifetime. And I'm talking about a dwarf's lifetime, at that!'

Above them, just beyond the dramatic curve at the edge of the frozen falls, Odin waited for his wolves to join him. The ravens, Hugin and Munin, perched upon his shoulders where he stood, his single eye ranging down upon the dwarfish citadel in the gorge beneath. Then he looked up at the sky, bright and starlit, and sighed to himself where he stood.

To the east, beginning to climb above the walls of Skroggrmagi, a black disc ringed with the merest hint of pallid light was rising from the horizon. In the gorge the wind was dropping, relaxing the cloaks of the four determined figures in the shadow of the arch.

'I've done all I can for you, Hather,' Odin whispered to the night. 'There's no other help I can give you without breaking my agreement with Mother Skuld and voiding the game altogether. . . . And I can't do that, Hather. Not even for you. You're worth a thousand Omunds, but you're not a Yngling. I still need them, Hather. I still need those mad, demented kings. Omund has to live, to raise sons who will continue the blood-line for a few years yet. I was permitted three times to offer some indirect intervention that might lead you through your weird. It could be said that I've broken that rule already. The first was Saeunna's dream. You've mastered the secret of the thirteenth heart now, though you'll refuse to believe it until the very last minute.

'The second was when I cut those runes upon the pine for you to find. You saw them. You remembered the name Crasyllus, though you didn't know then what it meant.

'The third was when I showed you the sign of Ginnir in the ice. Now you know that there are powers beyond those of mere men involved with your weird in this place.

'When I let my ravens show you the dwarfs, showing you the box which contains the powder of Crasyllus, I helped you a fourth time. At least, Mother Skuld could look at it that way. I prefer to think that you would have seen them anyway and remembered the powder on your own. And even if she chooses to say I've cheated, she won't void the game for that small infringement.

'Now, though, you and your friends are on your own. I can't help you any more.'

He stretched out a gloved hand for an approaching wolf to lick. I have my own game to play here at Skroggrmagi, he thought. Some might claim that we share interests in common, but they wouldn't be entirely right. It wouldn't occur to you to contemplate the betrayals I may be forced to before this night is over.

No, Hather, I can't help you any more. The rules forbid it. Even so, there's nothing in my agreement with Mother Skuld to prevent me from using whatever I have to in order to accomplish my own aims.

You see, Hather? Wherever you look, whenever you look for it, there is a betrayal waiting to be found. And if the gods and the Norns will betray each other, what hope can there be for mortals such as you?

207

With a sad smile playing about his lips, Odin turned away. Beneath him, in the gorge, upon the frozen surface of the river, Hather and his companions stepped beneath the shadow of the arch and approached the ice-bound ramp that led up into the stables. Trapped in the ice beside it, an ancient boat, its bottom somehow dry, except for a light sprinkling of frozen snow, its sides unholed despite the pressure of the frozen waters, was moored by a length of icicle-crusted rope.

Inside the fortress, in the inner chamber where it had spoken with the echo-voiced sorcerer, the vargr was pacing the dust-strewn floor. As Hundermann appeared, the drugged form of Hather's small son slung over his shoulder, it gestured impatiently towards the circular chamber with the ruined roof.

'On the stone table, in there,' it snapped.

Hundermann gestured to the following dogs to wait. He didn't like this work. It stank like a ship full of rotting corpses. Still, it had to be done. He'd known when he agreed to join the vargr that he would live through some stomach-turning times to earn his return to the Rhineland and a future life of ease.

He didn't like this room, either, he thought, as he laid Svipdag's unconscious form down on the marble. Those dwarfish figures supporting the slab didn't look right. Two of them seemed to have changed their form since he'd first seen them. It wasn't natural to have buildings upon bridges. And it wasn't natural to have either buildings or bridges built of stone.

Overhead, at one jagged edge of the sharded dome, a dark circle fringed with pallid light was climbing into the star-bright sky.

He emerged into the chamber where the vargr waited. 'The men are ready,' he said gruffly, one hand rubbing at the ears of the nearest dog. 'Hather and his friends have reached the archway. They'll be here very soon now.'

The vargr's golden wolf-mask nodded. The vargr-moon was rising in the sky and Hather Lambisson was coming. Soon he'd stand helplessly by and watch his son be slaughtered. Soon the vargr would consume the thirteenth heart and assume its full wizard-promised powers.

Very soon.

Warily, their weapons ready, Hather and his companions began to ascend the ramp, their eyes darting into the shadows. It's too easy, Hather and Vermund thought in the same instant. The way is open. They're waiting for us. Well, there's no way we'll disappoint them now.

Two dwarfs climbing a frozen waterfall with the powder of Crasyllus.

We're not alone, Hather comforted himself in his suspenseful anguish. There's something happening here beyond what either I or the vargr can expect. And where there's a surprise, where the sign of Ginnir can glisten in the depths of a frozen waterfall, my son and I have got some kind of chance.

CHAPTER FIVE

The naming of the vargr

THEY MADE their way through the stables where the out-laws' horses lay huddled in their straw against the cold. Treading carefully, with eyes and weapons alert, Hather, Saeunna, Vermund and Half-Foot entered the corridor beyond.

Whatever happened, whatever betrayals might lie ahead, an end to their search for all of them drew nearer.

'Bring me Tyrfing,' commanded the vargr.

They passed the small stone chamber where Svipdag had been imprisoned. Saeunna nudged the door open with her axe and peered into the darkness. The room smelled of a cresset newly extinguished. Someone had been in there recently.

The wrappings fell away. Tyrfing hummed along its shining, deadly length. It sensed a sheathing in living flesh. It sensed the lapping kiss of blood upon its blade. Tyrfing knew that it was going home, back into death.

Hundermann shuddered inwardly. A weapon of evil in the hands of evil incarnate.

Beneath its wolf-fanged mask the vargr's mouth creased into a wolf-fanged smile. Then a grin.

And after Hather and his brat it's your turn, mighty Yngling Omund.

The high hall showed signs of habitation but no

210

inhabitants. About its sides, around the glowing embers of its fires in the huge stone hearths, lay the fur blankets and bed-rolls of nearly thirty men. The long trestles were littered with fragments of food and wine and ale-vessels.

'They've lived well whilst we've been huddled in the cold,' Half-Foot snarled. He aimed a cut with his sword at an earthenware pitcher.

'Save your energy,' Vermund snapped. 'They're rested and fit. We're tired and little more than an eighth of their number. We'll need all the strength we have when we find them.'

His eyes flashed up to the cobwebbed roof-beams. Through a shattered window he glimpsed the rising circle of the new moon against the stars. 'Will we be in time?' he asked Hather.

'We have to be,' came the grim reply. 'If we're not, there's nothing left but bloody vengeance.'

Saeunna checked her tongue. For a moment she had forgotten Odin's promise. For a moment she almost said that there was nothing more than bloody vengeance left for her already.

Across the hall. Towards the door which hid the passageway and the spiral stairs beyond.

Thrudnir and Illugi grinned at each other. They sat beside the box, near the top of the waterfall. From here they could see down into the chamber with the broken, dome-shaped roof.

'When you see Tyrfing raised,' Kulubak Magri had ordered them, 'strike fire and light the rope that projects from the brazen box.'

'And then into the nearest tunnel,' Illugi grinned.

Mother Skuld smiled sadly. Odin was beginning to know her too well. Perhaps he'd abandoned Hather Lambisson to whatever fate awaited him at Skroggrmagi, but he certainly hadn't abandoned his own plans or intentions. But can you save Omund, Allfather? Can you stop Atyl Skin from killing him?

Alvis was sweating where he crouched beneath the slab. It wasn't effort. The two remaining petrified dwarfs were still taking the strain in their lifeless muscles. It was fear. If he came through this the first thing he'd do would be to find a way to get rid of Kulubak Magri.

'Won't the vargr expect your betrayal?' he'd asked the dwarfish sorcerer earlier.

Kulubak Magri's red eyes were burning with a fiery smile as he replied: 'The vargr will be too intent upon its own motives and purposes. It's a pity, really,' he continued with a sigh. 'I could have used that creature. That's why I originally agreed to create it.' And to get my hands on Tyrfing, he added silently. 'Still, the only way that Odin would agree to return Tyrfing to you was if I abandoned it. He loves his precious Ynglings a little too well for my taste.'

Hundermann frowned in the shadows, his dogs waiting silently beside him. It was a week now since the dying Graff had told him of an act performed many years before, yet the mystery of that tale persisted in his memory. It had to be true. Apart from the fact that a dying man had no purpose left to serve by lying, Graff's description of Tyrfing, a weapon he could never have seen unless his story was true, had been exact.

It must be true. If it is, it's terrible. Yet there's nothing new in terror. Only in truth.

Vargr, I've never seen your face, but I know now who you are.

Hather kicked open the door. It crashed back against the stone wall of the passageway. As the echoes of its opening died away into the unnatural stillness of the fortress they passed through towards the spiral staircase.

Saeunna, following Hather and Vermund, nodded to herself. She had found strength. Live or die now, it didn't matter. She knew that she loved Hather, that she would give her life for him, or for his son. Her family were gone and he was all she had, probably all that she would ever have, and for their few hard days together she was grateful.

If we have to die, Allfather, she prayed, let it be together. That's the only thing I have left to ask of you. I

212

know you betray your worshippers, but I still ask you this. Live or die, let us stand or fall together in this place.

The spiral staircase beckoned. They began the ascent.

'She . . . told me the signal . . . that she wanted . . . that I've told you . . . Hundermann. I'd taken . . . the sword from where she told me . . . it would be . . . I knew that when . . . I gave the signal . . . I was to wait, to be ready . . .'

And you were ready, Graff. You were ready, all those years ago. And now you're dead because you obeyed her all too well.

They entered the inner, windowless chamber. Beyond the tangled, tooth-gnawed ivory of a dwarfish skeleton a door stood open. It trapped their eyes, drawing them away from the shadows, away from the waiting, motionless, silent host that watched with glittering eyes from the darkness about the walls.

The cressets flickered in the draught from the broken dome. Through its sharded cavity the moon, the new moon, the vargr-moon, showed faint and deadly. The yellow, darting lights shone down upon the little figure on the marble slab.

'It's a trap,' Half-Foot snapped. 'It has to be a trap.'

'Trap or no,' Hather growled, 'that's my son in there.'

Hundermann felt a growl growing in the nearest wolf-like throat. He reached down and grabbed the dog by the back of its neck, twisting the flesh until the windpipe beneath was constricted into silence.

Alvis felt his body begin to numb with cramp and fear. On the opposite corner Kulubak Magri kept his eyes closed and his ears open. They had to wait a little longer. Then, with Tyrfing within grasp, he could meet, in his way, the two different bargains he had contracted.

'He's not moving,' Saeunna whispered.

'Drugged. Nothing more,' Vermund assured them. 'He's unharmed, Hather.'

Sword in hand, his eyes wary, his body alert, Hather entered the circular chamber and approached the marble slab. Carefully, their weapons firmly held, their faces lined with the constant strain of alertness, the others followed.

213

Somehow she came here, Graff. It took years, but she knew that someone, somewhere would want it. Would want it and strike a bargain that would suit her, a bargain that would accomplish everything she'd sought to have done. A complicated bargain, perhaps, but a bargain none-theless.

You came with her, no longer paid by anything other than your own fascination. You came with her and helped her to find me, to find the others. You waited for her whilst she met this sorcerer, whoever, wherever, he is. You waited and you served. And your loyalty cost you your life and your heart.

And still I serve, knowing what you knew. I shall always serve, as you did, Graff. I shall always remember the vargr, until the day I die. Hundermann will always serve, Graff. It's the only thing I still know how to do.

A little further, Hather. A little further, all of you. Just a little further.

Not long now.

He set down his sword on the veined marble and shook Svipdag gently. 'Son,' he said, his eyes bright with tears of joy. 'Can you hear me, Svipdag? It's your father. I've come for you.'

Of course it was a trap. It had to be. But they were together again. If they had to, they'd die together.

The vargr moved forward from the shadows, Tyrfing glittering in a paw-gloved hand. Hather and Svipdag. Die together, Hather and Svipdag. The others don't matter. But you do. Die together. Then I'll deal with Omund Yngling.

Vermund gasped. Leif cursed. Saeunna turned at the sounds, then backed away as the slavering jaws of Hundermann's dogs pinned her against the wall.

Hather snatched up his sword and roared towards the doorway. One dog leaped and seized his sword-arm. Another knocked his legs out from beneath him and stood, snarling at his throat, above his chest.

'Take their weapons,' the vargr ordered.

The others crowded into the chamber. They obeyed.

214

His heart sinking, his brain numb, Hather climbed to his feet as Hundermann called the dogs back. It had been so easy. Too easy. His love for his son had led his friends here to their deaths.

'And now I'm ready,' the vargr announced. 'The thirteenth heart is mine.'

As it spoke they raised their eyes to the ruined roof. Above them, directly overhead, the vargr-moon's pallid circle gleamed in the night.

Hather saw one thing and one thing only. Somehow the sword that his mother had given him all those years before, the sword that had killed Starkadder, that should be buried with Starkadder in his grave-mound on the plain at Roliung, was in the vargr's hand.

The vargr had Tyrfing. Or did Tyrfing have the vargr?

Above them the new moon misted over. Above them pale tendrils of unseasonable mist began to filter down towards the dome. They didn't notice. No one noticed. All that mattered was the sword in the vargr's hand. Tyrfing, in the vargr's hand.

Two men stepped forward. They ripped the clothing from the unconscious Svipdag's hairless chest. They left it bare. Vulnerable. Waiting.

Hather started forward but a naked blade forced him back against the wall of the circular chamber. Beside him, disarmed, Saeunna and Vermund and Half-Foot, similarly prisoned, awaited the fate that threatened to engulf them all.

This was why there had been no arrows in the gorge. To lure them here. To lure them to this roofless room where death could claim them for ever. Where the vargr's vengeance would be completed, at the cost of their lives.

'The thirteenth heart,' the vargr muttered. 'You'll follow your son, Hather Lambisson. But without him you have nothing left to live for, have you?'

It wasn't right. There had to be something he could do. Even if he leaped forward upon the swords that were at his throat and chest it might give the others a chance at the expense of his own life.

215

Mother Skuld scowled. 'I wasn't ready, Hather,' she muttered. 'I have no choice, though. Odin has surprised me. He's played fair in this game. I'm sorry, Hather. I'm truly sorry.'

Above them, on the frozen waterfall, Odin smiled.

The mist crept down the walls.

Thrudnir and Illugi watched for the raising of Tyrfing, for the cuts that would take Svipdag Hathersson's young life and signal the lighting of the rope.

'Watch me now, Hather. Watch me kill your son and eat his heart.'

Saeunna felt her legs grow weak beneath her. Was this the hope she had come here to give? Was this what Harbard, what Odin had promised in her dream? Had he betrayed her, then, as he had betrayed so many others?

Hather pushed forward towards the waiting sword-points. Better dead than watch the butchering of his son. Better dead with Odin in Valhalla.

The mist gathered. Tyrfing, firm in the vargr's grasp, began to rise.

Thrudnir struck flint to tinder.

Kulubak Magri tensed.

Tyrfing reached the zenith of its unholy journey. Thrudnir glanced at Illugi. Illugi nodded.

Thrudnir lit the fuse.

'Watch me kill your son and eat his heart, Hather.'

And then Hather spoke.

The bulk that blotted out the stars that night, so many years ago, was the ship she'd bought for you, Graff. You met her as arranged. You took Tyrfing from where you'd been told to, from where she'd hidden it after she took it from Starkadder's grave-mound, after Hather had placed it there but before it could be sealed. That's why she has it now. And they all want it, don't they, Graff? The dwarfs want it. That's why they lured her here. She wants it because it matches the evil she's become, the evil that I serve.

And Odin wants it too, to lie with Starkadder, as it should have done all along.

216

'He's not just *my* son,' Hather said. 'He's your son too, Astrid.'

The sudden silence became a tangible thing. They were too far from the waterfall to hear the sputtering of the fuse Crasyllus had plaited so many years before, or to hear the scuttering withdrawal of the dwarfs towards the nearest tunnel that could take them back to Trollheim.

The mist began to take on form

Tyrfing slashed down.

Nothing shall stop me becoming vargr, Astrid thought in her madness. Nothing cheats me of my revenge upon Hather's weakness and upon the Yngling dynasty he serves. Nothing.

Then Kulubak Magri snatched at her wrist. Tyrfing stopped.

'Now, Alvis!' the sorcerer screamed.

'NOW!' Vermund roared, kicking his distracted guard hard in the groin, grabbing the man's sword as he doubled up.

'Kill!' Hundermann roared to his dogs.

Hather knocked the wavering swords aside. He snapped a wrist across his knee and took the falling weapon before it could strike the stone-flagged floor. Continuing the same spurt of movement he decapitated the outlaw guarding Saeunna, snatched Svipdag out from beneath Tyrfing's trembling length and threw the boy from the slab across to her.

Kulubak Magri grabbed Tyrfing from Astrid's struggling fingers. Then he plunged it into Alvis, point first. 'The only weapon that could save you,' he sneered. 'And the only weapon that could kill you, king.'

Alvis stared up at his betrayer. His bloody fingers clawed at Tyrfing's length as he slid dying from the impaling blade.

The dogs started forward. Then saw the mist. Then howled with terror.

Leif Half-Foot smashed his guard on the jaw with a mail-gloved fist.

Rage and frustration burning from her eyes, Astrid tore

217

off the golden mask. The dogs backed off. They all backed off, outlaws and heroes alike. Even Kulubak Magri.

Alvis fell from Tyrfing's dripping point and slumped onto the floor.

A mist-formed hand stole Tyrfing from the sorcerer's grasp.

'Shall we play Odin's game, now?' asked a voice from Hather's past.

Astrid gasped, horrified herself as much as her appearance horrified the others. Her eyes were blackened pits, wider apart than any mortal's ought to be. Her nose and lower jaw had begun to lengthen, to take on the appearance of the wolfish mask she had worn for so many moons, the mask Kulubak Magri had so carefully fashioned to disguise her features and her voice. Her mouth was fanged, and Hather could no longer disbelieve in the power that could change his demented, lovely wife into a creature that could kill and rend and maim without compassion.

She wasn't Astrid any more. In her bestial way she was still as lovely, though more terrible, as Astrid. But now she was vargr, and all the horror of being vargr was hers for ever. . . . Or as long as for ever lasted at Skroggrmagi.

The mist had form. It was a person now, mere formless shapes no longer. It stood tall and strong and Tyrfing glittered in its hand. As Tyrfing had glittered there so many years before.

The mist-formed figure looked at Hather. 'Get your son out of here,' said a familiar voice.

Hather hesitated, staring in disbelief. 'How . . .' he asked. 'How have you . . ?'

The fuse burned down.

'You'll have to fight!'

'But . . . why . . . ?'

'Come on!' Vermund called, launching himself towards the doorway, the stolen sword scything before him, cutting outlaws from his path.

The fuse neared the powder, neared the ending of the

218

frozen waterfall's fragile majesty, banishing the sign of Ginnir from its depths for ever.

'GET OUT OF HERE!' Starkadder yelled, his deep-set blue eyes blazing. 'Odin's sent me here for Tyrfing, not for you!'

'Nooooo!'

Astrid launched her were-body at the gaunt, black-clad warrior. The fuse reached the mouth of the bronze box. Thrudnir and Illugi ran on towards the tunnel.

'Odin! You've tricked me! You've voided our bargain!' Kulubak Magri howled in disbelief.

Hundermann drew his sword. As his dogs hesitated in terror he shore through the passing Half-Foot just below his shoulder-blades, cutting him in half.

Odin grinned. In her own way, so did Mother Skuld.

Hundermann launched himself across the marble slab at Starkadder's back. From the back of his throat, growling even as they growled, he snarled to his beasts: 'Follow them! Kill them!'

Starkadder turned. Tyrfing sang with undisguised pleasure in his grasp. Hundermann shuddered to a startled halt.

Hather and Saeunna and Vermund cut their way through to the outer chamber, then towards the stairs. About their ears the pursuit began to rally.

Tyrfing's point, still singing, projected half-way down Hundermann's backbone. The blade tore out through his kidneys as he died upon it.

Astrid darted past the ghost of the man who had helped rescue her from the blacksmith, thirteen years before. Tyrfing hummed after her. And cut the empty air.

They leaped the stairs three, four at a time. Behind them, growing ever closer, the dogs and outlaws howled.

The fuse reached the powder of Crasyllus.

Starkadder grinned. Tyrfing sang its deadly song in the pressing host of the vargr's outlaws. It maimed, it killed, it lived before it sank for ever back into the grave to slow, rust-crusted death.

In a thousand flying, shattering, destroying, sharp-edged

fragments the ice-palace thundered outwards as the powder of Crasyllus did its work.

'But Odin promised me . . .' Kulubak Magri wailed. 'Allfather promised meee . . .'

His foot struck the fallen body of King Alvis. He fell on top of it, hard against one of the two dwarfish figures which still supported the empty marble slab, a figure which cracked and split.

The waterfall shattered. Beneath its frozen surface the water began to feel its liberation, to gather its strength in the moments of stark freedom that the coldness would allow.

'A promise is simply words,' Starkadder smiled grimly. 'And a promise from Allfather is no sort of promise at all.'

Even as he spoke the dwarfish citadel of Skroggrmagi began to tremble.

'My work is done,' Starkadder said bleakly. 'I have the sword Tyrfing. Now all that is left is the grave, and Valhalla. . . . Live for me, Hather. If you can.'

And then he faded back to mist, and Tyrfing faded with him.

CHAPTER SIX

The shattering
of Skroggrmagi

HATHER'S WORLD fell apart.

For the moments, the terrifying, confused moments that followed, it became a series of vivid, death-silent impressions, a chaos of falling stone and running feet, a haze of wondering and fighting, a maze of glistening, blood-dewed blades and cursing, horrified faces.

They ran.

Saeunna held little Svipdag close. Vermund, his eye bright, his sword ready, guarded their rear. Hather led, no longer afraid, no longer worried that they wouldn't keep up, that his son would somehow be lost in the mêlée of following, terror-fleeing outlaws and dogs that snapped close by their heels.

'Keep going!' he urged. 'Keep going. We have to keep going!'

Soon it would be over. Soon he could rest. Perhaps.

At one point he looked back, briefly. Saeunna tried to give him a reassuring smile as she ran behind, his son, still unconscious, across her shoulder. But he didn't dare to see. There was no time to see such things. There was only time to run, to make briefly sure that the others were behind him.

That was all that there was time for. Nothing more.

And Starkadder, his one-time friend, his twice-times saviour, was back there, was fighting for his peace, for his life in death, for his brief moment of returning from Valhalla, a moment that Odin, unspeaking, unrevealing, had planned all the way along.

Come back for Tyrfing. Perhaps he had, but there was more to life, to any life, than Tyrfing. Even Starkadder's.

It could only be the flimsiest of excuses. Tyrfing was nothing more than an excuse. It might have meaning to the dwarfs who forged it, to vanished Dvalin and sorcerer-murdered Alvis, but it mattered little to Odin whether it lay with Starkadder in the grave to rust or festered in the wolf-pawed grip of the murdering vargr that still pursued them.

If Tyrfing was an excuse, then so was their deliverance. It could still go wrong.

They reached the bottom of the staircase and leaped along the passageway into the high hall at the centre of the citadel. Above them, on the waterfall, the world was shattering and twisting down towards them in a glittering cascade of flying fragments bright beneath the vargr-moon.

Thrudnir and Illugi felt the universe shake within their ears. Stones and rocks rained from the roof. They fell beneath them to a slow, bone-shattered, suffocating death.

The marble slab cracked and slipped sideways. Kulubak Magri screamed as it crashed down upon his ribs, pushing them in upon his unprotected heart, sending his blood rushing up through throat and windpipe to bubble out in a frothing, fatal cascade that bathed his limbs.

You'll never be dwarf-king now, Kulubak Magri, came his dying thought. All the planning and scheming, all the plotting with Odin, all the creation of that elaborate apparatus you used to impress the vargr with your booming voice, a voice so fearsome and un-dwarf-like. All gone. All for nothing. All vanished beneath a falling marble slab . . .

222

The roof of the hall erupted inwards, enormous ice-splinters smashing the trestle-tables and their contents. As the fragments bedded into the door at the hall-end of the corridor Hather and Saeunna and Vermund, the helpless Svipdag motionless still across Saeunna's shoulder, were running towards the stables, unaware that the crashing, thundering horror within the dwarfish citadel was shattering the frozen river-bed outside, breaking its surface into a thousand separate, swiftly flowing ice-floes.

The dogs and the vargr ran on. The outlaws followed. The ice showered down.

The hall fell in upon itself. Men died. Dogs died. Still some pursued, barking and howling with their terror, fury and frustration.

It's not over yet, Hather. You're not out of here with your son yet.

They heard the destruction behind them. They felt the shaking of the stones of Skroggrmagi as the citadel shivered about them.

The vargr's still coming, Hather. Astrid's still behind you. She can still see you and Svipdag and Omund dead, Hather.

He ran on. Behind him, tiring, Saeunna and Vermund ran on as well.

Three of you left. Three and a sleeping child. And the world falling with the ice-palace beyond you, the world shattering into a million deadly pieces in the wake of Skroggrmagi.

Mother Skuld nodded to herself. Perhaps there was justice left in this world of ice and terror after all.

The ramp beyond the stables cracked. The age-moored boat broke free of its frozen rope. The horses reared, screaming and whinnying their fright. The river cracked. It broke up. It thundered, flinging ice and shearing splinters down the gorge.

He felt so tired, so tired. Behind him running feet slapped onto sharding stone. More feet than there should have been. Too many pursuers.

Astrid. And the rest. Was that thing still truly Astrid?

Wasn't Astrid just a name for something it once had been?

The dwarfs were dead. The fortress, like the river, was breaking up.

And Starkadder, he knew, was gone for ever.

They cut their way through the tangled legs and flying hoofs of the cracking stables. Hundermann was dead. Only the vargr, no longer Astrid, as it had never truly been Astrid, still pursued with its rag-tag following.

And the dogs, the whimpering, howling, fear-eyed, slavering dogs.

As he reached the ramp, feeling its frozen covering splinter beneath his heels, Hather turned to face Saeunna and Vermund. Behind them a cresset had fallen at the further end of the stables, setting light to the straw heaped in the byres. A blazing figure emerged, staggering wildly, falling beneath the fear-crazed hoofs of a tethered mount. Heavy splinters of flying ice rained through the roof, turning flames to steam where they met and interacted.

Desperate outlaws ran on, through the mêlée, the grim shapes of Hundermann's dogs following hesitantly through the whirling, swirling rubble of flying ice and fire and shattered stone.

Vermund surveyed the river. 'It's breaking up,' he called above the growing roar from within. 'We'll never make it back that way.'

'Into the boat. Now!' Saeunna ordered, scrambling down the ramp and picking her way across the cracking, separating ice, Svipdag's unconscious form still over her shoulder.

Hather nodded. Another, distant sound was beginning to reach his ears, a sound that came from outside the falling fortress, a sound that came from the waterfall itself. 'Follow her, Vermund,' he growled, determinedly.

The old marshal hesitated. 'Do it!' Hather snapped.

Three of the dogs passed the vargr. A flying hoof caught Astrid, sprawling her back across the remaining one. It leaped her falling body. So did her men.

It's not pursuit, Hather thought, standing at the base of

224

the ramp, sword in hand. It's flight. They're running for their lives.

The men and dogs reached the top of the ramp at the same moment. As a rider urged his horse through them, increasing the confusion around the entrance to the fortress, Hather glimpsed the source of the roaring from without through the gorge-spanning arch which supported the dwarfish citadel.

A huge mass, a mighty, moving wall of spray-lashed ice was gathering speed, piling higher as it drew nearer, scouring its frozen covering from the river, damming back the waters of the liberated falls.

Astrid struggled to her feet, her wolfish face snarling with pain and rage. The vargr-moon was still in the night sky, albeit blotted out by rising clouds of smoke and dust from her crumbling stronghold. The boy was still alive. Tyrfing might be gone, but that had only been a toy, a means of securing and keeping the patronage of the sorcerer she never knew to be a dwarf.

If her son was still alive the thirteenth heart could still be hers. If only she could reach it. . . .

The boat, still embedded in the ice, broke free of the bank with an ear-wrenching crack. In the bottom Saeunna huddled above Svipdag's body, Vermund covering her with his own.

'Hather! Come on!' he yelled above the tumult.

The mounted rider took off, leaping towards the breaking ice of the river. The dogs leaped for Hather's throat. Men stumbled down onto the ramp.

In mid-air the first flying ice from the moving wall struck both horse and rider, flinging them sideways, hurling them down the gorge to strike the frozen surface in a confusion of limbs and spraying black blood. Smaller fragments ploughed into and through the outlaws and dogs on the ramp as Hather dived low and sideways for the meagre shelter of the boat on the further side.

The ice-wall struck the fortress. For a moment it stopped. Then the centre buckled and a confusion of ice and stone and water thundered through the arch, pushing bodies and scrambling, screaming fugitives from the ramp, tearing furiously past the relative calm where the boat, held firm against the side of the gorge by surrounding ice-floes and sheltered from the worst of the rushing by the ramp, waited to join its flowing, destructive aftermath.

Astrid saw the sheet of frozen debris tearing endlessly past the entrance to the stables. Slightly behind her, away from the snorting horses, two of her men were glancing desperately back towards the inner corridor. The surviving dog, shaking its head groggily, sluggish blood trickling from the cut received from a falling stone, struggled upright on wide-splayed feet.

A trail of mutilated, crying, dead and dying bodies traced their escape from the broken-domed chamber where Kulubak Magri's centuried dreams had ended for ever.

No way back. No way forward. Outside, the ice and rubble pressed like a falling mountain on the stable wall. Mere moments remained before the fortress at Skroggrmagi fell for ever, like the dreaming and scheming of the dead dwarf overhead.

The mountain moved. The stone wall buckled. The dog stared at the wolf-muzzled vargr, sensing greater kinship with this unhuman being than with the frightened, scrambling men who were struggling to tear down a wooden stall-divider near the entrance.

Rubble and freezing water erupted into the stables, striking and smothering the struggling horses, hurtling towards the men and the dog and the vargr trapped within.

Rushing ice and water tore at the floes surrounding the creaking boat. They were cut and bruised by flying fragments, but they lived. With a sudden wrench the boat bucked and twisted as the ramp crumbled away, its loosened stones smashing through the securing ice. Clinging grimly to the gunwales they felt, rather than saw, the fragile craft hurled out into the storming chaos of the gorge.

Somewhere above them a one-eyed god and a veiled old

woman watched in silence. An instant later the arch began to buckle.

Hather glanced back through the spray of the torrent which was carrying them down the gorge. As if gigantic hands were pressing invisibly in upon it the citadel of Skroggrmagi twisted up towards the stars and the pallid circle of the hovering vargr-moon. The chasm-spanning archway narrowed. The tortured, shattering stones cried out their movement to the night. A fan of white spray arose above the base of the fortress, a spraying fan that grew and gathered, hurtling starkly up against the towering, gargoyle-crusted silhouette, a silhouette all the blacker for being set against the brightness of the liberated waterfall beyond.

The fan shattered as the stones separated and crashed through it. Stone dwarfs teetered from their ancient perches. For a moment longer the frozen silhouette of the rearing, jutting, dying fortress held together, then it sank slowly into the mêlée of spilled bodies, screaming horses and hissing flames, broken woodwork and glass-flying window-fragments.

Nothing could live through that, Hather thought. Not even the vargr that once was Astrid.

He was wrong.

CHAPTER SEVEN

The thirteenth heart

THE TINY boat hurtled on, the ice about its sides slowly diminishing with the buffeting of the rubble-strewn waters about it. Saeunna cradled Svipdag to her, pressing his face to her shoulder, staring ahead through the spray as the rock-walls hurtled past on either side.

They careened around the twist in the gorge, the boat rocking violently as its ice-guard caught the side, twisting it around, throwing it briefly back against the current. As they scrambled to maintain their fragile hold on life there came a distant roaring from behind them, the roar of falling masonry as the fortress they had left moments before collapsed into the gorge of Skroggrmagi.

The current began to slow.

'The fortress is damming the river,' Hather called. 'It won't last long. The waterfall will either sweep it away or flood over it.

'When we come to the horses try to jump ashore.'

They passed the place where Horsetail's body had lain upon the ice. It had long since been swept down towards the Dalalven on a tumbling, lifeless journey to the Baltic coast.

As the end of the gorge came into sight they struggled towards the bank, paddling desperately with their hands, willing the fragile craft towards firm land again. They came within feet, then within inches.

Beyond them, in the slowing current, the debris of men and animals and furnishings and stone-built citadel floated past. Vermund snatched out for the low branch of a stunted, leafless tree, its winter branches swept clear of snow by the flying, slashing spray that had preceded them. His fingers locked against the branch, sending a wrenching, searing pain up his arm, tearing open the healing wound. His body leaped from the effort, his knees banging against the gunwale as the effort threatened to pluck him from the boat. Hather lurched forward and grabbed him around the waist.

The boat stopped. Beyond them the debris floated on, fragments of the stables being washed on by the waters.

Somehow the dog still had its head above the water. It snarled at them as the current carried it past.

'I still have a trick or two left of my own, Allfather,' Mother Skuld said softly to her companion. 'Your precious Hather Lambisson's not safe yet.'

Hather took over the hold from Vermund, who scrambled ashore and reached out with his good arm to grip the gunwale. Unsteadily Saeunna rose to her feet and lifted Svipdag onto the bank. Then she stepped out of the boat and picked the child up in her arms, carrying it towards the waiting horses.

A broken stall from the stables floated towards them, grim eyes glaring from the huddled, sodden shape it carried.

Bone-weary, exhausted by their struggles against men and the elements themselves, Hather climbed out of the boat, letting the river carry it away to wherever it wanted.

They had faced the vargr at Skroggrmagi. They had rescued Svipdag. Drenched, frozen and tired beyond the power of their tongues to tell, they grinned their triumph, Vermund clutching his injured arm, Hather spreading his arms about their shoulders, kissing Saeunna and his son, clapping Vermund's good shoulder with a heartiness he was far from feeling.

Hather began to laugh with relief, but the humour died in his exhausted throat. A dark shape with darker, snarling eyes and long matted hair was hauling its dripping form out of the river.

'You have something that I want, Hather,' Astrid said menacingly.

'Mount up,' Hather told his companions determinedly.

'Will you run from me for ever?' the vargr asked. Its voice, like its face, no longer that of Hather's vanished wife.

'I don't have to. You only have tonight. Once the moon begins to wax again your work will have been for nothing. I only have to keep my son safe until then.'

Saeunna mounted and set little Svipdag, his eyes beginning to blink towards returning consciousness, before her. With a snarl the vargr launched itself towards them.

Vermund tried to interpose himself. The vargr thrust him viciously aside. He stumbled and fell, moaning, to the snow-covered ground.

Hather reached for his sword, only to find the scabbard empty. The weapon was gone, washed away with the fortress, abandoned when he leaped from the path of the moving ice-wall. Vermund twisted, trying to pluck the length of his own blade left-handed from its scabbard. Saeunna reared her horse, turning it, knocking Hather aside and towering flying hoofs above the advancing vargr.

Vermund freed his blade and threw it towards the fallen Hather. With a sharp pull on the reins Saeunna spun the horse away, carrying Svipdag out of range of the combatants.

'Kill it, Hather,' she cried. 'We'll never know peace unless you kill it!'

Hather grabbed Vermund's sword and struggled to his feet, holding the weapon out before him. A swift kick came up under his guard, sending the blade spinning harmlessly away. Another kick landed in the pit of his stomach, doubling him over.

The vargr sprang towards the nearest horse, which shied in terror as she climbed onto its back.

Vermund's hand closed over a stone beneath the snow.

230

He hauled his ageing, weary body into a kneeling position and aimed. The stone spun from his fingers towards its target. As it flew Hather scrambled after the fallen sword.

The stone struck Astrid between the shoulder-blades. Briefly she slumped forward with the force of the blow, then straightened and tightened her grip upon the reins.

Hather seized Vermund's weapon and lurched in front of the horse and its rider. As the vargr pushed forward he swept the point out in a wild and vicious arc. Its throat shorn through to the neck-bones, spurting blood from mouth and nostrils and wound, the beast collapsed and rolled, its legs thrashing as its life drained out, pinning the vargr helplessly beneath it.

Astrid glared up as Hather approached her, the dripping sword still clutched firmly in one hand, the other holding his aching stomach. With a scream of rage she struggled to free her legs, foam flecking her feral lips, the wolf-teeth in their fury champing bloodily down onto the tongue.

The eyes burned into his own. 'Bring . . . me . . . Svipdag's heart!' she commanded. 'Bring it to me, Hather. Bring it now!'

'Kill it, Hather,' Vermund growled, rising to his feet. 'Things like that shouldn't be alive. Kill it.'

He looked down, his tired, confused mind fighting to retain its hold upon reality. The wolf-muzzle seemed to fade, to dissolve back into the features, the lovely, human features, of the wife he had loved and lost so many years before.

He loved her so much. He'd do anything for her. Anything at all. His fingers relaxed their hold upon the sword-hilt. The weapon slipped to the ground.

'The thirteenth heart, Hather.' Her eyes, so brown, so hungry for him, flicked up towards the vargr-moon overhead. 'Bring it to your Astrid. Please?'

'Hather,' Vermund whispered, aghast. 'For Odin's sake, Hather. That isn't Astrid!'

When she saw the vargr's horse fall Saeunna had begun to edge back towards her friends. She saw Hather standing

231

over the fallen creature, saw the sword drop from his fingers, saw him turn, smiling, happy, and walk over towards her. Smiling back she dismounted and began to carry his awakening son towards him.

Vermund forced himself to one last effort and snatched up the fallen sword in his good hand. As he raised it for a decapitating stroke Hather's hand clamped about his wrist, slowly forcing the fingers of the marshal's weakened sword-arm to relax.

Hather took the sword. Vermund eyed him fearfully.

'Give me some room,' Hather said determinedly.

He looked down at the terribly altered features of his lovely Astrid. 'Old Tisti told me about the vargr,' he began, his voice calm, almost peaceful. 'She told me about the thirteenth heart, how it has to come from one who is blood-kin to the vargr.

'When we married, Astrid, you had no blood-kin left. Omund's father had killed them all, all your family, except for you alone. That's how I knew who you were, Astrid. You could only be keeping our son alive because you wanted that thirteenth heart which beats within his body. Your only blood-kin, Astrid. Our son, Svipdag.

'Yet are you not also blood-kin to yourself?'

The wolf-muzzle froze into a mask of terror. Once Vermund's sword had split her chest Hather dropped it and tore the blood-spattered bones apart. With feverish determination he ripped the living heart from her body, spraying them both as he held it high.

Vermund turned away, gagging. Saeunna shut her eyes tightly against the nightmare being enacted in front of her and hugged Svipdag's face into her body until the rings of her mail-shirt bit against his eyelids.

Even then, the power of the vargr wasn't broken.

Slowly, the muscles convulsing, the claw-like fingers twitching, the vargr reached up towards the torn-out heart. Its eyes were blazing with an unholy determination, a determination which, slowly but certainly, was pulling its legs free of the fallen horse. Its gaping chest made little difference. It should have been dead, but the last vestige of

232

Kulubak Magri's sorcery still preserved some form of life, some kind of jerky, necromantic movement.

Vermund steeled himself to glance back at the rising, ruined, wolf-like Astrid. He grasped his fallen sword.

She could still live. She could still become truly vargr. If only she could reach that heart.

And her power, the power of the vargr made beneath the vargr-moon, would be all the greater, all the more formidable, because of the torment of her making.

Hather swung around. The heart left his hand, hurtling in a gory arc towards the tumult of the river. As Astrid, finally free of the fallen horse, leaped after it, Vermund's stroke took the beast-snouted head clear of her shoulders.

CHAPTER EIGHT

Breaking the power of the Ynglings

THEY WERE so tired, but they rested little. They kept riding, cold and weary and hungry. At Dalalven they took food and shelter and the opportunity of a hot bath. Hather asked for news of King Omund's army and wasn't even slightly surprised to find his hosts uncertain about what he meant.

'As far as I know it's still camped outside Uppsala,' the fortress commander told him. 'From what I hear they'll be moving towards the border with Skane in a few days.'

Hather nodded wearily. It made good sense at last. Omund wanted war. That was why he'd been so eager to blame the vargr on the Danes.

'Would you like me to send a rider on ahead to tell the king of your victory over the vargr?' the commander asked.

'No,' Hather said. 'I'd rather give him the good news myself.'

He mustn't know I'm alive, he thought. Not yet. I want to see the look on his face when he learns he's lost an ally and gained an enemy instead. I want to see King Omund as frightened as I've been over the past few days. I want to see him tell his men I'm a traitor because I've killed the creature which wanted him dead.

I want to kill you, Omund, but I know I can't. If Odin's kept me alive this far it's so that I can save you from yourself, and from Atyl Skin. That's why we have to ride so hard, Omund. The Dane's got a day's start on me. I have to catch up. I have to save your worthless life, Omund, even if I have to kill a friend to do it.

'A few hours' sleep,' Hather grinned to his companions. 'Then we continue on towards Uppsala. And a reckoning of sorts.'

The following day they approached the city, falling travellers on falling horses. Vermund felt his mouth fall open as he saw the scale of the armed host assembled on the plain before the city. Hather grinned ruefully and rubbed his beard.

'Straight to King Omund?' Vermund asked.

Hather grinned. 'I don't think we have any choice about that,' he replied. 'If we don't win this one then we haven't won any of them at all. Straight to Omund, my friend. We still have work to do.'

They made their way through the huge encampment, then up through the town towards the palace gates. The gates stood open, but sentries challenged them.

'Get aside,' Vermund commanded. 'Don't you know the king's marshal, Vermund Bjarnisson, and Lord Hather of Sudrafell? Stand out of our way!'

The guards exchanged glances, then they stood aside.

Hather dismounted and lifted his son down from Saeunna's saddle. Then he held out his hand to help her dismount.

'The guards will give you guest-quarters,' he said. 'Wait for us there. This won't take long.'

'What are you going to do about Atyl Skin?' she asked. 'He was a good friend, Hather. It's not right to betray him for the sake of a worthless creature like Omund.'

'We'll do what we have to,' Hather replied. 'But if there's a way that we can protect him, we will. How would you feel about exile in Denmark, Saeunna?'

235

She smiled softly. 'If it will keep me near you, Hather of Sudrafell, I'd follow you even to Byzantium.'

He squeezed her hand. 'Perhaps you won't have to,' he comforted. 'Perhaps you'll marry a king instead.'

She didn't understand his words. There was only one king, and that was Omund. She'd never marry Omund, and, in the same way that Hather wouldn't kill him, he wouldn't depose him and take the throne himself either.

Vermund and Hather left her there with Svipdag. They walked away towards the royal apartments. From the shadows, wearing the uniform and holding the weapons of an archer of the king's guard, Atyl Skin watched them closely.

A dog ran through the camp beyond the city. A soldier tossed a pebble at it. The dog, unmarked except for a healing gash upon its wolf-like head, growled briefly, then ran on towards the gates of Uppsala.

In the vestibule before the royal apartments Hather and Vermund found their way blocked by Omund's guards.

'Would you keep out the king's marshal?' Hather demanded.

The one glanced at his companion. 'I shall announce you, sir,' he said firmly.

Vermund grinned. Hather grinned back. With sudden surges they hammered the guards' heads against the vestibule walls. Then they kicked open the inner door and strode inside.

The guards about the walls surged forward. Omund glared at them, then his grey eyes widened in surprise. And terror.

Hather slammed the door shut, sword in hand. Vermund whacked the nearest guard about the head with the flat of his blade. The man went down. The five remaining guards drew back around their king. Hather and Vermund strode forward.

'We're not here to kill you,' Vermund growled. 'We're still your men, King Omund. But unless you want your guards to hear what we have to say you'd be well advised to dismiss them.'

Omund wavered. They could be lying. And they should be dead. His dreams of empire began to crumble, like a shape of sand before the washing of the rising tide.

'Get rid of them or lose them!' Hather snarled. 'If we can survive the vargr we can survive five armed men.'

The dog reached the gates. Atyl Skin, an arrow nocked to his bow, stood before the vestibule.

Omund waved a hand. 'Get out of here,' he ordered the guards, suddenly weary. 'These gentlemen wish to speak to me alone.'

They filed out, leaving the door open behind them. In the vestibule they lifted their fallen comrades and carried them away.

The king slumped down into a chair. Hather and Vermund laid their swords upon the table, their points to Omund.

'The vargr is dead,' Vermund announced. 'We know that it was your creature, for as long as it suited you.'

Omund snorted defiantly. 'And what's that supposed to mean, Marshal Vermund?' he asked, his tones dripping with irony.

'It would have betrayed you, Omund,' Hather said quietly. 'It wanted you dead. Its whole purpose was to destroy the House of Yngling.'

Omund paled visibly. 'And yours isn't?' he asked, determined to brazen it out until the end, whatever that end might be.

A guard saw Atyl Skin with the arrow ready. 'Can you get a shot at them?' he asked.

The Dane nodded. 'I can get one of them,' he grinned, stepping silently into the vestibule. I know you want to keep him alive, Hather, he thought. But I've got to stop this war. And the only way I know is to kill King Omund. I hope you'll understand that.

'My work is to keep the House of Yngling going,' Hather said wearily. 'And that's what I'll do, if I can. We don't want you dead, Omund. You have to hold the throne for the future, whatever that future may be. Sweden needs the stability of Yngling rule. But ultimate power can never rest with the king again. It has to be spread, divided.'

'And how do we accomplish that?'

'By your royal decree,' Vermund responded. 'You will set up a system of petty kingdoms, each independent as far as its own matters are concerned, but answerable to a council of petty kings for national causes. You will assume the title of High King of Sweden.'

High King, Omund thought. At least they were permitting him to resign himself to servitude with honour. Then he saw the figure in the doorway, the figure with the bow ready in its hands, the figure wearing the uniform of his personal guard. He grinned at them, beyond them. The figure grinned back and began to raise the bow.

'And if I don't agree?'

Hather's hand brushed the hilt of his sword. He wouldn't kill Omund, but he couldn't let Omund know that. The bluff had to work. And then they had to find Atyl Skin and stop him.

'So, it would appear I have no choice,' Omund grunted.

'None at all,' Vermund answered. 'The Yngling name remains. Your own personal glory is enhanced, but the power is dispersed.'

'Did you really think an invasion of the Dane-Lands would work?' Hather demanded. 'King Gorm already has agents in this country, agents that will have reported the build-up of your forces. His own preparations are already under way. You'd face stiffer opposition in Skane than you could ever have imagined.'

The dog hesitated. It saw the man with the bow. It launched past him.

Atyl Skin sighted on Omund along the arrow.

The dog leaped, straight for Hather's throat.

Omund grinned evilly.

Mother Skuld smiled beneath her veil. I've kept my word to you, Garm, Hound of Hel. Your kin has its chance at Hather. I can do nothing more for you.

Atyl Skin loosed his arrow.

The dog twisted in mid-leap and fell. For a moment or

238

so its legs twitched convulsively, then it lay still, the feathered shaft projecting from its head.

The Dane lowered his bow and stepped forward. 'I owed you my life from the time at Vigaknoll,' he said to Hather. 'We're even now.'

Vermund smiled. 'We leave here now, King Omund,' he began, 'and you explain to the people that your army was raised for an invasion of the Dane-Lands that was foredoomed to failure. Or else you go ahead, providing Atyl Skin's next arrow doesn't kill you. The alternative is to hail Hather publicly as the killer of the vargr and make him the first of your petty kings. Then you can disband the army with honour, its purpose accomplished by a national hero. Hather deserves it. He's too modest to claim it for himself, but I'm here to claim his kingship for him. He knows. He's already agreed, albeit reluctantly.'

'And the other petty kings?' Omund asked.

'We shall choose them from the best and loyalest of your subjects,' Vermund answered. 'It's over, Omund. There's nothing you can do now but agree to our demands or die. You shouldn't have dismissed your guards so readily. You might have stopped us, if you'd had the nerve.'

Omund nodded slowly. He could come out of his predicament alive, with honour that he was far from deserving, or die. There was only one choice possible.

He picked Hather's sword up by the blade and handed it to him, hilt first.

'Hail King Hather,' he said slowly. 'The High King of Sweden, through the years to come, will value above all others your friendship and advice.'

The words were hollow, but they had been spoken. It was enough. Hather took the sword and laid it upon the trestle table, its hilt towards Omund.

'My sword is yours, King Omund,' he replied.

Vermund's single eye watched closely. His fingers strayed towards the hilt of his own weapon. Hather stood, impassive, his hand clutching Atyl Skin's wrist, preventing the Dane from nocking another arrow to his bow.

Omund took the weapon and stood up. For an instant

the point wavered before Hather's eyes. Then the king dug the point into the table and turned away.

'Hail, King Hather,' Atyl Skin said softly, his eyes upon the quivering blade.

'Hail, King Hather,' Vermund repeated. Then he smiled.

'Your son shall rule Tiundaland, the area around Uppsala,' Omund whispered. 'I think I owe him that.'

Hather sheathed his sword. 'You can still be a good king to your people, Omund,' he answered. 'May Allfather give you the glory that the Yngling line should have. For my part, I shall serve the Ynglings loyally.'

'So shall I,' Vermund added.

Atyl Skin said nothing, but beneath the elaborate nose-guard on his helmet his eyes were smiling brightly. Hather's loyal service to the Ynglings might yet see Omund in his grave.

Two wolves in the distance near the shore at Sudrafell

As THEY stood looking out across the sea he slipped his arm around her waist. She smiled and laid her head upon his shoulder, content to be with him there, content to see his son playing down upon the shore.

Together they had lived through Skroggrmagi. After that, Saeunna knew, they could live through anything.

Above them the gulls circled in the dusk, their whiteness bright against the roseate sky. Occasionally darker forms flitted between them, calling in a strident fashion which added discord to the mewing of the sea-birds.

Hather and Saeunna weren't watching the sky. They were watching Svipdag smile as he ran along the sand, pausing only to examine some new trophy provided by the pounding waves. Behind them the wooden walls of Sudrafell rose whole again, rebuilt and strengthened.

'He needs a nurse,' Hather said gently. 'You'll have quite enough to do as mistress of my estate.'

'As your queen, King Hather,' Saeunna prompted, smiling up at him.

He nodded and kissed her forehead. As soon as his

mourning for Gudrun was over he would marry her. Svipdag needed a mother, as well as a nurse.

'I think she should be a Lapp,' he continued. 'There's a lot that can be said for Lappish nurses. Don't you agree?'

She'd never known Old Tisti, but Hather had told her all about the old woman who had reached out beyond her years to keep them alive for each other. It was enough to make her agree. Their son, no longer simply Hather's son, should have the best that they could provide for him, as befitted the future King of Tiundaland.

'Have you told me you love me today?' she teased him.

He grinned and kissed her on the mouth. As they broke apart he said: 'I love you, Saeunna. I shall always love you.'

She returned his kiss. 'And I love you,' she replied. 'And this place. Sudrafell can be so beautiful in spring.'

The winter was past and the snows were fading from everywhere except the high lands and the mountains. Tiny flowers, Thor's helm, the aconite, and crocuses were blossoming into early life in the fields about them.

'We shall live here for ever and be very, very happy,' she smiled, encircling his waist with her arms.

The other figures standing nearby, the one-eyed man and the old, veiled woman, were beyond their power to see. They might have noticed the ravens that played and swooped with the gulls. They might have seen the dark, shaggy shapes of the wolves that prowled the hem of the one-eyed watcher's cloak. But they didn't. It wasn't written that they should.

Omund had kept his word. The petty kingships had been established. The first council of the petty kings was to be held at Uppsala in a few weeks' time. The army had disbanded to the provinces from which it had been assembled, the various contingents standing ready to come to the aid of their provincial ruler when they were asked to. Omund was no longer supreme commander. That role had fallen to his marshal, Vermund Bjarnisson, who stood at that moment further down the beach, fulfilling his role as Svipdag's honorary uncle.

242

Hather smiled down at Saeunna. 'As you say,' he grinned. 'We shall be very, very happy.'

Odin felt Mother Skuld's eyes upon him through the heavy wadmal veil. His own glare growled at her through the gathering darkness.

'You cheated, Allfather,' she said, smiling secretly.

Odin stopped scowling and shrugged. 'We both cheated, Mother. That's why we both won. There was nothing else that either of us could have done.

'Now,' he added, 'will you give them both some peace?'

He felt her smile, although he couldn't see it.

'Uncle Vermund,' Saeunna called, 'it's time Svipdag was in bed.'

The old warrior waved cheerfully and scooped the lad up in his arms. The right one still twinged a little from time to time, but the cut had healed and he held his honorary nephew easily.

'Come on, young'un,' he laughed. 'You heard what Saeunna said.'

He passed them where they stood, pausing to let Svipdag lean over and kiss his new mother good-night. Then he continued towards the stockade, still carrying his precious burden.

Saeunna took Hather's hands in her own. 'Let's have some peace, you and I,' she said softly. 'We've earned it, Hather.'

Odin turned so that his companion wouldn't see his smirk. 'It's up to you,' he muttered. 'It's always up to you, Mother Skuld. Will you let them have some happiness together, now?'

'They had happiness before,' she taunted. 'Now you want them to live quietly and enjoy the love they've found? Is that it, Allfather?'

'That's it, Norn. I don't think it's too much for me to ask.'

'And I'm supposed to leave your precious Ynglings to their own devices, Odin?'

'They might be the better for it if we both did that.'

'I'll make a bargain with you,' she countered.

243

Odin shook his head. 'No bargains,' he said. 'You know that we can never honour them.'

The ravens cawed and settled on his shoulders. The wolves, Geri and Freki, threw back their heads and called a welcome to the advancing night.

Hather and Saeunna heard them. Hand in hand, unhurried, they followed Uncle Vermund back to Sudrafell.